Revenge at the Bluebird Café

Doug Creamer

Revenge at the Bluebird Café

Copyright © 2014
Doug Creamer

Cover design by Andrew McCarn
Photo of author by Andrew McCarn & Sydney Byerly
Find them at: https://www.facebook.com/laurenandcathell

Painting on the back of the cover by Jean Smith
Find her at: https://jeansmithsrtist.com

Published by Faith Farm Publishing Company
PO Box 777
Faith, North Carolina 28041

ISBN: 0-9743935-2-5
ISBN-13: 978-0-9743935-2-0

Published and printed in the United States of America

Forward

I can't believe it has been ten years since I published The Bluebird Café and nearly twenty since I published Encouraging Thoughts. I knew as soon as I finished The Bluebird Café that I wanted to write a sequel. I never dreamed it would take ten years to accomplish that goal. I wrote the first twenty chapters for this book about eight years ago and thought I was done. I spent the next two summers editing it. I really liked the book but felt like it was incomplete. I struggled with that thought and then set it aside. I picked it up and put it down several times over the next couple of years.

About two years ago, I felt like the Lord said, "It's time." I was excited and pulled it out again. As I re-read and edited the book, I added five new chapters. I was confident that my book was ready to go. I shared it with some friends who felt the story wasn't quite right. Discouraged, I put the manuscript away again.

About a year ago, two sweet ladies from church, Mary and Paula, told me that they were praying for me and asking God to help me finish my book. They want to read it. How could I look at these two sweet women and tell them that I just didn't feel inspired to work on the book again? Besides, I was back to school teaching, and there is no energy left to work on a book after I get home from school. There is nothing like people telling you that they are storming heaven for you to help you discover motivation.

I sought the Lord, but my prayers were met with silence. Then gradually the Spirit of God began to stir in me. Creativity and inspiration blossomed. During a time when I normally feel drained, I was energized and I wrote five more chapters. I told these two sweet women of God that their prayers were working, which only ramped them up to pray harder.

Over the Christmas break, I asked the Lord for some guidance. I also asked Mary and Paula to pray that I would find a good editor. A few days later I was on the phone with an old friend, Wayne Finney. I shared my proposal which he agreed to pray about. After waiting on God, he agreed.

I worked hard editing the book once again before sending it to

Wayne. Then I had to work hard on getting all his corrections done. It took us about six months to work through the whole book. I thought I was done…

My wife wisely pointed out to me that my editor and I are both males, wouldn't it be a good idea to let a female read the book? Getting a female perspective on my characters and story could have an overall positive effect for my readers. I couldn't imagine another six month ordeal to get the book out.

The Lord works in mysterious ways. I had dinner with my Dad and Linda. She told me that she helped another author with her books. I thought about that and then one evening decided to give Linda a call; thankfully she agreed to read the book for me. I couldn't believe a week later when she brought me her feedback. It was fabulous. She offered me outstanding insights into my novel. I made the suggested changes and once again I thought I was done and ready to publish.

I began the process of feeding the book into the template that Amazon wants to publish through Create Space. I thought that would go quickly, but decided I would read the book one more time as I corrected formatting issues. My wife worked with me on some final editing to make sure we did the best job we could on the book. She helped me catch a few important things we agreed needed to be changed.

So now I am finally ready to launch… I learned quite a bit about writing and editing. I feel extremely excited about what you are about to read. I hope that you enjoy the journey back to the Bluebird Cafe. God bless you and thank you for your patronage.

Revenge at the Bluebird Café

Chapter One

Robb Thomas turned left onto Atlantic Avenue in Virginia Beach. Atlantic Avenue, known as "the strip" to locals, was lined with oceanfront hotels. He drove past the statue of Poseidon, which served to welcome weary travelers to the haven of the seashore. He pulled his car into the parking lot of the Cavalier Hotel. The Cavalier was located at the end of the hotel strip. Next to it began a residential zone, so its location gave a sense of peace and quiet while still being connected to all the beach has to offer.

He checked into his room on the twelfth floor for a two week stay. He ordered a bottle of the best champagne and poured himself a glass while he sat on his oceanfront balcony. Robb surveyed the beach, taking in all the beautifully tanned women and the occasional stark white tourist who filled the scene before him.

Robb drained his second glass of champagne and retreated to the coolness of his room, which was plush and oversized. A basket of fresh fruit waited to be raided on the table near the window. The room held a king-sized bed on the far wall and an intimate sitting area near the sliding glass doors that led to the balcony. The fifty-inch flat screen TV hung on the wall above the sitting area.

He poured himself a third glass of champagne and set it on the bedside table. He pulled out his notepad from his leather briefcase and looked over his notes again. He chuckled to himself feeling excessively proud of what he had accomplished on such short order. He picked up the phone and placed a call. Robb was still chuckling when the man at the other end answered,

"Hello, Boss. This is Robb. Reconnaissance mission complete."

"What?" came the surprised voice at the other end. "You only left this morning. How can your reconnaissance be complete?"

"Boss, I went to the old man's funeral. I couldn't have gotten better information if I had requested it from the local library."

"Be careful who you're calling 'old man' there, my boy. Now, I would like to hear some details, something to substantiate your claims."

"The preacher didn't give the regular eulogy at his funeral. He talked for a few minutes, but he also invited the mourners to share the impact the old man... uhhh... the guest of honor had on their lives. Many people stood up, introduced themselves, and then told how he had helped them," he said, laughing excitedly.

"No wonder I hear champagne bubbling in the background," he said. "I assume you have also started to make a plan of action for us."

"I picked up the local paper, *The Virginian-Pilot*, and plan to contact a real estate agent in the morning. I'll find us a nice executive suite and have the office set up within a week."

"Been rethinking that since you left this morning. I would like you to set up our office away from the beachfront. I pulled up a map on Google. Look out in the Kempsville area. Witchduck Road, Kempsville Road, Princess Anne Road and Providence Road. See if you can find a nice office space in that area. We will need more than one office set up to do the job right; so let's start with one in a more discreet location."

"Yes sir," he said, jotting himself a few notes on a legal pad.

"Now, give me some of those 'details' you picked up at the funeral."

"The toughest client will be a local real estate company, King Realty. The owner has a strong hold on the market. He sells in the Kings Grant, Cavalier Golf Club, Bird Neck area; most of his stuff is upscale, located on either golf courses or waterfront properties."

"Do you think we can take him down through established businesses?"

2

"No, I think we're going to have to open our own office. I'll study the market and see if we can buy anyone out. I've got a feeling it would be easier to build from the ground up on that one."

"You get started on that immediately. I want King Realty out of business within six months or at the outside a year."

"That could be a stretch, but we'll get to work on it."

"We've got some slick salespeople in Chicago, New York and LA; don't hesitate to call in some of the troops. Why don't we put a lawyer and a finance officer in that office? Make the real estate company one-stop shopping; you know, streamline the operation. I'm not interested in profit on this venture, just crushing the enemy."

"Gotcha, Boss. Next, you've got the girl and the Bluebird."

"Leave her to me. I have special plans for her."

"Check." Robb looked up from his notes to see a house finch land on his balcony and grab a peanut that had escaped the maid's cleaning. He chirped his victory as he flew away with it in his beak. Focusing on his notes again, "There's a doctor; he's a heart specialist. Then you got a banker, a branch manager in one of the local offices. And we can't forget the preacher. All these I imagine have pretty clean slates, you know, no skeletons in closets."

"Don't assume that. Everyone has things that they want to keep secret. You know, what we need there is a reporter who can dish up a good scoop on those three."

Robb popped on the big screen TV and hit the mute button. He flipped over to ESPN Sports and watched as he continued. "I guess we could try and find someone to trash these guys' reputations."

"Not just someone," the Boss said thoughtfully, "how about Eve?"

"You want to bring Eve in on this one?"

"I told you we are going to spare no expense to destroy all the good work this old man did. I want these people to turn their backs on God. We're bigger and we're more powerful than any old god they can dream up."

The highlights showed a player scoring a grand slam. He missed the hit but managed to see the player jump into the welcoming party at home plate. "I'll call Eve in the morning," he said, wishing he had seen the hit.

"Is the editor of the paper a male or female?"

"Uh, give me second," he said reaching for the paper and

flipping to the second page, "yeah it's a male."

"Then Eve is our man, or should I say woman? Bring her in as a journalist. She's a great writer and she's willing to do whatever it takes to get the job done."

"She really did a number on that CEO from California, didn't she?"

"I warned him, he just wouldn't keep his nose out of my business. And don't forget she helped alter the outcome of that New York senate race back in 2000."

"No one will ever forget her reporting on that one."

"Yeah. Eve will take care of those three, I'm sure of it."

"Beyond that, Boss, there are a few people with businesses which I will arrange to have competitors open up right beside them. With our resources, it shouldn't take too long to put most of them out of their misery."

"Good. We can open any kind of business as quick as you need it. Cars, retail, you name it, we can get you up and stocked quickly. Do you need some muscles to get things set up?"

"Yeah. Send me a few beefcakes to do the physical work. Then we'll need several guys who can manage some retail businesses. I'll need a sales manager for a car lot and a real estate broker, too. If I think of some others, I'll shoot you an email in the morning. Better send a truck of office furniture and equipment to get all these people up and running. I'll start renting the spaces this week and should have some of the businesses ready to go by the end of next week."

"Sounds like you have things under control."

"That's right, Boss, but I've got a couple odd ones I'm not sure how to approach. The first stood up and told a story of getting pregnant in high school. This woman was no high school student. She looked to be in her fifties. Said she gave the baby up for adoption. Not much to go on there."

"Yeah, I agree. When Eve gets in town, let her dig around. Not even sure what kind of story she could write at this point to affect her. Might have to let that one go. What's the other one?"

"There is a cop that seems to be hanging around Jenny, the girl who owns the café."

"Did you talk to him?"

"Yeah, he helped play host at a reception that was held at the Bluebird after the memorial service."

"Does he seem connected to the girl?"

"Yeah, I think there might be something there."

"I want him out of the picture right away, top priority," he said vehemently. "I don't need a cop sniffing around there."

"When you say, 'out of the picture,' do you mean permanently, like an accident?"

"No. I don't want to raise any suspicions. I was thinking along the line of a career move."

Robb reached for the map that was lying on his bed. "Um… There is Richmond, which looks to be about two hours away. Then, of course, you have DC, which is about four hours away."

"I was thinking about a place a little smaller, a place where we might be able to influence a sheriff, if you know what I mean?"

"Well, you've got three universities about three or four hours away, James Madison University, University of Virginia, and Virginia Tech."

"A college campus could be very distracting for a young man. I was thinking about something a little closer so we could drag out the heartbreak. You know how difficult it is to keep a long distance relationship alive."

"Well, there is a little town about an hour and a half away that's right on Interstate 95 called Emporia."

"Sounds like a place to check out. Drive out there one day early this week and check it out. Report back to me before you contact the sheriff."

"Boss, I have to say, that I'm not so sure this guy will go out there."

"We may have to sweeten the pot some, but I'm sure we can convince this young man to go. I want to make sure he's out of the picture before too much happens. He might have the smarts to put all this together. As for the rest of those church-goers, I want them squashed like bugs."

"Operation 'flyswatter' is underway."

"Oh, I love that name," the boss responded. "Now don't let that champagne get warm. Make sure you keep focused, and don't let those bikinis get you too distracted from your main purpose there."

"I think I can handle some bikinis and get my job accomplished too," Robb laughed.

"You always seem to. Keep me informed of your progress, and I don't mean with the bikinis." Robb laughed and the line went dead. The boss sat quietly in his dark office. He reviewed the conversation in his mind and smiled. "OK, Charlie," he said out loud, "now that you're in the grave, I'm going to destroy all your good work." He slapped his desk as if he was squashing an ugly bug.

Meanwhile, Robb drained his third glass of champagne and put on his swimsuit. He headed down to the beach where he hoped to find a few young ladies who were looking for a good time. Although Robb didn't possess six pack abs, he was in great physical shape. It took Robb less than an hour to find a couple of young ladies to come up to his room. Several guests turned and stared at the girls in their skimpy bikinis. Robb's smile only grew bigger with each passing glare.

In the room, the Jacuzzi bubbled just like the champagne. Room service brought steaks and more champagne for all three of them. Robb smiled and laughed because he knew he was on his way to a memorable evening and a resounding bug-squashing success.

Chapter Two

Margaret Johnson ran the flower shop in an old, worn-down strip shopping center on Virginia Beach Boulevard. Margaret kept the shop and the area outside it looking beautiful. She was located on the end and she even kept the landscape maintained on her end. Margaret and her late husband had owned the shop for thirty years. Her reputation in the area was one of the best. Locals loved her and patronized her business faithfully.

Pulling up to her store always affected her customers' senses. In spring, the lilacs and daffodils were always a welcoming sight. Summer brought roses into full bloom, and fall was always greeted with mums. Winter wasn't left out, because she always kept pansies in front of her store. Besides her beautiful flowers, she was known to help out strays of all kinds. If a dog or cat was lost and hungry, it could always find some love and food from Margaret. On more than one occasion, she took pity on the homeless. She always had some kind of food in the shop, and she never turned anyone, man or beast, away hungry.

On this particular morning, Margaret was working on some funeral arrangements for Sylvia Smith, who had passed away the night before. Sylvia had attended church with Margaret, but they weren't very close. That didn't keep her from putting together an arrangement of the most aromatic roses from her own collection, though. Sylvia loved roses and found time to stop and see Margaret's rose beds each summer. Margaret also made an arrangement of Asiatic Lilies, another of Sylvia's favorites.

Margaret stopped to take a short break and to feed some stray cats when Grace, the local gossip, pulled up. Margaret tried to be nice to Grace, but she could talk for hours and that wasn't good for business. Margaret could tell by how quickly Grace was moving her squatty body that she was particularly pleased with the gossip she was serving today. She looked like a mother duck waddling in with her news. Margaret attempted to play innocent while she worked on an arrangement for Sylvia. Grace told several juicy tidbits, served like hors d'oeuvres on a warm summer's day. She could tell that Grace had finally arrived at her point when she asked,

"Have you heard the latest about your shopping center?"

"No, I haven't. I do know, however, that I'm getting a new neighbor."

"Do you know where?" she asked.

"In the old A&P building. I don't know who's coming, but I hope it's a drug store or some other kind of chain that will help bring more customers into the shopping center. It would also be nice if they fixed up that end of the shopping center, too."

"So you have no idea who is coming?"

"No, but I suppose you do," she admitted with a sigh.

"As a matter of fact, I do," Grace said with some pride. "It's a florist!"

"A what? Get out of here," she said walking over to the window to look over at the old A&P. "That place is way too big for a florist. Besides, who would want to compete with me?"

"They're opening up a wholesale operation! They're going to have public access and wholesale prices. They're going to have three or four florists in there using real and artificial flowers. They're even going to sell flowers on the internet."

"Computers," she said, stunned by the information. "How are they going to use computers to sell flowers?"

"People will be able to send orders in on their computers, and they're even going to allow the customers to create their own arrangements using some computer program."

"Oh, my God." she said. "I hope you're wrong."

"You know me. Grace always tells the truth." She said raising herself up with pride. That made Margaret chuckle, while Grace got mad. "What? Do you think I make stuff up?"

"No. No," she said pulling herself back together. "I just can't believe it."

"Well, you better believe it," Grace said with a huff. Then she got up to leave.

"No, Grace. I'm sorry. I didn't mean to…" but she was already out the door. Margaret stood and looked at the workers going into the A&P building. "What are those guys doing over there?" she thought. "Maybe I should just go over there and have myself a look. A florist in a huge building like the A&P. Who ever heard of such a thing?"

****

Jenny opened the door and turned on the lights at the Bluebird Café. Within minutes the smell of freshly perked coffee permeated the place. She went about her morning routine: mixing up the pancake batter and making some buttermilk biscuits. She needed to prepare for customers who soon would be arriving.

The disc jockey on the old radio talked about another hot day beginning in Virginia Beach. The new air conditioner hummed quietly while the traffic reporter on the radio talked about a stalled car on Interstate 64 and a wreck at the corner of Kempsville and Princess Anne Roads.

The bell on the door rang out the arrival of the first customers of the day. Jenny looked up just as she had every day for the last month to see if it was Uncle Charlie. Her heart sank every time, even though she knew it wouldn't be him. She looked over at the calendar and realized that he had been gone for more than a month, and yet she still looked for him every day. She missed him so much. She was only now beginning to realize how much he had done to help her in her business venture at the Bluebird. He had worked the grill almost every morning since he sold her the cafe. His pay was only a pittance of what he was worth.

Thankfully Uncle Charlie had started to train Carlos on the grill before he passed away. Carlos was doing a great job getting the food ready and interacting with the customers. He was still a bit slower than Uncle Charlie, but he hadn't been doing it quite as long, either.

Carlos had arrived twenty minutes before the first customer and had the bacon and sausage cooking before they arrived. Many of the regulars arrived early to enjoy the aroma of the food being prepared on the grill and to take advantage of the Early Bird Special: two eggs, bacon or sausage, and two slices of toast served with a piping hot cup of coffee.

The morning rush filled the Bluebird like clockwork. Carlos and Jenny were learning to work together and were finally developing a rhythm. About 8:30, as the morning crowd began to dwindle, Joe walked in.

"Morning, Aunt Jenny," he said giving her a kiss on the cheek. Jenny rolled her eyes as usual, patted him on the back, and sent him to the backroom to get started on the dishes. Meanwhile, Carlos and Jenny finished serving the remainder of the morning crowd.

About 10:00 o'clock, Joe came out from the backroom, poured himself a cup of coffee and headed for the corner booth. Carlos grabbed a plate, threw some sausage and bacon on it and grabbed his own cup of coffee and joined Joe. After wiping the counter one last time, Jenny got herself a cup and joined the other two. It had become the 10:00 o'clock ritual; the three of them talking and resting for about forty-five minutes between the morning and lunch rush.

"What's going to happen to this place come the end of September?" Joe asked Jenny.

"Wintertime is really different around here," she said, not really wanting to think about it. "Once these tourists head for home, we get quiet." The wind began to gust, blowing sand and trash around in whirlwinds. A seagull landed in the parking lot to grab a discarded piece of biscuit.

"I guess that means I need to be looking for another job," Joe said. The rain began to beat against the glass and run down in sheets.

"I don't know what to tell you. When Uncle Charlie and I ran this place, he would always take the first two weeks of October off, and I would take the first two weeks of November. We always closed for a week at Thanksgiving and Christmas. We would each take a week in the middle of winter, and then we would pray for an early spring."

"Where did you go during your time off?" Carlos asked. Lightning flashed and the thunder rolled, causing the lights to flicker momentarily.

"When I was young like you two, I used to head for the beaches in Florida. I would hit the bar scene way too heavy. I would get home red as a lobster and would be unable to remember much of what had happened. Kind of a dangerous way to live."

"Sounds like you were a wild chick," Carlos said.

"Let's just say I have my fair share of memories mixed with

regrets." The thunder crashed again; but the clouds were beginning to break up; a small thunderstorm dropping the sweet blessings of rain but filling the air with unbridled humidity.

"Where do you go now that you are old?" Joe asked sarcastically.

"I'm not that old!" she said hitting him on the arm. "I've enjoyed a few cruises, gone to see the Grand Canyon, gone backpacking in Yellowstone National Park and on the Appalachian Trail, toured some of the Civil War battlefields, and sometimes just headed up to Williamsburg for a couple days."

"Do you ever miss your partying days?" quizzed Joe.

"No. My 'old' body couldn't take it anyway." There was silence around the table. The seagull returned looking for the rest of his lunch, but the brief shower didn't leave anything in its wake. Carlos lit up a cigarette, and Joe faked a few coughs. Jenny got up to get some more coffee and freshened up the two guys' cups while she was up. When she returned to her place, Joe started in again.

"When do you think I'll be finished up, Aunt Jenny?" Joe asked.

"What's with this Aunt Jenny stuff?"

"I like to think of you as my aunt, because I don't know too many people who care about me as much as you do."

"Oh, yuck. He's going to get all mushy on us!" Carlos said thumping the table with his fist.

"That's enough out of you," Jenny said to Carlos. "That was real sweet, Joe." She said, kissing him nicely on the cheek. Joe stuck his tongue out at Carlos.

"Oh, double yuck," Carlos said turning his attention outside. The sun was back out in full force. The sunbathers were making their way back to the beach, and sounds of kids screaming could be heard in spite of the traffic

"You're avoiding the question, Aunt Jenny," Joe prodded.

"I know. I was hoping you wouldn't notice," Jenny sighed and looked out the window. The lone seagull was joined by a few friends who scoured the parking lot for some morsels. The steam rose off the pavement and danced its way back up into the sky. The moment of silence was finally broken when Jenny said, "Joe, you've come a long way since you walked in that door two months ago. You did well at the rehab center, and you've worked hard to pay me back what you owe me. But things will start slowing down soon. As soon as we get past Labor Day, my customer base drops dramatically.

"To make a long story short," she continued, "I want to make you a selfish offer. If I go ahead and take my vacation starting the last two weeks of September, would you be willing to hang around and help Carlos run the place?"

"Are you kidding, that would be great!" Joe said, giving Carlos a high-five. The two of them laughed and started to chant, "Party! Party! Party!"

"Now you two cut that out. I will be trusting you with this place."

"Don't worry, Jenny," Carlos said. "We'll clean up after the party."

Joe laughed out loud, which earned him another slap on the arm. Carlos and Joe did another high-five.

"Can I trust you guys?" Jenny asked in a motherly tone.

"I promise, Aunt Jenny, everything will be OK. You know us; we love this place and its customers about as much as you do."

Jenny smiled as she looked at the two of them, because she realized it was true. While they loved giving her a hard time, they loved treating the customers right more. Jenny sighed heavily and leaned back in the booth. Joe leaned across the table and whispered loudly,

"Do you think we can get a keg on that counter?"

"Get up and get back to work, both of you!" she scolded, popping them both on the arm as they passed her. They laughed and talked about the party they would throw while heading into the backroom, and Jenny returned to her seat in the booth.

Jenny faced the ocean and enjoyed the comforting sound of the waves crashing in on the shore. She watched as people headed out to stake their place on the sand. With the storm passed and the warm summer sun beckoning, the sun worshippers were answering the call. This would be her first fall and winter without Uncle Charlie. She missed the long talks they shared between the breakfast and lunch crowds, but she was growing fond of the friendships she was developing with Carlos and Joe.

Chapter Three

It was the Monday before Labor Day. Summer was coming to an official end. Jenny approached the weekend with mixed feelings. On the one hand, this was her last busy weekend for a long time; but on the other hand, she knew it was almost vacation time and she was looking forward to a break. While Jenny had no definite plans, she was considering a trip to the mountains. Although she never grew tired of the ocean, she loved seeing the mountains, especially when they exploded with the beauty of fall colors.

Al, Joe, and Jack sat in their usual places at the counter of the cafe. Jenny was busy cooking up the morning delights for the customers who had filled the place to capacity. Carlos was taking his turn waiting on the customers. The aroma of bacon and freshly brewed coffee filled the air. The noise of clanging dishes and barked orders couldn't overcome the sound of the conversations and laughter that made the cafe feel alive.

Slowly the morning rush died down to a trickle. Jenny took the last couple of orders, and Carlos helped Jenny start the routine of cleaning the grill and putting the breakfast things away. Al, Joe, and Jack finished arguing over which baseball players were the best and who had made the worst errors in last evening's games. They had now taken up their favorite topic of the year: football.

All three men, who were from diverse backgrounds and who had retired from teaching in different high schools, believed that their former school's team was on the way to being the city champs. The area high schools had finally begun fall training, and the football season was something these three men lived for each year. Jack still helped the coach at his school and could be found on the sidelines of every game. Al helped out in the boosters' concession stand of his school, and Joe just liked watching his old team play the game.

Jack had to admit that maybe Princess Anne High School might be going through a growing year since they graduated ten seniors off their city champion team from the previous year. That slight sign of weakness was all that Al and Joe needed to attack like sharks.

Jenny looked up just in time to see Mike walk through the café door. She wiped her hands and walked over to give him a kiss. Their lips parted without the slightest comment from the three old men who sat at the counter. They kissed again and this time Al commented,

"All right you two, cool the engines down," which made them both smile. They gazed into each other's eyes and seemed to get lost in the moment.

"A little more coffee down here," Joe added to help Al.

"You know where the coffee pot is," Jenny answered and turned back to Mike to give him another kiss.

"Have you ever seen so much sappy affection in all your life?" Joe asked while getting himself that cup of coffee. "What's the world coming to with such a lack of service?"

"You've gotten yourself plenty of cups of coffee," she said as she smacked him on the shoulder. She gave Mike one more quick kiss and returned to her work behind the counter. Mike sat down next to the old men at the counter and asked,

"Have you solved all the world's problems yet?"

"Oh no," Jenny injected, "but they did decide that Princess Anne would not be city champs this year." That got the three of them going and Jenny winked at Mike. Mike asked Jenny if she would make him some breakfast even though she was starting to get ready for lunch, which Jenny gladly whipped up for him while the three old men argued about high school football. They tried to get Mike's opinion, but he wasn't foolish enough to get involved in that debate.

"All I do is work the games for the extra pay. I don't take sides. I just enjoy watching close games, not those ones that are totally lopsided." All the men agreed with Mike on that point. Since they couldn't draw him into their conversation, they went on arguing without him. Mike turned his attention back to Jenny,

"It's hard to believe that it's almost Labor Day weekend," Mike said as Jenny placed his food in front of him. "It won't be long and this place will be deserted."

"I know," Jenny said as she poured herself a cup of coffee and sat down with Mike. "I'll really miss the crowds when things finally slowdown. But, I'll still have my regulars to keep me busy until next summer," she said, tilting her head towards the three old men still arguing high school football.

"When do things really start to slowdown around here?"

"There is a big drop off after Labor Day, then we have a steady slowdown until the middle of November. When the golfers can't hit the local golf courses, then things seem deathly quiet. But thankfully it doesn't last too long. We always get a few warm weekends in late January or early February. The golfers flood to town and many stop in for a bite."

"So it's really only about two to three months, depending on the kind of winter we get around here?" Mike asked.

"Yeah, I'd say that's about right. But that gives me a chance to take some much needed vacation time. I'll do a little traveling, catch up on my reading, and try to whittle down the long to-do list that sits on my refrigerator."

"I guess it's a well-deserved rest after a long and hot summer."

"It hasn't been too hot this summer with that new air conditioner." They both turned and looked at it and they both thought of Uncle Charlie. "I almost didn't get that because of you," she said with a smile. Mike turned to her and gave her a kiss.

"Well, if you had to choose between the two, which would you rather have?" Mike asked. Jenny took too long to answer. Mike dropped his fork loudly. Jenny smiled, hugged him and gave him a big kiss on the cheek.

Mike finished up his breakfast, and Jenny returned to the other side of the counter and to her work. Mike and Jenny continued to chat. The Bluebird emptied out; even the old men went on their way.

Carlos and Joe fixed themselves something to eat and headed for a corner booth. Jenny refilled Mike's coffee and poured herself a cup and they headed for the corner booth at the other end of the cafe. They sipped their coffee and sat back quietly.

"Jenny, I need to let you know that I have to go out of town next week on Wednesday. I'll probably be gone overnight, but I'll be home to take you out on Saturday night for sure."

"OK." she said. "What's up?" she asked with mild curiosity as she pondered what things she needed to add to her to do list.

"Nothing much. I just have to take care of some family business."

"Oh, well, I hope it's a good trip," she said absentmindedly as she stirred her coffee. "Do you need me to take you to the airport?"

"No, I'll be driving, but thank you for offering."

Jenny took a sip of coffee and allowed her mind to wander.

"Aren't you interested in what I am going to do while I'm out of town?" Mike asked, interrupting her thoughts.

"Well no. Should I be concerned?"

"Absolutely not. I would just be curious, if I were you."

"Mike, I trust you. You said you had to take care of some family business. I figured you would tell me if you wanted me to know."

"Wow, you aren't like most girls I've known. They would have given me the fifth degree over something like that."

"You've given me no reason to doubt you. But on the other hand, maybe I should be concerned that you are meeting someone out of town and you are having a secret affair with her."

"You know that's not true." Mike countered with a smile.

"Yeah. That's why I said I'm not worried about you going out of town."

"Thanks, I appreciate that." They both took a sip of their coffee and looked out the window at the packed beach. Mike watched some seagulls floating in the air above some kids who were throwing bread up in the air to them. Jenny saw it too and she laughed. Mike looked at Jenny, who was smiling at him. They shared a kiss and talked about their work until they had drained their coffee.

Mike picked up his cap and prepared to head out on patrol. Jenny put their coffee cups behind the counter and came back around to Mike for a hug good-bye. They embraced, kissed, and Mike headed out the door.

Mike drove down the road concerned that Jenny might find out what he was really doing. He was also worried about doing it. He wondered if it would affect their relationship, and if so, how? Mike hated being secretive about anything, particularly since Jenny trusted him so completely. Mike had to put all the worry aside and concentrate on what he had to get done while he was out of town.

Chapter Four

"I hope we can move some more houses before the market cools off from this hot summer streak. I'm about ten houses short of an all-time record year. Why does Labor Day have to get here so darn fast?" George King of King Realty complained to his secretary. He brushed past her desk, picking up his messages on the way to his office. George dropped the armful of papers he was carrying in the chair beside his desk. He leafed through his messages and hollered out to Mrs. Fairbanks,

"Have we heard back from the Johnsons on the Baxter's place?"

"There's a message in your stack."

"Damn it!" he yelled from his office. "What do they mean they're going to think about it while they're gone on vacation? I had them this close to closing on that house; how did I mess up? Hey, Barb," he yelled out to Mrs. Fairbanks, "can you get them on the line before they go on vacation?"

Mrs. Fairbanks appeared at the door; her perfectly permed hair in place and her face red with anger. "The name is Mrs. Fairbanks. You think you would learn that after the last ten years of hard work. And secondly, I don't appreciate the profanity in this office!"

George took a deep breath. "I'm sorry, Mrs. Fairbanks, I occasionally forget in my excitement that you prefer to be called Mrs. Fairbanks. And I apologize for the profanity; I know better and I appreciate your bringing it to my attention. I'll work on it." He was sincere and Mrs. Fairbanks could tell he meant it.

"Apology accepted, but I'm afraid the Johnsons have left for their vacation."

"Da…" Mrs. Fairbanks raised her eyebrows at him. "I mean darn it!" he said with a slight smile to Mrs. Fairbanks.

Mrs. Fairbanks returned to her desk to answer the phone, and George started in on his work. The King Realty Company office was located on the corner of Newtown Road and Virginia Beach Boulevard. The office sat elegantly on a professionally landscaped piece of prime real estate. Every detail concerning the appearance of the place both inside and out was attended to by Mrs. Fairbanks. She wanted nothing to tarnish the appearance of the business.

She watched the landscaping and yard maintenance crews like a warden watching prisoners at work. She demanded perfection and she got it. She required the janitorial company to clean while she was there. She gave the office a white glove inspection before they left each time. When a customer turned into the parking lot of King Realty, he could see the money and most people would swear that it could be smelled when one walked inside.

All the couches and chairs were covered in leather. The desks and bookshelves were solid oak. The bathroom had brass fixtures, and the office that was used for signings had a gas fireplace. Nothing was left to chance. The place was impeccable, and Mrs. Fairbanks was proud of it.

There were four agents who worked for Mr. King in his office. There was Amy Hollow, who was the newest agent and a bit green. Mrs. Fairbanks was training her to become more professional and helping her learn the ropes. She honestly didn't understand why Mr. King would hire someone so young and inexperienced. When she stopped to think about it, she knew exactly why Mr. King had hired her. She was a very attractive young lady, and she thought that maybe he was a little too attracted to her, being a married man and all. While Mr. King taught her the art of selling houses, she guided her through the details of real estate work and made it her business to make sure no hanky-panky went on while she was on duty.

The other three agents were experienced sellers who kept up their sales quotas, which helped to grow the agency. Mr. King always made sure that they knew he appreciated their hard work and dedication. Because of their combined efforts, King Realty dominated the housing market within five miles of the oceanfront. They also controlled several of the area's elite golf clubs, waterfront property, and they were beginning to test the waters in other areas of the local business sector.

It seemed the King Realty Company had the Midas touch. Whatever they touched just seemed to turn into gold. George King knew it wasn't his ability alone that made things happen; it was a team effort. Each member of the team pulled his weight to make the company a success.

At lunchtime, Mr. King came out of his office and sat down on the couch in the main lobby where Mrs. Fairbanks' desk was located. They talked about work and he asked her about her kids. That always opened her up because she loved her kids, and she loved to tell anyone who would listen what was happening in their lives. It was the only time Mrs. Fairbanks lowered her guard and let her professional distance drop. When Mr. King felt she had shared all the big news, he decided he would head for lunch. He picked up the paper and headed for the door.

"I circled an article in the business section I thought would interest you," she said as he reached the door.

"I'll check it out, Mrs. Fairbanks," he said as he left. He flipped the paper open as he walked to the car. There was her distinctive green ink circling an article. The headline read, "New Real Estate Agency to Open". The short article told of an individual who had been in real estate up north and wanted to come to a warmer climate. His office would be opening on Pacific Avenue in Virginia Beach. "I hope to capture the country club markets and homes located along the many beautiful waterways in the area. I hope to get involved in doing some development, too," Randy Stumps, the new owner, was quoted in the article.

"Good luck, chump," George thought as he folded the paper. "He's trying to compete for my territory, and I've got a lock on that market. He's a nobody, an outsider," he continued, "no one would list their home with him. They want a name they can trust, a reputation. They want me." With that George threw the paper in the passenger seat of his car. He turned the key and the engine revved to life. He had already forgotten about Randy Stumps, as he merged out into the lunchtime traffic.

Chapter Five

"I moved you into the assistant editor's position, because I thought you would keep the errors out of the paper. Do you see that glaring headline error? How did that happen?" he yelled so everyone in the office could hear.

"I don't know, Mr. Birch," Mary Roberts responded quietly.

"You know that this will make its way to Jay Leno, and we'll be the laughing stock of America."

"I hope not," she responded.

"Get in my office," he yelled at her. She moved quickly and quietly like a mouse.

Craig Birch towered above his peers at six feet, six inches tall, and he had a booming voice to match his size. He ate way more than he should, and he ate all the wrong stuff. He was beginning to wear his food around his middle even though he tried to deny it. Craig entered his office and slammed the door shut. Everyone made themselves busy; they figured Mary was in for it. While Craig was a big blow-hard, they didn't think Mary would lose her job over the error.

Craig threw himself in his seat and glared across the desk at Mary. He sighed and sunk into his chair as he examined the paper more closely. He turned his chair around and began looking out the window. A long moment of silence passed as Mary considered how her resume might look. Craig turned his chair slightly and picked up his phone,

"Jane," he yelled into the receiver, "get in here immediately." Three seconds later the door opened and she came in. "Take this to David and bring me an answer on the double," he said after scrawling a note on a piece of paper. Jane ran out and was back in less than thirty seconds. "Thank you," he said, taking the note back from her, "you can leave and close that door behind you." There was another long moment of silence, as Craig rubbed his temples and pushed his brown hair back off his face. He regained his composure and looked at Mary with softer eyes. Meanwhile Mary's heart almost beat right out of her chest.

"Mary," a subdued Craig began, "it wasn't your mistake. It was mine. I want to apologize to you for blowing up at you out there."

"What?" she said, not believing her ears.

"That article was written by David. He gave it to me, and I approved it and the headline… It was my fault." Mary's racing heart began to slow down. "You'll have to forgive me," Craig continued. "My girlfriend and I are going through a rough patch. To be totally honest, she moved out. I just took all my frustration out on you," he sighed.

"I'm sorry to hear that," Mary managed to get out.

"Thanks, if you can't tell, I'm not dealing with it very well. We're having dinner on Friday and I think she's going to end it. I don't know what to do to fix it."

"I hope you can find a way to make it work."

"Thanks. Sorry to dump on you like that. After working with you for the last couple of years, I feel so comfortable talking to you. You are a friend and a good colleague."

"Thanks. The feeling is mutual." Mary said beginning to relax. "You are kind of like a big brother to me, even though I know you are my boss. I like talking to you, well, except when you have an episode."

"Again, I'm sorry about that. We've got another problem on our hands. Everyone out there thinks I'm in here balling you out. I know I have a reputation for blowing off some steam from time-to-time."

He sighed hard and continued, "You see, it's my way of keeping everyone on their toes. As for you personally, I want you to know that you are my right hand man…uh…I mean woman. I know I couldn't get this job done around here without you. But," Craig continued, "I've got to make it look good. I don't want to ruin my tough image. Oh," he said snapping his finger, "I know what I'll do." He picked up the phone and punched in a number. The conversation seemed very disjointed to Mary as she tried to figure out what was happening. He smiled and hung the phone up.

"Here's the deal. I'm going to start yelling at you again in a minute. I will continue yelling at you as I open the door. I'll tell you that you have the rest of the day off to think about your mistake."

"But you just said it wasn't my mistake," Mary countered.

"I know," he said impatiently. "But listen to the rest of the plan. My brother has a limo service. He's going to come by and pick you up and take you and your date out for an evening on the town, at my expense."

"But I'll lose a half day's pay!" she said, not sure if she was following him.

"No, no, you won't. I'll take care of all that. Look, it's like this. I need you, particularly with my personal life in a shambles, to help cover my tracks, at least until things settle down again. You're good at what you do. I chewed your ear off, and it was my fault; therefore the limo and the afternoon off. I'm asking you to let me yell at you on the way out so I can look good in front of the staff. I know it puts you in a little bit of a tough spot; but maybe while you are out on the town, you can forget all about it. You know everything's OK between you and me."

"Let me get this straight," Mary started, her head swirling around. "I'm not in trouble. We're going to open the door, and you're going to yell at me, and then I'm going out for a night on the town at your expense. Then, tomorrow, I come in, possibly a little late, and everything is alright."

"Oh, I like how you added, 'possibly a little late,'" he said with a smile. "I guess if I had a night on the town in a limo I might be a little late for work the next day, too. But yeah, I think you got it."

"Great. I need to hurry and get some shopping done," she said, almost opening the door to rush out.

"Wait!" he yelled. "I have to start yelling at you," he said.

"Oh yeah, I almost forgot."

"Do you think you could shed a few tears? You know make it more realistic." She rolled her eyes at him. "OK, here just take the tissue and look upset," he said handing her the tissue. "Ready?"

"You know," she said, "if you took this kind of time with your girlfriend, I bet things would work out."

He paused to consider that. "You see, that's why you're my assistant." He smiled and patted her on the shoulder, "Are you ready?" She nodded. He opened the door and let it rip, "Don't you ever make a mistake like that again, do you read me? Now, you go home and take the rest of the day off and think about this!" Mary made crying sounds and pretended to wipe her eyes as she ran for her cubicle. "And hey, I want you back in here tomorrow with your priorities straight." He returned to his office and slammed the door. Mary ran from the office pretending to cry and all the while trying to think where she would find a dress for the evening.

****

Three days later everything seemed back to normal. Craig was barking out demands from his office, and everyone was doing their best to keep him happy. Mary had found a lot of support from the other workers who felt badly about the way she had been treated. She accepted their support, but never told them what really happened behind closed doors.

At 11:30, Craig and Mary were making preliminary decisions about how the paper would lay out for the day. Competing for top billing were a shooting on the south side of Norfolk, the newest tax plan by the governor, a chemical leak in Richmond and its possible effects on the drinking water and the environment, and a car theft ring that was operating in the Larkspur neighborhood of Virginia Beach.

Each writer pitched his story to Craig and Mary, hoping he would obtain the lead for the day. The egotistical pitches of the writers made the room feel stuffy as they pitched their stories. Each writer knew that any breaking story could knock his off page one. Each of them staunchly believed he had the top story, but would discard it like rotten meat if he could find something hotter. Craig and Mary would decide the layout of the paper by four-thirty, and the presses would be rolling by midnight.

"Hey, Craig," Jane said poking her head into his office, "you might want to come see this story that Channel 10 is running."

"What is it?"

"Hostage situation in downtown Norfolk."

Craig and the writers pushed their way to the rack of TV's in the middle of the newsroom. People were starting to gather around to listen to what was going on. A twenty-nine year old male was holding 45 people hostage in the Freedom National Bank. He claimed to have enough explosives with him to bring the building crashing down. His demands were not immediately available to the press. Within thirty minutes, CNN and Headline News were running live feeds from the site. At one o'clock, the three major networks started broadcasting the story to the nation with small news briefs breaking into regular programming.

The newsroom exploded with life. Reporters were calling every source they knew attempting to gain information or insight into the situation as it unfolded. Craig barked out orders to the reporters and photographers. Mary consulted with writers, confirming information and trying to avoid speculation. By four o'clock, all the major networks had set up satellite trucks and were ready to produce live footage for their evening news broadcasts. At six-thirty, the national networks opened the evening news showing FBI agents and SWAT team members surrounding the building. At midnight, the presses began to roll at *The Virginian-Pilot* with the headline reading, **Disgruntled Employee Holds Bank Employees Hostage.**

At ten, the next morning the stand-off continued. The media had taken up positions surrounding the Freedom National Bank on every side. The only major incident through the night had occurred when the gunman shot his supervisor in the butt. The gunman then allowed a doctor and nurse to come in and tend to the wound but insisted that the boss be left on the scene. The doctor removed the bullet and stabilized the supervisor. The late night talk show hosts had a blast with this part of the story.

Craig called a meeting of the writing staff at 10:00 AM. Everyone reported to the conference room on time, carrying some type of caffeine. "I can tell," he said looking around the room, "that many of you haven't made it home for a shower or even some shut eye. I do appreciate your dedication to getting this story out there. I think we did a great job," he said dropping a copy of the paper on the table. "After this meeting I want everyone to head home for a little rest. I want you back here by four, refreshed and ready to get the paper out tonight."

"In the meantime, we have to figure out some different angles from which to cover this story, to keep it fresh. Has anyone got a connection with the family of the gunman?" The groans and sighs from the crowd were all the evidence that Craig needed that no one had made that connection. "What's the trouble?" There was a short silence.

"Craig," Mary ventured, "we've all exhausted every avenue to try and get to this kid's parents. I've even gone to the mailroom and asked the staff down there. No one here knows the family. Besides, the police have them so insulated from the public that no one is going to get near them."

"We've got to work harder," Craig countered to a room full of sighs.

"Craig," Jane injected, "the major media are sending their top brass down here and even they can't get to the family."

"Where there is a will, there is a way!" Craig responded. The room remained silent, and everyone's eyes focused down at the table. "Alright. Alright. Keep calling friends and friends of friends. There must be some good stories there," he said, backing off. "You're writing some good stuff in a crucial time. I want you to know that I appreciate that. Keep it up. We need to pick up on some of the other lead stories throughout the area too. Let's not forget that there are some other things happening around town. Get me some copy and we'll work in those stories too. Now you all get out of here and get cleaned up and rested. Be back here at four, we'll have our meeting at six. If we need to, we can push printing back until 2:00 a.m. to try and get the very latest on the situation." With that, the meeting ended and everyone made a beeline for the elevators.

Craig went back to his office to sort through a few papers and make a few phone calls. The office area was sparsely populated with writers from other departments getting a jump on their daily assignments. Jane poked her head around the door and waited for Craig to acknowledge her. "There is a woman out here who would like to speak with you."

"Unless it's the mother of that hostage taker, I'm not interested."

"I think you may want to meet this woman," Jane answered as she stepped away from the door. Craig begrudgingly got out of his seat and went to the door. From there he saw Jane talking to an incredibly beautiful woman. He quickly dodged behind his door and straightened his hair and tucked in his shirt. Then with all the sweetness he could muster, he called to Jane.

"Jane, I changed my mind. I'll make time to see her right now." Craig checked her out from head to toe. Her white blouse was so tight it appeared to be painted on and he couldn't avoid noticing the plunging neckline. Her skirt was a bit short revealing her nicely tanned legs. She had light brown hair that hung straight down barely touching her collar. Her radiant blue eyes captivated Craig, and her smile revealed pearly white teeth. Jane introduced her,

"Eve Sinclair, this is Craig Birch, our chief editor," she said but he missed the introduction.

"I'm sorry, what's your name?" he asked reaching out his hand.

"Eve Sinclair," she said. "It's nice to meet you."

"Likewise. Please come in and make yourself comfortable." His gaze followed her as she slipped past him and found a seat. Her plunging neckline revealed her blemish-free, gold tanned skin. She looked away granting him a brief glance that he savored for a long moment.

"What could I do for you today, Eve?" he asked seating himself in the chair next to her.

"I have watched this huge story unfold and wondered if I could do a little writing here at this paper?"

"Have you got any experience?" he asked.

"Yes, I brought you my resume," she said, reaching down for a folder she had placed on the floor. Craig took the opportunity to take in more of her intoxicating beauty. "Here," she said, handing him her resume. Taking her resume he seemed to stare straight through it to her.

"What is that perfume she's wearing?" he thought.

"…think…"

"Wh.. What?" he asked, being shaken back to reality.

"What do you think of my resume?"

"Oh," he said, making a big effort to focus his eyes on the paper. "What's this, you've worked at the *Washington Post*, the *New York Times*, the *Chicago Tribune*, and you've had some things published in *The New Yorker* magazine?"

"Yeah, I've had a little success."

"Well, I can see that," he said as he read on. "This is impressive. So, what brings you to the Tidewater area?"

"My mother lives here, and she is ill and needs someone to look after her. I've taken a leave of absence from the *Washington Post,* but I'd like to do some writing while I am here taking care of my mother."

"I really don't think I have the budget to add on another reporter," he said, hating every word.

"I'm sorry, I didn't make myself clear. I only want to do some freelance work. I'll work at home so I can take care of Mom, and bring you my work. I'm known for doing outstanding work, particularly on hard-hitting stuff."

"I've got a lot of reporters out there who might resent you taking the spotlight off their careers."

"I understand," she said. "How about this hostage story?" she asked. "It's what motivated me to come see you," she nodded. "I guess you've got an interview with the parents of this guy?"

"Heck no. That's a million-dollar story right there. If you could get that interview, you'd have a job with any news agency in the country."

"Even here? Freelancing several days a week?"

"I'll see what I can do if, and that's a big if, you can land an interview with that boy's parents. I want the copy on my desk by four o'clock."

"Five o'clock, AND it's a deal," she said extending her hand.

He shook her hand and smiled at her, "Good luck."

"See you at five," she said as she got up to leave his office. He stood at his office door and watched her until she was out of sight. He looked back at his desk and then shook his head and started for the elevators himself.

"Hey, Jane," he yelled over his shoulder, "call me at home if anything breaks on this hostage situation. I'll be back by four at the latest."

"Yes, sir!" she yelled back.

****

Eve got back in her car and pulled out her cell phone. She dialed a number and when she heard the man's voice she said,

"He bought the package. You watching the news at all?" she queried listening for his affirmative response. "I need some money to get the job done. He wants an interview with the parents."

"Anything you want or need is available," came the response.

"I also need to know where the police are hiding the family, and I need pictures of the family."

"You should be able to upload that information in less than an hour. Anything else?"

"That should do it. I'll be in touch once I'm officially in."

"I'll be waiting for the call."

The line went dead and Eve went to work.

****

At 4:30, Craig was back at his desk trying to figure out how the front page was going to get laid out. The reporters had returned to their desks refreshed and invigorated making calls to anyone who might shed new light on the hostage situation. Everyone was trying to find a way to get the scoop on this hostage story. The cigarette smoke was heavy in the air, especially when the adrenaline and excitement of a big story rolled around.

Mary was busy in her cubicle helping writers edit their pieces and letting them know the odds of whether their story would be chosen as the front page lead. Jane came over to Mary's cube and started talking about what was going on in the office.

"So you think things are better between you and Craig?" she asked.

"Oh, I think so," she said smiling to herself. Mary allowed herself the pleasure of remembering the night on the town at Craig's expense. "Craig's a tough cookie, but he knows I do good work and that's what will save my butt."

"Have you asked him about moving into that nice big cubicle right outside his office?"

"Not yet. You know with the big blow up and then this huge story there hasn't been any time. I think I'll get it through," she said.

"That's good. You deserve it."

Mary looked out over the office and noticed that all the men had stopped working and were looking up towards Craig's office. Mary jumped to her feet to see what was going on. What she saw was a very attractive woman approaching Craig's door. "What's going on?" Mary asked Jane as she looked back at all the men.

"You have to admit she's pretty good looking," said Jane. "In fact, Craig talked to her this afternoon about a job."

"About a what?" Mary retorted.

"A job."

"She doesn't look qualified for any kind of job that requires writing," Mary hissed.

"You're right about that," Jane agreed. "She does look like a tramp. And judging by the looks of these men, she's good at playing her part."

"What's she got that I don't have?" Mary asked puffing out her chest.

"You honey," Jane began, "are the kind of woman any man would be proud to take home to Mom. You are daughter-in-law material. You're the kind of woman who will bring home grandchildren. Now that is the kind of woman every man wants hidden away to bring out for "get-away" weekends. She's mistress material, using her assets to wind men around her little finger," Jane said as they watched her enter Craig's office and close the door.

****

"I know I'm a little early," Eve began as Craig stood up from behind his desk, "And to top it off, I think you're going to like what you see."

"Have you got the story?" Craig asked with anticipation.

"Before I answer that, I want to be sure our deal is still in place."

"What deal?"

"Several days a week freelance work with my own by-line. Also you'll keep me abreast of breaking stories that you want me to cover. I am planning to work freelance, but my price may be a bit higher than you are used to paying."

"Wait a minute there. I'm not promising anything until I read the story."

"Fine," she said getting up to leave. "I assume a TV station would be glad to put me on the air within minutes with this story," she said holding up a flash drive and several typed pages.

"Let me see that," Craig demanded.

"Uh, uh, uh," she chided, "do we have a deal?"

"Two days a week, paid by the piece and no benefits," he responded.

"Three days a week." she responded holding the story just out of his reach.

"Deal," he said taking the story from her hands. She sat back down while he read it.

"This is incredible," he said while reading it. He pushed a button on his phone and said, "Get in here," to the person who answered. In a minute, Mary walked through the door. "Mary, this is Eve," he said not even looking up from what he was reading. "She's got an exclusive story that we are running on the front page. Here is the flash drive, get it set to run."

"Can I ask what the story is about?"

"She got an interview with the parents of the hostage taker."

"You what?" said Mary. "We've been trying every angle we know to get to them. Give me some of that to read Craig." Craig handed her the first page and she sat down to read. "This is outstanding," she exclaimed, after only a few paragraphs. Eve just sat back and smiled as they both were mesmerized by what she wrote.

"Wow!" Craig said, as he handed the last page to Mary to read. "That is powerful stuff."

"You think you might sell a few papers with that story?" Eve asked.

"Are you kidding? We won't be able to print the paper fast enough."

"Can I shake your hand?" Mary asked as she finished the piece. "That is incredible writing. I'm honored to meet someone who can write so well."

"Thank you," Eve said shaking her hand.

"Craig, I'm going to go out and get to work on this thing."

"You do just that. But I have an idea. Let's try to plug the leaks and keep this one under wraps until after the press runs. I think it would be fun to hand deliver the paper to all those media giants out there!"

"Oh yeah," Mary laughed. "You want to join us?" Mary said turning to Eve.

"No, I'll let you two have the fun. I've had a tough day, and I think I need to get home and check on my mother. "

"I understand," Craig said.

"That flash drive contains photos of the family and the hostage taker."

"Great," said Mary as she rushed out of the office to her cube and began working. The door closed behind her leaving Eve alone in the office with Craig.

"Do you mind if I ask you, how did you do it?"

She leaned back against the door striking a sexy pose. He picked up on her move immediately drinking in her natural beauty. She eased over to his desk and leaned across pulling his face close to her own. Her perfume intoxicated him. She ran her finger around his ear and down under his chin, lifting his head so they would make perfect eye contact.

"That," she whispered "is exactly how I did the job. Men can be quite taken in, you know. Take you, for example," she purred like a cat playing with a mouse. "You weren't going to interview me until you saw me waiting out there. You just had to meet me," she said, releasing his chin and allowing him the pleasure of taking in her beauty as she straightened back up. "I find a weakness, and I exploit it," she said as she picked up her purse and started to leave. "I'll see you in the morning," she said with a cheerful lilt in her voice. "By the way, I'm glad you enjoyed the story. I hope you will also enjoy the view you'll get as I leave," she winked at him and walked out of the office.

Craig watched her every move as she made her way to the elevator, then he shook his head and got back to work. It was going to be a long night, but one he would thoroughly enjoy in the morning as the paper made its way throughout the area.

Eve made her way to her car and clicked out a number on her cell phone, "I'm in!" she proclaimed to the listener.

Chapter Six

It was a quiet Monday afternoon at the Bluebird. The lunch crowd had come and gone with fewer customers as the hot summer had finally given way to some cooler fall days. Jenny watched the numbers as business slowed down which was a mixed blessing. She needed a vacation, but she knew that ultimately she would have to lay off one of her workers.

Joe and Carlos had worked hard with her all summer. Joe had been working to repay Jenny for his rehab treatment. She felt an obligation to keep him employed so he could pay off his debt and hopefully keep an eye on him so he wouldn't slip back into old patterns. Joe was starting to learn to work the grill. Working with the customers came naturally because he worked in his father's Italian restaurant chain while he was growing up. He would be a tough asset to lose.

Carlos was also an excellent employee. He had been at the Bluebird a little longer than Joe, which gave him seniority. Jenny had continued the training on the grill that Uncle Charlie had begun before he passed away. He was doing a great job. He didn't have as much personality as Joe, but he was efficient and a good guy. Both were fun to have around, and they were always pulling jokes on her. Just the thought of the two of them made her laugh.

"Everything is cleaned up in the back," came Carlos's voice from around the corner.

"Did you two have another water fight back there?" Jenny chided him.

"Who us?" asked Carlos. Jenny looked at the two of them with their shirts soaking wet.

"What am I going to do with you?"

"What, do you think this wet shirt is water from a water fight? This is pure sweat. We have worked our fingers to the bone back here." Joe mocked as he pulled his shirt away from his body.

"You better not have gotten water all over back there." she said, sounding more like a mother than an employer.

"Oh, you are in big trouble." Joe said to Carlos as he pulled a squirt gun out and gave him a few blasts. Carlos returned fire and dove behind the counter for cover.

"Now, you two, cut that out!" she yelled. "I need to talk to you about something serious and all you two ever do is play around."

They both looked at each other. Carlos gave Joe a little wink. They both turned their guns on Jenny. "Ready..." Carlos yelled.

"Aim..." responded Joe.

"You better not." Jenny yelled, but it was too late.

"Fire!" they yelled together and Jenny was hit. Jenny grabbed the hose at the sink and returned fire. The water fight only lasted a moment, but the three were left on the floor, laughing hysterically.

"What am I going to do with you two?" Jenny asked.

"Keep us." Carlos answered.

"That's the trouble. I can't."

"We know that." said Joe as he rounded the corner to help Jenny to her feet. "That's why I've decided to leave."

"You've decided what?" she asked.

"Look, Jenny," Joe said as he sat down at the counter, "I know that Carlos has been here longer and I've decided he should stay and I should go."

"Did you know about this?" Jenny asked Carlos. He shrugged his shoulders and sat down next to Joe. "What are you going to do?" Jenny asked Joe.

"Look, I've already contacted this ski lodge my family goes to up in the mountains of West Virginia. The manager thinks I could work as a ski instructor or maybe in the kitchen at the hotel. Either way, I'll be fine. They have free boarding up there and I'll be fine. Besides, I need to get away from all my 'friends' around here. There are too many temptations for me to go back to my old lifestyle here. I've not come all this far to go back."

"Well, that's great, but I hate to lose you."

"One of us has to go, right?" Jenny nodded. "Okay, I've made the decision easier for you."

"We'll miss you."

"Thanks. Any idea when you want my last day to be at this point?"

"No. I was kind of hoping you would stay here with Carlos while I take a much needed vacation. We talked about that before, remember?"

"Yeah, I remember. I just need to let them know when I can be up there. There's no real rush, I mean it will be a while before they see some snow."

"I'll take a look at the calendar tonight and try to make some tentative plans for when I want to be off. I'll let you know something tomorrow."

"That will be fine."

"You mean," Carlos jumped in, "you are going to leave this place in our hands?" Joe and Carlos high-fived each other and pulled their squirt guns out.

"Maybe I'll close the place while I'm gone." Both guys pointed their guns at Jenny. "Or maybe if I think I can trust you, I might let you two run the place. God help me." Both guys laid their guns on the counter and reached across and gave Jenny a hug. "Oh, you guys." Jenny sighed. "What am I going to do with you?"

"I don't know." Joe said while picking up his gun, "But you better run for cover." Before Jenny could reach down for the sink hose she was being hit with streams of water from both guys' squirt guns. A water fight ensued that left all three soaked to the skin and laughing heartily. When it was over, the three of them spent an extra hour cleaning up from the rampage.

When Jenny finished up and locked the Bluebird for the day, she wished she hadn't had the water fight because the north wind was blowing and there was a little nip in the air. When she got in the warmth of her car, she changed her mind again. She wouldn't have had it any other way.

****

Mike was driving home from his interview tingling with excitement. Things had gone well, and he felt like he might be receiving an offer. He couldn't wait to see Jenny and share the good news. He was on his way to becoming a deputy sheriff. On the seat beside him was a camera filled with a special surprise for Jenny.

****

"Mr. and Mrs. Morris I really appreciate the opportunity you are giving me to represent your house on the market. I promise you that I'll work hard to get you a buyer in here soon."

"I know what it's like to be the new kid on the block. When I started my cleaning business six years ago, someone had to give me a shot. Now we've got four stores and we're moving to a new neighborhood. When you get ours sold, we'll get you to help us close on our new home too." Mr. Morris said.

"Thank you again." Mr. Stumps said. With that, he pounded his first sign in the ground. It was the only different realty sign in the neighborhood. All the other signs were for one real estate agent, George King.

Chapter Seven

The beautiful autumn leaves drifted from the trees to the earth, creating a rainbow of fall colors that danced in the breeze. Virginia Beach was beginning to look like the ghost town it always was during the dead of winter. Leaves were blowing down Atlantic and Pacific Avenue much like the cars do in the middle of summer. The beach was deserted except for the die-hard runners, several fishermen, and a few lonely shell hunters searching for treasure.

The Bluebird's breakfast and lunch crowd were as sparse as scattered frost. Fall was a slow-paced time filled with the laughter of the regulars enjoying the peacefulness that comes when the tourists have gone for the season. No one was in a hurry, and people lingered over their coffee for what seemed like hours.

The old men who sat at the counter laughed, joked and argued about football now. The high schools where they each taught were in the middle of their conference schedules, and each man hoped his team would win the championship. The old guys often stayed for hours in the morning, but they brought a strange comfort to Jenny as she worked around them. Sometimes she caught herself thinking about Uncle Charlie and how he would be right in there arguing for the Kempsville Chiefs.

Jenny had enjoyed a ten-day vacation from the Bluebird. It was the longest she had been away in the five years since she had bought the place. She had spent some time around the house getting her to-do list caught up. She had also escaped to the mountains for a few days hiking along the Appalachian Trail. The vacation did her some good, but she knew that the end of her vacation signaled the end of

Joe's time at the Bluebird. She was not looking forward to his departure at all.

Jenny had become fond of Joe since she rescued him from his life of addiction to drugs and alcohol. She discovered that he was full of life and that everyone had a good time when Joe was around. In a way, he reminded her of Uncle Charlie. His life seemed so full of hope and promise now that he had defeated the drugs and alcohol. But as life always does, it was going to take a new turn for Joe as he headed up to the mountains for his new job. Friday was to be Joe's last day. Carlos and Jenny planned to take him out to dinner to celebrate.

The regulars sustained life at the café for the winter. While the chill was making itself felt in the air, there were still warm days which was a reminder that Virginia Beach was in the South. This was one of those warm days where people came from all around to enjoy a walk on the beach. The guys cleaned up and wasted little time getting out of there for the day. Joe took a walk along the boardwalk before heading home.

Jenny stayed behind to get her weekly ordering completed. She finished the inventory, created her orders from her various vendors, called the suppliers and had just poured herself a cold glass of tea and was settling in a booth to relax. She took a few sips and peeked out the side window at the ocean waves crashing onto the shore. The boardwalk seemed deserted compared to when summer tourists would have packed it at that time of day. There was only the lone runner and a passing seagull to distract her from the view.

Jenny really was looking forward to the winter's passage and hoping for an early spring. Business was glacially slow. The only thing good about business being slow was that she would have more energy to put into her relationship with Mike. They had grown close and intimate over the couple of months that they had been dating. Jenny couldn't believe that she was giving her heart away to a police officer, but she couldn't deny the truth.

Tap, Tap, Tap came a noise that interrupted her thinking. It was Mike at the window.

"Speak of the devil," she said, getting up.

"What?" came his response from the other side of the glass.

"I was just thinking about you," she said as she opened the door for him.

"Were they good thoughts or bad thoughts?"

"Good, of course," she said giving him a hug. "Can I get you an iced tea?"

"Yeah, that would be great." Jenny got the tea and the two of them sat at the booth where Jenny had been resting. They talked for a while about their day and what had happened since last they saw each other. When Jenny had finished her tea, she got up and retrieved a pitcher from the refrigerator. She returned to the table and refilled Mike's glass. She set the pitcher down and sat back down.

"Jenny," Mike said, "I've got something I want to talk to you about."

"You sound serious. You're not planning to break up with me are you?"

"Are you kidding? After the nice conversation we have been enjoying, why would I want to break up with you?"

"I don't know. You just sounded serious all of a sudden."

"No. I want to talk to you about something wonderful that happened to me."

"Well that's good, bring it on."

"Jenny, I've been offered a job, a really good job."

"Well, congratulations! That's great Mike."

"I'm really excited about this opportunity."

"What's the job?"

"What's not the problem, where is." Mike started. "Let me back up. Remember about three weeks ago I told you I had to go out of town on some family business?" Jenny nodded. "Well, actually I went to an interview for a job."

"You went to an interview out of town and you didn't bother telling me?" Jenny asked with surprise.

"Yeah," Mike responded.

"Where is this job opportunity?" she asked with a quizzical look.

"It's in Emporia."

"Oh." Jenny said letting her head hang slightly.

"It's a great opportunity for me Jenny. I would be hired as a deputy sheriff and the pay is great…no, it's out of this world."

"Well," Jenny sighed, "it sounds like you want to take the job."

"I do, Jenny. I really do. But this is the best part," he said taking her hand in his, "I want you to come with me."

"What?"

"Even though it's a great opportunity, I don't want it if you won't go with me."

"Are you asking me to marry you?"

"I haven't thought of it that way. I might be, but I'm not sure."

"Well, you're definitely no Romeo and that was far from a romantic proposal. Besides Mike, I've got the Bluebird Café to run."

"It gets better Jenny. I've found a café for you out there," Mike said almost bursting out of his skin with excitement. "The owner passed away about six months ago, and none of her children wanted to run it, so they just closed it. I talked to a real estate agent and he assured me that it was a profitable place. I even went and took a look at the place," he said reaching for a pack of pictures sitting beside him. He laid the pictures on the table, and Jenny looked at them in shock. "Isn't it great? It looks in pretty good shape. I would be willing to help you get whatever you want done to get it ready to open. Isn't it exciting?"

"But Mike," Jenny tried to begin, "I already have a café."

"You could sell it and move out there with me."

"Sell the Bluebird? I love this place. I wouldn't know what to do without it. I've worked here since I was sixteen years old, Mike. You don't just walk away from that. Besides, where would we live? And maybe we'll get married? Those are huge steps. I really like you Mike, but you are asking me to take an incredible leap of faith."

"Don't the pictures of the café look nice?" Mike asked, deflated.

"Oh, don't get me wrong, they're great. But, Mike, starting over in the restaurant business is not easy. You've got to build a customer base and loyalty. In the beginning you just don't make a profit."

"I could help with the bills until you get established."

"It's not just that, Mike. What happens in a few months or maybe a year or two when you discover you hate your job? What will happen with me? I'll be stuck with a new café in a town I don't know anything about and I will have lost the Bluebird. Then think about us? We've only been dating for less than three months, and you're ready to tie the knot with me. You don't even know me that well."

"What I know about you, I really like."

"Me too, Mike, me too. But marriage, that's huge. And giving up this café, that's almost impossible. I love this place."

"I understand." Mike said, sitting back and looking discouraged. Certain he had the perfect plan, the thought that she might not agree hadn't even crossed his mind until that very moment. The dream, like a bubble, popped right in his face. He looked at the pictures on the table, the dreams he had thought they would share, all went up in flames.

There was silence between them. Jenny picked up the pictures and looked through them. "This is all very sweet Mike, but I can't leave the Bluebird. This is my home away from home. But you, you aren't tied down. The job sounds like a big step up for you and quite honestly a good opportunity." She reached across the table and took his hand in hers. "You need to think seriously about taking it."

He looked directly in her eyes, "Not without you," he said sadly.

"Oh, Mike. You obviously think this is a good opportunity for yourself. You also think a great deal about me," she said looking at all the pictures on the table. "It makes me feel good that you care that much. But Mike, sometimes our careers take us to strange new places. I don't know why, but maybe God's got something for you out there, and you need to go and discover it."

"Maybe I need to come to work for you, here at the Bluebird."

"No, Mike, that would be a big mistake. You have a servant's heart, a heart to serve the public through law enforcement. That's a high calling. I know I couldn't do it. Besides, the café would bore you to tears."

"Jenny, I don't want to go without you."

"Mike, I'm not telling you to go. You are the best thing to happen to me in a long time, but I don't want to hold you back either."

"What will happen to us?"

"We've only been in this relationship for three months. Don't misunderstand, it has been a wonderful three months. It's probably been the best three months I've ever had with a guy. I know what will happen, we'll stay in contact for a while, but then you'll go your way and I'll go mine." Jenny said with a sigh. A tear fell from the corner of Mike's eye. Jenny lowered her head because she could feel the tears stinging her own cheeks.

"So, what do I do?" Mike asked between the tears.

"Pray, Mike. Pray."

****

Two weeks later Mike pulled into the parking lot of the Bluebird Café at three in the afternoon. Jenny came out and met him. They embraced and headed down to the beach for a walk. It was a breezy but warm fall afternoon. They walked along the beach for over an hour before heading back to Mike's car.

There was a long embrace, a few kisses, and many tears. When their embrace finally broke, Mike got into the car, which was packed with his belongings, and he drove off for his new job in Emporia. Jenny went back inside the Bluebird and sat in a booth and cried.

Chapter Eight

Steve Leaks was a strong young man; standing an impressive six-foot-two, he was solid muscle. He could have been a star for one of those Pepsi ads where the women all turn to watch the man taking off his shirt. His six-pack abdomen looked like it was chiseled out of solid rock. His eyes and his face revealed his tender side, which made his allure to women all the more powerful.

Steve was working a temporary job on the docks in New Jersey. He carried heavy loads with the ease of a locomotive going down hill. Most of the guys working the docks used profanity as often as they took a breath. Steve, however, kept control of his tongue. This self-control mirrored his tender heart. This gentle giant volunteered at the local homeless shelter and often worked with the guys to help them find employment. The irony being that he was currently working a temp job himself.

It was near the end of his shift when his supervisor called him into the office. Steve reported immediately.

"Yes sir, Mr. Griggsby." he said as he walked into the office.

"The big boss says he wants to see you in the morning."

"You mean the temp agency or the big boss?"

"The big boss; says he's got a special assignment for you."

"OK. Where do I go?"

"Here." he said handing him an address written on a piece of paper. "It's an office downtown, the Big Apple. Be there 9:00 AM sharp. Don't be late, kid. By the way, clean up before you go down there, you want to look good for the boss." Mr. Griggsby left the office chasing someone who had just passed by. Steve stood there just staring down at the address.

At 8:45 the next morning, Steve found himself walking down the streets of New York City. He didn't know why he was being called to the boss's office. He just had an address and an office number. He didn't even know the man's name. For that matter he wasn't sure it was a man at all. In today's world his boss could just as easily have been a woman. Steve approached the building and looked at his reflection in the glass. He made sure his hair and his tie were straight, then he entered the building.

He rode the elevator to the tenth floor and arrived at the nondescript office door at five minutes until nine. He hesitated before entering unsure if he might be walking right into someone's office, but then realized that there must be a secretary on the other side of the door. He pushed the door open, and to his relief, there indeed was a secretary sitting at her computer terminal just inside the door. He realized as he approached her that he wasn't sure what he should say,

"You must be Mr. Leaks." came her pleasant voice, much to his relief.

"Yes, ma'am."

"Please have a seat, the Boss will be right with you." Steve sat down and leafed through one of the magazines on the coffee table. At precisely nine o'clock, the door that led to the main office opened. The secretary spoke once again,

"You can go in now, Mr. Leaks." Steve got up and went through the door, which seemed to close on its own behind him. The office was dark so it took Steve's eyes a moment to adjust. He wasn't sure if it was the dark mahogany furniture, the fact the drapes were closed, or that there was only one light on in the office, but Steve had a hard time making out anything in the office besides the small circle the light was making on the desk. The light offered only a glimmer of an older gentleman sitting behind the desk. In the dim light, Steve could not make out the older man's features.

"Please, come have a seat." came the deep, graveled voice of the man behind the desk. "Relax. You're not in any trouble. Can I get you anything?"

"No, sir." Steve responded carefully sitting himself in the seat across the desk from the mysterious man. "My supervisor told me to report here this morning, said something about a job."

"I like that about you, getting right down to business. Your work down at the pier is just temporary, that right?"

"Yes, sir."

"I understand you have an interest in acting."

"That's right, but how did you know that?"

"I have my sources." Steve caught the outline of the old man's smile. Steve tried to make out more of the old man's features, but the lighting just didn't permit him to do any better. "I would like to know if you would consider doing an acting job for me?"

"Well sure. What's the part? Would the production be done here in New York?"

"No." the old man chuckled. "This acting is a little more involved. Your stage is the world."

"Huh?" Steve responded.

"I need someone to play the role of a boyfriend to a pretty attractive young woman."

"You mean, we would be working together to accomplish some goal?"

"No. She will be unaware that you are acting."

"I don't understand. Am I spying on her?"

"Ooh, interesting word." the old man chuckled again. "I don't like the word spy. I prefer to think of you as someone who is opening her eyes to the possibilities."

"What possibilities would that be?"

"The possibility that there are other fish in the sea."

"I think I could do that, but would it interfere with my work down at the pier?"

"This role would require all your effort; I am afraid you won't be working at your job down at the pier. But don't worry; your job will be there for you when you finish your acting job, if you decide to accept it. As a bonus, you will be compensated nicely, and you will have an expense account while on 'location'."

"Wow." Steve responded.

"Steve, the truth is your role goes much deeper than you are now imagining. Let me explain. You are going to take on the role of someone who is planning to open your own restaurant. You will become close friends with the woman in question. Your goal is to let her believe she is mentoring you in your new venture."

"That doesn't sound too hard. Where would this take place?"

"Norfolk, Virginia."

"That sounds like a warmer place to spend the winter."

"Such a positive attitude in one so young."

"So all I have to do is report back to you occasionally about what she is doing, right?"

"In a way, but you wouldn't be reporting directly to me. I have a person down there to whom you will report."

"That doesn't sound too hard." Steve started to relax.

"Well, there is a little bit more to the job than it sounds on the surface. You see, I want you to transform and develop the relationship into something more than just two colleagues," he said with strong emphasis.

"I think I understand." Steve said.

"Good. Good. Do you think you would have trouble with the assignment?"

"No, I think I can handle it. I assume you are using me to break her up with her current boyfriend, am I right?"

"Yeah, something like that. You catch on quickly."

"Thanks."

"First, you will need to look over the assignment." the old man continued. He reached into his desk and pulled out a folder and handed it to Steve. "Here is the information you will need to complete your role. It has your background, her background, and all the details about your restaurant." Steve flipped through the folder and scanned the information. He found a check written out to him for fifty-thousand dollars. His eyes nearly popped out of his head as he looked over at the old man who just smiled back. Then he saw the picture of the woman standing in front of what he assumed was her restaurant.

"She's pretty." Steve commented.

"I'm glad you think so. It should enhance your acting ability."

"The details of your flight plan and where you need to report are listed in the folder. As I said, you'll be reporting to my man who's already in place down there. You'll find his name and contact information in the folder. You've got about a week before you'll need to leave. I don't want you to make contact with her for another week after you arrive. We don't want to rush things."

"I understand." Steve said closing the folder.

"When you arrive down there, you'll get a new cell phone, checking account, car, and apartment. Have you got any questions?"

"No sir."

"So you think you could carry out this acting job without any problems?"

Steve hesitated, "I understand your goal is to break her and her boyfriend up, but what if she isn't interested in me? I mean, if he is around, why would she want to go out with me?"

"Good question. He is currently working out of town. I am hoping the distance will provide a weakness that you will exploit."

"What if I develop feelings for this girl, do I get to stay in the relationship?"

"No, I am afraid this is a temporary assignment. It calls upon your acting ability to convey your feelings which are obviously not true."

"I don't want to see her get hurt."

"Don't worry; there are plenty of fish in the sea. Once you are out of the picture, she will find other interests."

"She could go back to her old boyfriend."

"That is a distinct possibility, and then I will have to come up with a plan B."

"Why are you so interested in breaking these two up? Is she your daughter or is he your son?"

"I am not related to either one. The reason for my actions is not open for discussion."

"Let me see if I understand the situation right. You are paying me quite a bit of money and setting me up to live down there which is also costing you a pretty penny. Your purpose for my going down there is to help her forget about her current boyfriend. You want me to help her see that there are other people out there to be interested in besides this current guy.

"I am to take on the role of a restaurant owner and use that to get her to help me get things started. She is to become my advisor, and I will be her apprentice. I will use that to manipulate her feelings and entice her into a relationship with me. All the while I am to maintain an actor's objective while playing the role and not allow my own emotions to get involved. Does that sum it up?"

"Yes, I think you have the gist of it."

There was a long silence in the room as Steve looked down at the check and the picture of the young lady. "It's a lot of money," he mumbled. The silence continued as Steve leafed through the folder.

The man reached into his wallet and pulled out two crisp one hundred dollar bills. He laid them on the desk and said, "I think I have given you quite a bit to think about. Why don't you take this money and go to Coney Island for the day. Relax, walk the park, enjoy the rides, eat one of their famous hotdogs and think about things. I need you to be all in on the assignment. I don't have time for second chances. This has to be convincing and it has to work."

"Thanks, I would appreciate the time to consider this." Steve said.

"Take everything with you, and plan to come back and see me in the morning, say nine o'clock, with your answer."

Steve reached for the money on the desk and tried to get a better look at the man behind the desk. He could see the white hair and thought he made out either blue or green eyes. The rest of his features remained a mystery. Steve got up and made his way to the door. As he reached for the handle, he thought he noticed someone standing in the shadows, but he couldn't be sure. "I'll see you in the morning then, sir." Steve closed the door behind him and said good-bye to the secretary.

"You think we made the right choice there?" asked the voice of the man who was indeed hiding in the shadows.

"I think so." the old man responded. "If he takes the job, she'll fall for him hook, line, and sinker. He's believable and I bet he gets the job done right."

"If you say so, Boss."

"Yep, now that Mike is out of the picture, Jenny should fall head over heels for him." the old man chuckled.

Chapter Nine

Chuck Johnson was driving his Mercedes down Virginia Beach Boulevard to his office on Arctic Avenue. It was a raw, rainy day, but the sun seemed to be shining in Chuck's heart. Chuck tried to always keep a positive spin on things, even on a rainy day. Chuck signaled and turned into the parking lot of the Virginia Federal Bank, where he was the branch manager.

Chuck walked in the bank and greeted the tellers and other office staff with hearty hellos. He had a good staff with little turnover at his branch. Chuck entered his corner office and looked over his calendar of appointments. It looked like it would be an easy day. He had a few car loans, one home loan, and a luncheon with some of the brass from the main office. The luncheon was a routine visit to make sure things were going well, and Chuck was looking forward to their time together.

"Mr. Johnson," his secretary's voice came over the intercom, "you have a call on line two."

"Thanks, Judy." he responded and picked up the phone. "Hello, this is Chuck Johnson, how may I help you?"

"Mr. Johnson, this is Marty Mason from the Hughes Johnson Accounting office. I am calling to see if we can push up our annual audit of the books by a couple of weeks. We finished our last job a little early, and we were wondering if we could get a jump on yours. I understand that yours are usually in great shape and was hoping to be out of there in time for an extended holiday break."

"We weren't expecting you for at least another couple of weeks. We don't have all the paperwork together that you'll need. But if you want to come on, we can get you started on some of the preliminary stuff while we finish up our other reports for you."

"That would be fine. I understand that you won't have everything ready, but I know your efficient manner will facilitate our work in your office."

"Thanks, we'll get right on it. When can we expect you?"

"How about Monday?"

"That would be helpful in giving us a little more time. We'll see you Monday, Mr. Mason."

Marty hung up the phone. "I think he went for it, Boss. I didn't feel like he threw up any red flags."

"You get down there Monday. You know what your assignment is, don't you?"

"Oh yes, boss. There will be some problems in their books before I leave, you can be sure of that."

"Don't forget to leak the information to Eve. You have her number, right?"

"Right here in my cell phone, Boss."

"Have a pleasant trip," said the Boss sitting behind his desk chuckling to himself.

****

Two weeks passed and the audit was going well as far as Chuck Johnson knew. His office staff was able to pull all the paperwork together and get it to Mr. Mason in record time. He seemed very appreciative. Mr. Johnson had noticed that Mr. Mason had been staying quiet and avoided having lunch with him. Most auditors would go out to eat several times while they were working at the bank. He didn't think much about it because Mr. Mason had made it clear he was trying to get finished early to enjoy the holidays.

It was a Friday morning, and Mr. Johnson entered the office his normal cheery self. He greeted his staff and headed for the coffee machine. He noticed the light wasn't on in Mr. Mason's temporary office, which was unusual, as he had beat Chuck to the office every day that week. Chuck poured his coffee and headed for his office.

Chucked listened to his messages while he brought his computer up and checked his email. There was an email message from Hughes Johnson Accounting office. He clicked on it, and it was from Jerry Hughes, the office manager. Jerry and Chuck had become good friends over the years, and they tried to set aside at least four afternoons a year to play a round a golf together. The email read,

"Chuck, I hope you have your clubs all polished up, it's about time we hit a course together. I'm sorry we are running late getting our people over there to work on your audit, but I know your books are meticulously kept. Our staff should be setting up office in a couple more days. Thanks for your patience. Let's aim for next Friday for the golf match, weather permitting."

"What is this email?" Chuck thought. It must be a joke; the audit is almost complete. Chuck picked up the phone and dialed Jerry's number. Jerry picked up on the second ring,

"Jerry Hughes, can I help you?"

"Yeah, you can stop sending joke emails." Chuck began and laughed.

"I know you don't polish your clubs, but they always look brand new." Jerry answered with a laugh.

"Oh, they'll be all polished up for you. You want to play the Cavalier this time?"

"Yeah, that sounds good to me."

"I'll set the tee time for two o'clock. Now what's this crap about sending your team over here, Marty seems to be a hard worker, and I think he's doing a good job."

"Who is Marty?" Jerry asked.

"Marty Mason, from your office."

"We don't have a Marty Mason on our staff."

"Stop playing around. He's a good guy, kind of quiet."

"Now you're pulling my leg."

"Huh?"

"The auditor scheduled to do your books hasn't left our office yet. He's been tied up on a previous job."

"Then who the hell is this guy down the hall?"

"I don't know."

"Hold on." he said, his heart rate jumping up. Chuck walked down to the office that Marty Mason had been using. It was empty and the light was still out. There was no sign of the man who had once worked there. "Judy, have you seen Marty this morning?" he asked his voice sounding a bit excited.

"No, sir. What's wrong?"

He picked the phone back up, "Jerry can you get over here? Something fishy is going on, and I don't know what."

"Yeah, I can be there in less than thirty minutes."

"Thanks, Jerry." and he hung up dumbfounded.

Within thirty minutes, Jerry and a crew of four others were combing through the books and the bank's database to try and determine what happened. Chuck pulled his entire staff except a skeleton crew to help with the process. Judy walked in the conference room where they were working and told Chuck that the Vice President was on the phone for him,

"Thanks, Judy. Jerry, I'm going to go to my office to talk to him."

"That's fine, you go, we'll keep working."

Harry Wilson was the Vice President of the Virginia Federal Bank. He and Chuck were friends, but Harry could be a bit hot under the collar at times. He had been known to fly off the handle and shoot from the hip on some of his decisions.

"Good morning Harry, how are you?"

"I'm not sure. Have you seen the paper this morning?"

"To be quite honest, we've had a crisis over here, and no, I haven't."

"I'll say you have a crisis over there."

"But how do you know what's going on over here?"

"Read the front page of the business section Chuck." Chuck reached into his briefcase and pulled the paper out. Flipping through he pulled the business section out only to discover his picture on the front cover and the headline reading, "100,000 dollars in missing funds are unaccounted for by branch manager Chuck Johnson."

"Oh my God." he said out loud. "Judy," he yelled, "take this into Jerry." and he handed her the paper. Judy's eyes almost jumped out of her head as she read the headline.

"Harry, I've got Jerry Hughes, the VP from Hughes Johnson Accounting office, here. We're trying to get to the bottom of this now. He said that auditor wasn't from his office."

"Are you telling me that you allowed unauthorized access to our books and our computer system?"

"I don't know what I'm telling you right now, Harry. I need to work on this a little bit."

"Hey buddy, your head's on the line. You may not have a job this afternoon. At the very least, you'll be suspended."

Chuck shook at the thought. "Give me some time. I'll get to the bottom of this somehow."

"I want to hear from you before lunch."

"Yes sir," he said and hung the phone up. He glanced out the window only to see a Channel 10 news truck pulling into the lot. "Oh, great," he thought, "just what I needed this morning."

By 11:00 Harry Wilson had decided he needed to be at the branch office which was surrounded by the media. The police had been called to keep the media back so customers could use the bank. Harry, Chuck and Jerry were in Chuck's office discussing their strategy.

"Look Harry, I really believe Chuck is innocent here. I am prepared to make a statement to the media to that effect. Even though the 100,000 is still unaccounted for at this time, I think we'll be OK. I believe my team will be able to find it when we go through all the accounts."

"I imagine you are right." Harry said. "But the media and the public won't let this go until you do find the money." The three men agreed on that point. "I think we are going to need to put you on administrative leave for a while, Chuck."

"Oh, come on Harry. You know I wouldn't touch the money."

"I know it, but look at that media out there." he exploded. "We have to think about our reputation as a bank." He brought his temper back under control. "Look," he sighed, "I think you need to leave and get out of Dodge until we can figure out what happened here. When I say leave, I mean go see some family who live far away. Stay away from the media, and don't make any statements."

"That makes me look guilty," Chuck countered.

"Don't you think I know that?"

"Don't you think it would be better if I was here trying to help get to the bottom of this mess?"

"Chuck, I think Harry's right." Jerry injected. "You know I'm going to personally work on this one. I'll get to the bottom of this, but I think you need to distance yourself from the whole thing. I'll email you and keep you up to date on our progress."

"I'm innocent," he said looking to both men for support.

"We know that," Harry said with the first signs of compassion in his voice. "You need to give us time to figure this whole thing out."

Chuck got up, a defeated man. He picked up his jacket and his briefcase and headed for the door. "I'm depending on you two." he said in a low voice. Everyone in the branch saw the defeated man walking for the door. When he exited the building, the media mobbed him. He had to get two police officers to get him safely to his car.

Harry Wilson followed Chuck out of the bank taking away the media's attention from Chuck. He read a prepared statement to the media and took no questions. The statement, although brief, promised the public that a full investigation was already underway and that officials at the bank were sure that they would get to the bottom of the problem. He also announced that Chuck Johnson was placed on administrative leave until the investigation was complete. He offered no support for Chuck in his statement.

Chuck drove several blocks before picking up the cellphone and calling his wife. He gave her a short synopsis of the events and explained that they needed to get away for a few days. He told her to start packing and that he would pick up the children from school. He arrived home within the hour and helped his wife pack the car. They were on the road to Pennsylvania before the evening rush hour began.

****

At eight o'clock that evening, the phone rang in Eve's apartment. "Hello." she said answering it. "Oh, hello Boss. Did you see my story about the bank manager?"

"It was great," he responded. "Did any of the other media pick it up?"

"All of them. It was the lead story all day."

"Oh, how sweet!" he let out a huge laugh.

"You should have seen the pictures of him running to his car."

"I love it. Did you tail him to see what happened?"

"Yes, Boss. He packed up and left town."

"Good job. Keep in touch."

"I will," she said and hung up.

The door opened in the Boss's office. It was Marty Mason. "Sounds like you did a good job," the boss said as he came in and sat down.

"Thank you. I wiped my fingerprints off everything. I left that place clean. Now Boss, as far as the money goes, I left it there. It will take those accountants weeks to find it all. I buried it so well that I am not sure I could find it all."

"That's outstanding. I wanted the money left in the bank. I don't have any need of their money. Did you make some copies of any of the personnel records?"

"Yeah, Boss. It's right here on this flash drive," he said handing it to the Boss.

"Great. This will help keep the story alive and help to destroy Chuck Johnson's career in banking. Let's see some god rescue him from this one. Well, my friend, it looks like you have done your usual good job. I think we can declare this one, mission accomplished."

Chapter Ten

It was Friday morning, and Pastor Andrews had just pulled into the parking lot of Hilltop Presbyterian Church, a place where he had been pastor for ten years. He parked his car and allowed the sun to bathe him through the windshield. While it was December, the weathermen had predicted a warm day with highs reaching into the sixties.

Pastor Andrews got out of his car and headed for the building when he was struck by the thought that he hadn't been in the garden in quite a while. Zipping his light jacket, he went out to the chapel area. Most of the garden had died back for the winter, but someone had taken the time to plant pansies. He stopped to look at them as they glistened in the sunlight. A slight breeze blew, causing them to dance like ballerinas.

Suddenly he began to smile as he thought of his old friend, Uncle Charlie. Uncle Charlie liked this peaceful place, and standing here now Pastor Andrews understood why. "Hey old buddy," he thought, "I could really use some of your wisdom right about now. There are some people in my congregation who are beginning to go through some rough times. You were always so good at encouraging the discouraged. Wish you were here right now." The thought of his old friend warmed him inside. Pastor Andrews sat down in the sunny courtyard and connected with his Father in heaven while he took in the beautiful morning.

When he broke himself away and headed into the building, his secretary gave him a cheerful greeting. She reviewed his schedule with him and then offered to get him a cup of coffee. When she took it to him in his office, she asked,

"Have you heard about Chuck Johnson?"

"I've been trying to call him all night. I think I might try emailing him."

"I heard he picked his kids up from school and hasn't been heard from since."

"I better get that email out right away. I want him to know that we are here for him. Is there anything else happening that I should know about?"

"No." she said, "Seems like a lot of our folks are going through some tough times here lately." He looked up into her compassionate blue eyes and nodded his agreement. She smiled at him and pulled the door closed behind her.

Pastor Andrews sent an email to Chuck and took care of several other things before getting back to work on his Sunday sermon. He only needed to add a few final touches to the sermon, and it would be ready for Sunday morning.

By 11:30, he had finished his sermon notes and had met with a few of his parishioners privately. The morning had been uneventful. His secretary came to the door and asked if he had a moment to talk to someone from the local newspaper. He closed down his email and walked to the outer office. There was a very attractive woman standing at the counter who reached out her hand to greet him,

"Hello, my name is Eve Sinclair. I write some articles that appear in *The Virginian-Pilot*, and I was wondering if I might talk to you for a few moments."

"Sure. Would you like to come in my office?"

"That would be very nice." They entered the office and Pastor Andrews sat in one of the overstuffed chairs across from Eve. He noticed that she was an attractive woman with her blond hair cascading to the shoulders of her tight red dress, but he did not allow that to distract him.

"What can I do to help you?"

"As I said, I do some freelance writing for *The Virginian-Pilot* and as a matter of fact I've written for a number of the larger national papers. Anyway, I want to write a story on the church today. It will be something that will be covered for several weeks, and it will look at the church from several perspectives. I want to work with several of the major denominations, a Catholic priest, a pastor of a non-traditional church like Rock Church, some youth and some elderly people. I want to take the pulse of the modern church and create a series that lets the readers know what's happening today."

"Wow, sounds ambitious. Have you ever attempted anything like this before?"

"Yes, but on a broader scale. I want this piece to focus on the local church."

"How can I help?"

"I would like to interview you privately at length one day, and then I was hoping to get you to participate in a round table discussion with some local pastors and some lay-people in the area."

"Do you think you'll get their cooperation?"

"I was kind of hoping you could help with that, too," she said sheepishly. "I was hoping you might suggest a few people and then possibly use your influence to get them involved," she said, knowing she was stroking his ego.

"I might be able to suggest a few people who would be willing to participate, but I think you should talk to them yourself. It's important for you to sell your idea."

"That sounds fair. So I take it you're interested?"

"Yeah," he said, "I am."

She smiled and rose from her seat and headed for the door. "I'll make an appointment with your secretary to do your individual interview. After that, I'll schedule a time for the group discussion."

"Sounds good to me." he said walking her to the door. Eve went out and made an appointment with the secretary, and Pastor Andrews returned to his office. He noticed the faint aroma of her perfume when he closed the door. It was intoxicating, which made him decide to open the office door and allow it to air out.

Eve went to her car took out her cell phone and punched in the number. "Hello Boss, this is Eve. I hooked the pastor."

"Good job," he responded with a hearty laugh. "Keep up the good work. Are you having any trouble with the editor?"

"None. He's like putty in my hands."

"I don't know any man who wouldn't be putty in your hands. All I know is that I am glad you are on my side or I'd be in big trouble."

"Keep that in mind." she said letting out her own hearty laugh.

"Keep me informed, Eve."

****

Winter was closing in, and Mike felt its icy grip on his life. The gloomy low hanging clouds seemed to match Mike's mood. He missed Virginia Beach and his old stomping grounds; but more than that, Mike missed Jenny. His thoughts were consumed with her. He thought about her every day, cooking at the Bluebird, sitting out on the beach, eating a quiet dinner with her, and just hanging out at her place.

While his job was going well and he was receiving positive feedback from the sheriff on his job performance, he still longed to be back on the force in Virginia Beach. Even though he knew he could never make this kind of money with his experience, or be given this much freedom, he still longed for home. He had made a few good friends with some of the guys on the force in Emporia, but he missed the comfort and companionship of Jenny.

Mike and Jenny had talked quite a bit just after Mike had left for Emporia; but as time passed, they called less frequently and almost stopped texting completely. Mike asked Jenny if they could spend some time together over the upcoming holidays; Jenny was slow to commit. Mike could see the signs that the relationship was coming to an end. The thought of that about killed him. He tried to suppress it, but it still lurked in the back of his mind.

Mike stopped in at Wendy's for a meal one day when Scarlette approached him. "Hey, Mike." came her syrupy sweet voice. "Are you eating all alone?"

"Yes, ma'am. But why don't you join me and change that."

"That would be nice," she said sitting down across from him. Mike noticed immediately that her blouse was opened a little too wide and her cleavage was pushed up a bit too high. He forced himself to look away.

"Have you caught any bad guys today?" she asked before stuffing a few french fries in her mouth.

"None today, Scarlette. I've just pulled a few speeders and changed a flat for an elderly gentleman."

"Well, that was nice of you," she commented. "Have you seen any good movies lately?" she asked. Mike saw right through the obvious come-on. His only thought was to turn her down because his heart ached even more for Jenny.

"No, I haven't." he answered in the cheeriest voice he could muster. "What about you, seen anything good?"

"Well, there is a new romantic comedy I want to see. You think you would enjoy going sometime?"

"I'm not sure my girlfriend would really like me to see the movie with another girl, if you know what I mean." he answered with a smile.

"Oh, I'm sorry. I didn't mean to…"

"Don't worry, you couldn't know." He gave her an easy out. Even though Mike knew her intentions, he still thought she was a nice girl and didn't want to hurt her feelings. The conversation was very platonic after that, and Mike actually found himself enjoying her company. It sort of took the sting out of being away from Jenny.

****

"Yes, Mrs. Glassburg I understand completely. I just wish you would give me a couple more months. I really believe I can move your home if you give me the chance." George King was trying not to lose another customer. But it was hopeless, her head had been turned, and she was beyond the point of no return.

George slammed the phone down and yelled out, "We lost another one to that bastard. That brings the total to twelve who have jumped ship since that jerk came to town."

"People's heads are being turned by that one percent savings in commission," his secretary responded.

"It doesn't help that that woman reporter gave him that nice glowing report on how efficient and caring he is with his customers. Did you see that article the paper did on him? It was almost a full-page story."

"I did think that was a little excessive. There are a lot of real estate people in the area, just because he's new doesn't give the paper any right to spotlight him."

"Yeah, you're right. Especially when you consider how much advertising we do in that paper. I think I might fire off an email to that reporter, give her a piece of my mind."

"Now you know that won't do any good."

"Yeah, but maybe if I talked to the guys in the advertising department, that might do a little good."

"That may not hurt, particularly if several agencies wrote in at the same time."

"That's a good idea. Maybe I can give a few of my counterparts a call and see if we can put some pressure on them." That was exactly the way George spent his afternoon: calling other agents who would join in his fight. He was only interrupted once by another client who had decided to jump ship to the new agency. That was only additional fuel for his fire.

****

"What can I get for you?" Jenny asked a tall, strong young man who came into the Bluebird and took a seat at the counter. Jenny was taken aback by his nearly perfect physique and had to force herself to concentrate on what he was saying. He wanted a burger all the way with fries and a drink. He talked with Jenny while she prepared his order on the grill. She served him his meal but continued to talk to him while she made the other customers' meals.

The next day he was back again having another burger all the way. Jenny picked up the conversation with him right where they left off the day before. The old men sitting at the counter began to tease

Jenny about her flirting with the young man who just blushed and turned away.

When the young man walked in for the third day in a row, the old men couldn't help themselves. They began to tease him and ask him if he was trying to make a move on Jenny.

"Now you guys just hush," Jenny said giving Al a pop on the arm. "Don't pay them any mind," she told the young man.

"I'm sorry if I embarrassed you." the young man at the counter said. The three old men got really quiet and looked directly at Jenny to see how she planned to answer the young man.

"These three clowns couldn't embarrass me. They just want to know if I am going to take up for my boyfriend…or should I say a guy who is a friend. He's someone I was seeing last summer." she responded.

"Ouch, poor Mike. Put out like the cat." Joe said shaking his head.

"Don't mind them," Jenny said. "They're a bunch of busybody gossips."

"OOOHHH!" Al countered.

"Slide down here away from those old goats." she said, encouraging him to move to the opposite end of the counter. The old men gave up on their game and went back to their own conversation. "What brings you in here three days in a row, anyway?"

"If I said it was cause I thought you were attractive, you would probably be suspicious of me, wouldn't you?"

"Are you suggesting that I'm not attractive?" Jenny said knowing she was toying with him.

"Oh, for heaven sakes no!" he responded, getting flustered.

"I would hope not," Jenny said, posing with her hands on her hips.

"Oh boy, I might as well crawl in a hole and die," he said.

"No, I'm just playing. Let me start again. Hi, my name is Jenny and I'm the owner of this fine eating establishment. And you would be?"

"Hi, I'm Steve Leaks and it's very nice to make your acquaintance. And yes, I really do believe you are attractive, but that's not my reason for coming back here three days in a row. Actually, if you want to know the truth, I'm a spy."

"A what?"

"I'm your competition. Oh, don't worry, I'm not opening anything around here. I'm planning to open a restaurant, café, or luncheonette in an office building in downtown Norfolk. One day I was talking to one of the construction workers about the business and he told me about your place down here. He said you have the best burgers in town, and to be honest with you, I agree. That's why I've been here three days in a row."

"Where are you planning to put your business?"

"The plan is to open it on the ground level of this newly remodeled office building near the MacArthur Center. I'm renting the space and I think I can make a go of it with the right luck and maybe the right recipe for delicious burgers, dogs and sandwiches."

"That's interesting. So you really are spying on me?"

"Yeah, guilty as charged," he said hanging his head briefly, and then returning his gaze to her.

"I suppose you want some insider information that might help you be more successful in your venture. Do you have any experience working with food?"

"My uncle has a full-serve restaurant up in the Chicago area, and I worked for him during the summers when I was growing up. Now I want to strike out on my own."

"So you're not totally naive about restaurants."

"No, I'm well aware that it will be hard work."

"Well, maybe I could offer you a few pointers since you won't be offering me direct competition. Let's say Tuesday afternoon."

"Wow, you're kidding? You're going to help me? I can't believe it. Thank you. Thank you, Jenny," he said, shaking her hand.

"In the meantime, you can enjoy the menu and the view from that side of the counter." she said with a smile. He blushed and smiled back at her.

"I will."

Chapter Eleven

The holidays came and they went. Jenny made a trip out to see Mike in Emporia, and Mike made a trip back to Virginia Beach. It was obvious to both that the spark had gone out of their budding relationship. While they both pined for a deeper relationship, neither was willing to give up his or her career for the other. Jenny had hoped that Mike would want to move back to Virginia Beach; but after seeing how much he enjoyed his job in Emporia, it was obvious that he wasn't making plans to leave anytime soon.

Mike hoped that Jenny might want to leave the Bluebird and make an attempt at running the diner in Emporia. But even a trip to see the diner didn't change Jenny's mind. He knew when he kissed her good-bye after New Year's, he was kissing her good-bye for good. The tears stung his cheek as they rolled down his face.

Scarlette wasted no time trying to help Mike lick his wounds. Instead of pushing her away, he started to spend some time with her. She was flirting and since he didn't see many other prospects in the area, he began to let his guard down. Seeing him weaken slightly, she put on the full-court press to develop a relationship with Mike. It took Mike a while, but he finally started to go out with Scarlette.

Back in Virginia Beach, Jenny had been spending a great deal of her free time with Steve. She was helping and guiding him through the decisions he needed to make to get started in his business. Steve finally asked Jenny to go out to a movie with him; and having nothing better to do, she agreed. During the movie, they kissed for the first time. Jenny felt her heart tearing as she noticed that all thoughts of Mike were being washed away.

After two weeks of dating every night, Jenny asked Steve to spend the night, which he did. Jenny woke up happy and excited about where things were going. Here was a guy who shared the same dreams and understood the love she felt for serving others. Jenny slipped into the shower and worked on getting ready for the day at the café. Steve jumped into the shower behind her and was dressed when Jenny finished her breakfast. They kissed while he got his coffee, then Jenny scurried off to finish getting ready for work.

Steve asked Jenny if she had a minute to talk before she left for work. She explained that she was already running late. But he embraced her and convinced her to sit on the bed for a minute so they could talk.

"I was wondering something," he whispered in her ear.

"No, I have to go to work now," she said with a giggle.

Steve smiled and tickled her. "That wasn't what I wanted, but thanks for clearing that up. What I really wanted to know is if you would be willing to go away with me?"

"What? You can't go away now. Your restaurant is getting close to being finished, and you need to be there to keep an eye on things."

"The way I see it, once I'm open for business, I'll be so busy that I won't be able to get away. Now, I am not tied down, I could actually slip away for a few days and keep in contact by phone. Jenny, we've had some really nice times together; and I would just like to share some quiet, special time with you before I get too busy to do that."

"Where do you want to go?"

"I was thinking about the Florida Keys. I've never been down there, and I bet it would be great at this time of the year."

"I would have some things to work out myself; when do you think you would like to go?"

"I was thinking about a week from Monday, during the week. I thought that would be a less busy time for you. I figure the weekends are the busiest for you now."

"Yeah, that's right. So you want to take me away, huh?"

"Jenny, I'll pay for everything, plane fare, car rental, the hotel, the works…"

"Where are you getting all this money to take me away? You are just starting a new business."

"Don't you worry about that, just say, 'yes'…"

"OK," she said pushing him back on the bed. She gave him a sweet and passionate kiss, "but I need to get going. I do have a restaurant to run." She kissed his cheek and got up to leave.

"Thank you," he said softly from the bed.

"No," she said turning back to him, "Thank you."

For the next week, Steve started to come in the café to help with the lunch crowd. Jenny was giving him some practice on the grill, and he helped Carlos in the back with the cleanup. He felt that helping out was a practical way to really learn the business first hand. Jenny could see some previous experience shining through as he worked the grill and the customers, but he was still a bit green. He would have a lot to learn once he got started on his own, but she could help him.

It was obvious to the three old men that Jenny was falling for this guy. Carlos watched as the two carried on before, during and after the rush. He had a hard time being excited for Jenny. Something just didn't seem right to him. He couldn't put his finger on it, but something was wrong with this guy. Jenny was blinded by him.

For the next week, Jenny just seemed to float around work. It was a good thing that business was slow because Carlos didn't think Jenny was concentrating well enough for heavy summer traffic at the café. The old guys were giving her a hard time about her flightiness. She was so happy their comments just rolled off her back.

"Hey, sweetheart, how about floating down here and refilling my coffee." Al called to Jenny one day.

"I think I can handle that," she said squeezing his cheek. "How's that?"

"Sick. You are just sick, girl. I think you need the love doctor to cure you."

"Oh, that's okay." she said twirling around, "I feel great."

"I think I like you better when you are between boyfriends." Jack commented. "At least, then we don't have to put up with so much sappy, happy stuff."

"I love you, too," she said blowing him a kiss from across the counter.

"Yuck, I think I'll go home for the day before she starts to break into song. Then I'll lose the breakfast I just paid for."

"Love is a wonderful thing," she said.

"It's sick, if you ask me," Jack said.

The three old guys left and behind them the rest of the lunch crowd. Carlos, Steve, and Jenny worked on cleaning up. Steve took off before Jenny and Carlos finished and headed for his café in Norfolk. When Carlos was done, he came out to let Jenny know he was leaving.

"Hey, wait a minute," she called out. "I wanted to ask you something. Do you still keep in contact with Joe at all?"

"Yeah, we text each other. Why?"

"Well, I was wondering if he might be interested in coming down and helping you out for a couple days next week."

"Why, what's up?"

"Steve invited me to go away with him for a few days."

"What? And you're thinking of going?"

"Well, yeah! I think it would be fun."

"Do you think you might be rushing this thing a little, Jenny?"

"What?"

"I'm just worried about you, that's all." Carlos said.

"Well, thank you." Jenny said, taken aback a bit. "But don't worry, Steve is a nice guy. And besides, we're both adults."

"Are you sure Steve's alright? I have a bad feeling about him."

"Steve's great, so don't you worry. We have so much in common especially since we both own restaurants. The conversation is never dull. Anyway, do you think you can get a hold of Joe for me?"

"I'll text him and let you know what he says."

"Great, see if he can come down for four days."

"Alright. I'll see you tomorrow," he said, wishing he could change her mind.

****

Joe arrived late on Sunday night. He was ready to go on Monday morning. Jenny was packed and ready to go to the Keys for a four-day trip. Carlos told Joe about his concerns, but Joe only said it was Jenny's life, and she could choose to live it any way she wanted. Carlos and Joe had a great four days at the Bluebird. It was just like summer when the place was filled with laughter.

Jenny returned from the trip a little tired, but smiling from ear to ear. She had picked up a nice tan and a few little gifts for Carlos, Joe and the old men. She beamed with the delight of early romance. Joe wanted to hang around through the weekend, but the forecasters were calling for a few inches of fresh powder up in the mountains. That meant he really needed to be back for the crowd.

Jenny and Steve spent the next couple of weeks working the Bluebird for breakfast and lunch and then going to Steve's café and putting the finishing touches on his place. They were almost inseparable.

****

Scarlette was getting hard to resist. Mike tried to hold her back, but she was coming on strong. One Friday night after a long week, Mike took Scarlette out for Pizza and beer. He lost count on the number of beers he had consumed and he was feeling pretty good. Scarlette picked up on this, and stepped up her campaign to press the relationship to the next level.

Mike invited Scarlette back to his place; and since the roads had become icy, she asked if she could spend the night there. Mike hesitated, looked out the window and then decided she could stay. She flew back to his bedroom and jumped into bed. Mike made his way to the linen closet and got a blanket and a pillow and headed for the couch.

"What are you doing?"

"I'm getting out some bedding so I can sleep on the couch."

"Oh no, you don't," she said pulling him into the bedroom and throwing him on the bed. "I've waited long enough for you, and tonight you are mine!" she said as she pulled off his shirt and removed her own. His defenses were down and she was taking full advantage of it. Mike lost all his resistance and allowed his hormones to make the decisions. Things were moving along just as Scarlette had hoped when his phone rang.

"Don't answer it," she whispered in his ear.

"Don't worry about it. I don't plan to answer it." The answering machine kicked on and the voice on the other end spoke,

"Mike? Are you there? This is an emergency, pick up the phone, man. Hey Mike…"

"Yeah. Yeah. I'm here, what's up, Chip?"

"Oh, man, we've got a terrible accident out here on 95. There are at least six vehicles involved and there may be fatalities. Oh God!" he yelled. "There goes another vehicle into the pile. You need to get out here as quick as you can."

"Uh, well uh…"

"Tell Scarlette you'll see her later. We need you out here now!"

"Yeah, man. I'll be out there as soon as I can. Are you north or south bound?"

"North. Less than a mile from the exit. Hey, Mike, stop and pick up several coffees and a few blankets; it's going to be a long, cold night."

"Right." And with that Mike was dressing for a cold night outside. Scarlette just lay back in bed.

"I guess we'll have to save this for later, huh?" she said in siren-like tones.

"Yeah, I guess so," he said reluctantly, looking down at her warm and tempting body. Within five minutes he was out scraping ice off his cruiser and warming it up. He carefully made his way to the crash site and began to help with the cleanup and directing traffic.

The dense clouds obscured the rising sun over the horizon before things were finally finishing up out at the wreck scene. The captain ordered everyone to Myrtle's Diner on highway 58. They were all glad to see the inside of the greasy place where they could thaw out and get a hot meal. Myrtle's was nothing like the Bluebird; but when you are cold and hungry, anything can taste good. Each guy drank what seemed like a pot of coffee trying to warm up. It had been a long night for the guys, and they all longed for a hot shower and some sleep.

Some of the guys finished up and headed for home. Mike slid down next to Chip, and they talked for a few minutes about the wreck before Mike asked,

"Chip, how did you know Scarlette was up my place tonight?"

"You're the new blood in town, and she likes new blood. I have to admit it has taken her a while to hook you, but it sounds like she's got you now."

"What do you mean, 'new blood' and 'got me now'?"

"Don't tell me you're falling for this, 'I just want to settle down with someone like you' crap?"

"She's told me that, yeah."

"Don't believe it. She'll chew you up for the next couple of months then spit you out like yesterday's news."

"Scarlette?"

"Hey, guys," Chip said to the rest of the officers at the table, "how many of you have been with Scarlette?" Over half raised their hands and then went right back to their conversations. "You're her temporary squeeze. Don't get me wrong, it's probably the best you'll get around here, but it's temporary."

Mike was visibly stunned. He took a long sip of his coffee.

"Hey, man, haven't you ever had any girls like that in Virginia Beach?" The mere mention of the place made Mike think of Jenny. His heart ached for her.

"No," he said quietly. "I didn't know Scarlette was that way. Thanks for warning me. I don't give my heart away that easily."

"It's not your heart she's after," he said punching him in the arm.

****

Several weeks had passed and the endless cold of winter had gripped Virginia Beach. Jenny was glad to see the six inch snowfall close things down for a couple of days. She spent them resting and thinking she was fighting a stomach bug.

"Carlos, I need your help up here on the grill man." Jenny's voice called from out front. Carlos came quickly, and Al and Jack started to lend a hand. Jenny made a mad dash for the bathroom. When she came back, she said, "I must have gotten into some bad food somewhere. We've been eating so much takeout lately that I couldn't even begin to guess where I got it."

"Yeah, right." said Carlos, as he headed back to the backroom. "Call me if you need me again."

"What's up with him? Hadn't he ever had a stomach bug that seemed to hold on for a while?"

"Hey, it's alright." Jack said. "But in his defense, you should have gotten over it by now. Maybe you got something else. You should go to the doctor."

"I've thought about it, but I go through periods of feeling good then I feel sick all over again."

"Just don't let it go too long," Jack said.

When the lunch crowd had eaten and gone, Carlos and Jenny went about their usual cleaning routines. Carlos stayed in the back while Jenny got the grill broken down and cleaned up. When Carlos had finished, he poked his head out and announced,

"I'm done back here so I think I'll head for home."

"Wait a minute. You seem out of order, like something is bothering you."

"I'm alright. I just got to go today."

"No, something's up. You've never kept anything from me before, so don't start now. What's up?"

"I told you nothing," he said looking down.

"Now hold on there," she said grabbing hold of his hand and pulling him over to a stool. "Tell me what's bothering you."

"It's you, alright!"

"Me! What have I done?"

"You've been sick and you're not using your head."

"What do you mean?"

"Look, you're sick mainly in the mornings, and you feel better in the afternoons."

"Hey, if you've got to be sick isn't that the way to do it?" she said with a laugh.

"You just don't get it," he said, exasperated.

"What? I'm sick in the mornings…Oh my God. You think I'm pregnant!"

"Well, you're showing the signs."

"Oh my God," said Jenny, "that's not funny. I told you I got into some bad food or the stomach bug that is going around.."

"You'd be over either one of those in a couple of days, if that was the case."

"Well, maybe. But I'm not pregnant. We use protection and I am on the pill. So, will you stop worrying about me and get out of here for the day. Pregnant! God."

"Whatever you say. See you tomorrow." Carlos headed for the door, took one last look back at her, shook his head and was gone.

"Pregnant. I can't be pregnant," she thought to herself. Jenny wiped the counter thinking things over. He was right about her feeling badly in the morning and then feeling better as the day wore on. But pregnant?

Jenny finished up at the restaurant and locked the door on her way out. The north wind blew, and the clouds hung heavily in the sky. Some light snow was in the forecast again. She made a couple of stops on the way home, but once there she succumbed to an afternoon nap.

When she woke up, she lay in bed for a long while before getting up. Finally, she got up and went to the kitchen and picked up a bag that lay on the counter. She pulled out the pregnancy kit and carefully read the instructions. Ten minutes later she was sitting on the couch waiting for the timer to go off. When she heard it beep she shut it off. With a deep breath she reached out and took hold of the test stick. She looked down and found the positive result staring her right in the face.

****

Mike went to the sheriff and asked if he might have a couple of days off. He agreed as long as Mike didn't take his time on the weekend. On a Tuesday morning, Mike packed up a few things and headed to Virginia Beach. He couldn't wait to see Jenny. He missed her and wanted to see if they could work things out. Mike had also contacted his old supervisor with the Virginia Beach police force to set up an appointment. He wanted to know if he could get his old job back. Mike could hardly wait to get there.

****

Jenny left several messages in Steve's voicemail, but Steve hadn't returned any of her calls. She wanted to talk to him, to tell him the news. Finally, she decided she would drive down to Norfolk and see him at his café. When she pulled up to the building, she saw a group of construction workers working in the café, which confused her because she thought they were almost done the last time she came down to see the place.

"Excuse me," she said to one of the workers, "can you tell me where Steve is?"

"Who's Steve?"

"He's the owner of this restaurant."

"Ha, you're funny, lady. This ain't no restaurant, it's a movie set. The movie company shot their film and now we're tearing it down."

"No, Steve Leaks owns this place, and I've been helping him get it ready for business."

"Lady, you're confused. I've never heard of a Steve Leaks and I've got a job to finish." and he turned his back on Jenny and returned to work.

"Excuse me," she said "here is his picture on my cell phone. This is Steve Leaks. Have you seen him?"

"Yeah, that is the star of the movie they shot here. He finished up and left town already. No wonder I didn't recognize that name you said."

Jenny went back to her car and just stared at the men as they tore apart the restaurant that she thought she was helping Steve build. She picked up her cell phone and dialed his number once again,

"Steve, if you are there, I really need to talk to you. Give me a call. Love you. Bye." Jenny sat and watched the demolition crew tear the place apart. After ten minutes, she turned the key in her ignition and headed for home.

****

"Boss, it's Robb. I just heard from one of the guys down at the restaurant. They've been tearing it down and this lady showed up, it was Jenny. The guys told her it was a Hollywood set and that Steve was an actor in a major film. She left the site blubbering. So I think she is putting some of the pieces together. She is also leaving some desperate-sounding voicemail for our boy."

"Sounds good to me. Keep up the good work."

****

Jenny pulled into her place, an emotional wreck. Even the warm winter sun setting in the western sky couldn't lift Jenny's dark clouds. She didn't know what to do. Steve had always come to her place; she had never been to his. She had no idea how to get in contact with him and let him know that he was going to be a father. "Oh, no," she thought, "I'm going to be a mother." She sat in her car and cried.

Jenny pulled herself together and got herself inside where she started to cry all over again. She didn't know what to do or where to turn. She called Steve's number again and left another message. Then she threw herself on her bed and cried. About twenty minutes later, there was a knock on her door. Jenny ran to the door and said,

"Steve, I've been trying to get a hold of you…. Oh my God, Mike! What are you doing here?"

"Obviously, I wasn't the one you expected. Maybe I should leave."

"No! Are you kidding? Please don't leave." she hugged him, clung to him and began to cry almost uncontrollably.

"Jenny," he said picking her up and carrying her inside, "what's wrong?"

"Oh, everything." she said through her tears.

"It can't be all bad. Besides, I'm here."

"Oh, Mike, you are a sight for sore eyes."

"Thank you. You look great, too."

"I must look a mess. I've been crying. My world is coming unglued, and I don't know what I'm going to do."

"Just sit back and tell me all about it. Maybe I can help you sort through the details." Jenny did just that. She told him about meeting Steve and helping him plan for his business, which ended up not being a business after all. When she told Mike that she went to the Florida Keys with Steve, she noticed that he stiffened up, so she decided not to tell him she was pregnant.

Mike asked Jenny for a description of Steve. When she was done, he called a friend from the police force in Virginia Beach and asked if they could do a little background check and find out something about the business/movie set in downtown Norfolk. Mike's friend said he would get back to him. Mike and Jenny spent the rest of the evening catching up.

Mike told Jenny about the police force in Emporia. He told her about some people he met in the new church he was attending and how he spent his days off. Mike decided he should tell Jenny about meeting Scarlette. He even admitted to going on a few dates with her, but that was it.

The night grew long, and they both were enjoying each other's company. Mike's friend called back and told him he was drawing a blank with the information about Steve. He told Mike that he would continue to look into it, but not to expect much. Because of the late hour, Jenny invited Mike to spend the night on the couch, which he accepted.

In the morning, Jenny took off for the café as usual, and Mike showered and came down for breakfast later. After breakfast, Mike met with his former boss down at police headquarters in Virginia

Beach. The meeting went well, but there were no openings on the police force at the time. Mike was disappointed, but he understood. Mike also checked with his friend to see if he found out anything else about Steve and the business/movie set in Norfolk. The friend came up empty.

When Jenny got home from work, Mike was there waiting for her. Jenny lay down for about an hour; then she got up and took a shower. She got herself ready to go out to dinner with Mike.

"Are you sure you want to go out?" he asked. "I saw you got sick this morning at the café."

"Yeah, thanks, I do want to go out. My stomach is probably upset from all this stress and worry over what happened to Steve." With that assurance they headed out the door to a nice dinner. It was a clear and cold night. The stars overhead were dancing like fairies in the frigid dark sky. They considered a walk on the beach, but opted instead for staying in to watch a movie. They chose a light romantic comedy, which helped to take their minds off their problems. When the DVD was over, Jenny started the conversation,

"Mike," she said hesitantly, "I am afraid I haven't been totally honest with you about one thing."

"What is it?" he said after he put the DVD back in the case and put his glass and the popcorn bowl in the kitchen sink.

"It's personal and scary. I'm afraid you'll hate me," she said and a tear fell from her cheek. Mike returned to the couch and gently wiped the tear away.

"You can tell me. It'll be alright." She felt safe in his big, strong arms.

"Well, it's about Steve and me. I told you we went to the Keys together."

"Yes," he said and stiffened slightly, sitting back on the couch.

"Well, when two people are away like that, you know…"

"Yes, Jenny. I kind of figured you two had been together."

"Well, that's not the worst part. Mike, I got pregnant."

"What?" he reacted strongly.

"Don't be upset. I don't know how it happened. I mean we were being safe and used protection."

"Well, evidently it didn't work."

"No, you're kidding." she said sarcastically.

"I don't believe what I am hearing," he said, getting up and walking around the room. "How could you?" Jenny started to cry. "I thought we had something here." Jenny started to cry harder.

"I'm sorry, but you've been gone to Emporia and what am I supposed to do, wait around for you?"

"I don't know. Do you know I looked into my old job today? I was willing to leave what I had out there because I wanted to be with you."

"What?" she said between her tears.

"That's right. I was planning on coming back here because I wanted to be with you." Jenny looked up at him, tears streaming down her face. "You know, I could have dealt with the fact that you two had been together, but a baby. What am I supposed to do with another guy's baby? A guy you can't even find anymore!" There was a moment of silence before Mike continued, "I can't handle this. I'm out of here!"

With that, Mike grabbed his things and threw them into his suitcase. Jenny pleaded with Mike to stay. Mike didn't even respond to her. He picked up everything and rushed to his car. Jenny cried and begged Mike to stay, but he was gone. Jenny fell down on the driveway and cried uncontrollably. It was the emptiest and loneliest she had ever felt in her whole life.

Mike flew down the road on his way back to Emporia. It was a good thing for him that there were no cops on the road. When he was about five miles from Emporia, he pulled out his phone and punched in a number.

"Hello," came the voice from the other end.

"Are you up to some company?" Mike asked.

"Yeah, come on over."

"I'll be there in less than ten minutes." Mike pulled into the Texaco and grabbed a twelve pack of beer. He consumed three before he knocked on the door. Scarlette answered, wearing a silky red chemise. Mike kissed her and opened his fourth beer, chugging most of it in the first gulp. Tossing the can aside, he picked up Scarlette and carried her back to her bedroom.

Chapter Twelve

The next afternoon Jenny was in Pastor Andrews's office talking to him about all that had happened. She found him to be much less judgmental than Mike and thanked him for his understanding. He reminded Jenny that the church frowns upon sex before marriage. She freely admitted that was an area that she needed to work on and wished she had started earlier. She told Pastor Andrews that she was sorry for what she had done and wished it hadn't happened. He explained to Jenny there was grace for sins where there was repentance, but that there were consequences for sin. In her situation, it was the baby, and she had to face up to the responsibility.

Jenny sighed as she realized that she had a tough road ahead of her, especially if she was going to be a single mom. The thought scared her, but she had made an adult mistake, and she had to own up to the consequences. About thirty minutes into their conversation, Jenny noticed that Pastor Andrews was distracted. She made three really off the wall comments hoping he would respond to them, but he didn't. He was obviously no longer listening to Jenny.

"Pastor, what's the matter?"

"Huh, what?"

"You're distracted about something. What's up?"

"Oh, nothing. I'm sorry."

"What are you looking at?"

"Nothing," he said hiding a piece of newspaper.

"What's that?" Jenny demanded. And like a little boy caught with his hand in the cookie jar, Pastor Andrews handed Jenny the newspaper.

"Oh, it's the series of articles that lady has been writing about the modern church. I haven't had the chance to read this week's installment. Is it good?"

"It's troubling," he responded. "She took some things I said and either twisted them slightly or took them completely out of context."

"I thought she had been fair with her assessment up until this point. Here, let me read it and see what I think." Jenny began to read the article. When she had finished, she looked at the pastor, who looked like he was miles away and said; "I can see your concern. Some of those statements could reflect badly on our church and on you in particular."

"I think so, too. I've read that article five times, and I've come up with the same conclusions. She was so nice to me, to all of us in the church community. I just can't believe she would misrepresent us and, in particular, me in this way."

"Have you called her?"

"I've left several messages, but no response."

"Well, you're very articulate. Why don't you write a response to what she wrote? You know, give yourself a chance to clear up a few things."

"You know, Jenny, that's a great idea. Marge," he said picking up the phone, "do I have any appointments for the rest of the day?" She confirmed that his calendar was clear. "Good, I have something I need to do. Thanks," he said hanging up the phone. "And thanks to you too, Jenny. You've helped me a great deal." He said helping her to her feet.

"But I'm not finished talking with you..."

"We'll talk more later. I need to get to work on this response," he said escorting her out of his office and closing the door behind her. Jenny stood in the hall just staring at the door shocked by being put out like the cat. She shook her head and left the church. Jenny felt somewhat consoled but at the same time put out, literally, by the pastor.

****

It was about noon when Mike woke up in a strange place. He immediately noticed that his head was throbbing and his mouth felt dry. Mike sat up and found a couple of empty beer cans on the nightstand and several more on the floor. That explained the throbbing head. Now, he needed to figure out where he was. He tried to get his mind to focus when, all of a sudden, a voice spoke to him,

"Good morning, sleepy head. I thought you were going to sleep all day." He suddenly remembered where he was and whose voice he was hearing. It was Scarlette, and he was at her place. Mike allowed his feet to hang over the edge of the bed, and then he pulled the sheet back…and quickly pulled the sheet back over himself.

"Oh, don't be bashful." Scarlette said. "You were wonderful." It was all falling back into place for him. He could hardly think because his head was throbbing so badly. "Would you like some breakfast? Or would you prefer lunch? Or maybe we can go straight for some more dessert," she purred, while caressing his chest.

"Breakfast would be nice," he said in a groggy voice that was not quite his own.

"There are some fresh towels under the sink, help yourself. I'll get breakfast started."

Mike stumbled to the shower and allowed the water to massage his hung-over body. The water had a therapeutic effect on the cobwebs in his mind even though his head continued to pound from the effects of the alcohol. Mike quickly ate his breakfast and escaped before Scarlette could get her talons deeper into him.

****

Craig yelled out from his office, "Hey, Eve. Get yourself in here, please." She quickly made her way to his office and closed the door as she entered. "Sit down." He barked. "This piece you've been doing on the church has been great. It's been even-handed journalism up to this point and I applaud your effort."

"Well, thank you," she said with false humility.

"However."

"Somehow I thought there might be a 'however'," she said.

"However, this last one was way too sharp. It's like you were throwing daggers at this guy, uh…Pastor Andrews. I've reread your piece, and I can see how your statements could have been focusing on the church as a whole and not on his specific church. The problem is it could also be interpreted that your comments were referring to him and his church."

"Oh, I did not mean for that to happen at all," she said, knowing it was a lie.

"Well, he called and emailed me a response; and while it is a bit long, it's good. I am going to edit it and get it in tomorrow's paper. I just wanted you to know, I'm not undermining you, but I also want you to be more careful when you write."

"Can I read his response?"

"Yeah, it's right there," she picked it up and quickly scanned it.

"Look," she said after scanning it, "I see what he's trying to say. Since I messed up on the article, how about I edit his response and save you the time."

"No, I'm going to edit it myself. It wouldn't be right for you to do it."

"Right and wrong." she said coming around his desk and twirling him in his chair to face her. "They're such abstract concepts in newspapers." She sat down on his lap, allowing her perfume to intoxicate him. "Some things," she said while caressing his broad shoulders, "seem just out of our reach. We desire it, but we just can't seem to have it. Do you know what I mean?" He nodded while lightly caressing her arm and shoulder.

"Now the way I see it, there is something you wish you could have, and there is something that I wish I could do," her voice hissed softly like a snake in his ear. "Now I wonder if we might work out some kind of compromise?"

She leaned forward and allowed him to kiss her neck. She pulled back, smiled and winked at him. She reached onto his desk and picked up the email. She kissed him on the cheek and walked over to the door. Before she left, she turned and smiled at him.

"Thanks," she said suductively, "you won't be disappointed." She winked at him and walked out.

****

Mike drove over to Lake Gaston and found a private place where he could release some of the anger he had towards himself.

"How could you let yourself do that, you idiot!" he yelled, hurling a rock at a tree. "You weren't thinking; you were just reacting to Jenny's news of an upcoming baby. What's the matter with you? You know better!" as he flung a stick at another tree. "You would think you would have better self-control than that. Jenny was hurting and in trouble and all you did was think about yourself. You are just a selfish idiot. Now Scarlette has her talons in you, what do you plan to do about that…you jerk!"

Mike walked and seethed at himself for an hour before he allowed himself to sit quietly by the water. "Oh, God, you must be terribly disappointed in me. I am so sorry that I let you down." Mike stayed by the river allowing the peace in nature to work on the whirlwind in his heart. While he was mad at himself, he knew God's forgiveness was greater than his sin.

Mike knew he had to forgive Jenny and not blame her for his stupidity. He also knew he needed to apologize for his behavior. She needed a friend, and he abandoned her in an hour of great need. He knew he needed to call and apologize to Jenny and to find a way to forgive himself for his selfish behavior.

****

The morning paper arrived, and Pastor Andrews was up early to look at it. He skipped the front-page news and the sports page. He wanted to see the editorials. He opened the page and saw what he hoped to see, his name above an editorial. He smiled with pleasure as he sat down and began to read it. But his smile disappeared when he realized that these words were not his, but they were a twisted version of what he had written so eloquently. The more he read, the more his heart sank, and the more anger rose up within him. Someone had taken his words and made him look like a babbling baboon.

By nine o'clock in the morning, there were ten calls from angry parishioners on his answering machine. He called the church and told Marge that he wasn't coming in for the day. She immediately knew why. The phone hadn't stopped ringing all morning. Pastor Andrews decided that he needed to confront the editor of the paper in person.

Pastor Andrews arrived at the newspaper building and asked to speak with the editor. He only had to wait a few minutes before he was escorted to his office. He expressed his anger at how his response had been butchered in the paper and asked that his subscription be cancelled. The editor tried to apologize and explained that his response was a little long so they decided to edit it a little. Pastor Andrews asked why they didn't tell him and give him the chance to shorten his piece. The editor explained that there wasn't really time to call everyone who sent in something they wanted in the paper.

"Look, Mr. Andrews, I haven't read the response yet, let me take a look at it now."

"What? I thought you said that you would personally handle this for me."

"Something came up, and I gave it to one of my assistants."

"I'd like a few words with that flunky."

"Hold on, let me read this thing." Craig went and got a copy of the paper and within minutes understood why Pastor Andrews was in his office. He returned sullen and angry himself. "Look, we will do something about this."

"I would hope so."

"I'll try to run your entire original response tomorrow."

"You'll try? Or you WILL!"

"Look, I said I am sorry. We'll get it in the paper in the morning." Craig worked to smooth out the feathers that he agreed should be ruffled. Craig looked around and noticed that Eve was conspicuously missing.

After confronting the editor, Pastor Andrews decided to take a walk on the beach. The sun felt warm, but the air was brisk so he zipped up his jacket. He walked along the beach and periodically sat and watched the pounding surf. All the while he complained to God about how unfair things were and focused all his thoughts on himself. But after an hour of fussing and fuming, he got quiet before God.

That's when he began to think of other people in his congregation who were also going through hard times. The longer he considered it, the more he realized that it wasn't just a random bad thing that happened to them. There was a whole group of people who were going through bad times, good people who were facing larger than life crises. He started to make a mental list of people who had called him over the past six months suffering from some type of outside pressure. When he was done, he had come up with over twenty names.

Pastor Andrews was getting a revelation, but he didn't know what to do with this newfound insight. He kept walking and praying, asking God to give him wisdom. The only thought he had was that he should try to get the group together and figure out what they all had in common and see if they could figure out the source of these… these… attacks.

"Lord," he said, "these people won't get together with me, particularly after they read the article in the paper today. I need a sign from you that this is your plan." There was silence. "Please God show me a sign, so I don't think I am crazy." He looked up and in the distance he saw the answer to his prayer, the Bluebird Café.

Ding-a-ling, rang the bell over the door. Jenny looked up to see Pastor Andrews entering the cafe.

"Hey, Pastor," she said. "How are you?"

"I'm better than I was this morning," he said excitedly. That's when he noticed he was hungry, or maybe it was the wonderful aroma of the food cooking on the grill that made him hungry. "Can I get one of your world-famous burgers, Jenny?"

"Coming right up," she said. It was obvious to Jenny that the pastor had something on his mind; so she was glad when the crowd cleared out and they could have a chance to talk.

"Have you had the chance to read the morning paper?" Pastor Andrews asked.

"I glanced through the front section and sports between the breakfast and lunch rush, if you want to call the few customers I've had today a rush."

"I guess you haven't read my 'response' to the article the other day."

"No, but I'm sure it's good."

"You would be wrong about that. Someone down there edited what I wrote and made me look pretty bad. I don't even want to think about it. But that's not what I want to talk to you about anyway. Well it is, but it isn't."

"Slow down," Jenny said getting herself a glass of tea. "Let's go sit in a booth, and you can start over, from the beginning."

Pastor Andrews picked up his plate and drink, and Jenny carried a slice of pie to go with her tea. Jenny locked the door and turned the sign around that said, "closed." She slid into the booth across from Pastor Andrews and gave him a big smile.

"OK, now let's start from the beginning," she said.

"The first thing I need to do is apologize to you."

"What are you talking about?"

"I was self-centered and focusing on my own problems the other day when you came by my office. It's easy to do, and I want to ask your forgiveness."

"I did feel a little put out by you, so thank you. But what's going on that has you all excited?"

"Jenny, I think there is something bigger going on than some hit-and-miss stuff. I think we may be under some kind of spiritual attack."

"Who's the 'we'?"

"Jenny, there are about twenty people who have been in my office over the past six months who are facing larger than life problems. To have one or two big problems in a congregation our size would be normal, but twenty? To be honest with you and as delicate as I can be, I don't think Steve showing up right after Mike left for Emporia was an accident. I don't think this article in the paper is an accident. I think it might be an orchestrated attack."

"Wow, I don't know what to think. Are all the people you are thinking about from our church?"

"Most, but not all of them and that's interesting too. The people who are not members chose to talk with me, isn't that interesting? I didn't start putting it all together until today. I don't know what the connection is; but if we can find that, then we can find the source of all these problems."

"How do you propose doing that?"

"That's where I'm stuck. I want to call all these people and see if they would agree to meet with me as a group. They've all met with me individually, but a group setting would be different. What do you think?"

"I don't know. In a way, you would be breaking their confidentiality."

"I've thought about that, but it's a risk I think I have to take. Do you think it's a crazy idea?"

"Not really, although I don't know what everyone else will think. Where would you try to meet?"

"I hate to intrude upon you, but I was thinking about here at the Bluebird. We would meet in the evening when you are closed so we wouldn't interfere with your business. We could meet at my church, but I may not have a job after next Sunday."

"Now, Pastor, no one is going to kick you out. You will stand up and talk to your congregation on Sunday and explain what happened and people will fall in behind you. It won't be easy, but I have full confidence in you."

"Thanks, Jenny. I needed to hear that."

"And if you want to have this meeting, let's hold it here at the Bluebird."

"Thank you, Jenny. I could kiss you right now, but that wouldn't be appropriate," he said, trying to contain his enthusiasm.

"Yeah, I would say so, particularly in my condition," she said rubbing her tummy.

"Oh, I'm sorry Jenny. I didn't mean to…"

"I was just joking. So when do you want to plan this little meeting?"

"Next week. Can I call you later with the details?"

"That would be fine." With that Pastor Andrews was on his feet heading for the door. He stopped and turned back to Jenny and gave her a big hug.

"Thanks, I really appreciate your support. You're an answer to prayer."

"You're welcome. I'll be praying for you."

"Bye, Jenny," he said as the door closed behind him. He got half way around the building when another thought struck him. He returned to the café and asked Jenny, "Is there any chance you could help me with another problem?"

"What is it?"

"I've been walking the beach most of the morning. I think my car might be four or five miles down the beach…"

"Say no more, I'll get my purse." Jenny gave the Pastor a lift to his car and then returned to finish cleaning up the café.

****

Robb Thomas picked up his cell phone and punched in a number. "Hello, Boss. I just saw something and thought I should make you aware. I saw that girl who owns the café driving down the road with the pastor in her car."

"Too bad you didn't have a camera; we could really have some fun with that."

"Yeah, the pastor and his mistress, the young café owner." The two men laughed out loud.

"Thanks for the call and the laugh. I don't think it's anything to worry about. The plan seems to be moving right along. I think we are about ready for a special appearance, don't you?"

"I believe we are just about ready."

"Good. I'll book a flight for next week. Set the rest up on your end."

"I'll take care of it, Boss."

Chapter Thirteen

Pastor Andrews always went to bed early on Saturday night so he would be as fresh as possible for Sunday morning services. This particular Saturday night was different. He was writing and re-writing his sermon to carefully convey his thoughts to what he figured would be a hostile crowd. He hadn't returned any of the sixty calls he had received from the parishioners. He had, however, talked to the elders individually to try to explain what had happened. They were not happy with him, but they understood the situation.

The paper, for its part, did print Pastor Andrews's response in its entirety, but waited until Sunday morning to do so. That meant that most of the parishioners hadn't read it yet. Needless to say, they had all read the earlier edition. It was quite obvious to Pastor Andrews that his congregation had come to church this particular morning loaded for bear.

The choir sang its hymns and the people joined in; but Pastor Andrews felt all eyes were on him, and they felt like needles in the back of his head. When the choir began their last song, Pastor Andrews took the opportunity to say a little prayer. The last note was played, the offering received, and the moment of truth arrived.

"Good morning," Pastor Andrews began. "Thank you for coming this morning. I imagine that many of you in this room are very upset with me. To be quite honest with you, if I were you, I would be angry with me too. But the truth is, the words you read in the paper were not my words at all.

"This morning the newspaper has run my response in full to the article that started this whole thing. There was no apology, just a statement that the previous response was edited, and that it might have made some minor differences in the meaning of what I was trying to communicate. Let me tell you, there are major differences. So big are the differences that I made copies for each of you to read. If the ushers would come forward to distribute them, I would appreciate it. I hope you will take time to read what I really said in response.

"I know you are angry. To be totally honest with you, I'm angry too. I am so angry that I have contacted a lawyer, and we are considering a liable suit." He saw shock in the faces of some of the people. "Does that surprise you? I was misquoted and this congregation has been maliciously hurt by the twisting of my words in the paper. You are my flock, and a wolf has tried to come in and separate you from me. I love you all; and if you know me, you know I would never say the things that were printed in the paper about you." He could see that he was winning some hearts back. At this point everyone had received a copy of his response, and he gave the congregation a few moments to read it. Then he continued,

"Let me talk to you about how I really feel about you and about where I think our church is going." With that, he launched into a warm and inviting presentation. He spoke with passion and a deep love for his people. When it was over, he felt the tide had changed. He hadn't won everyone over to his thinking, but he was well on the way. He knew he had won the opportunity to at least be in the pulpit the next Sunday, and he hoped he would be able to win this battle.

After church, there were still those who were less than pleased with the pastor. The most vocal was a woman who had only been attending for about a month. She was in her seventies and had gathered a crowd to complain to. People enjoy complaining, and she was stoking what fires she could. She dropped the suggestion that maybe they needed a new pastor around there. Most of those in the group around her agreed with her up to a point. While they thought he should pay for his mistakes, getting rid of him seemed a bit extreme. Besides, finding a new pastor was always a difficult job, and he had been doing a pretty good job up until this point.

After the plump little woman had stirred the pot, she got into her Buick and headed for home. She walked into her apartment and immediately unzipped her dress allowing it to fall to the floor. Then she unzipped a rubberized fat suit to reveal perfectly smooth skin. Then the woman went over to the mirror and pulled at the wrinkled face until it released from her skin. She pulled the mask off to reveal her youthful, tan skin. Eve looked at herself in the mirror and smiled.

****

"Boss, this is Robb. I have your travel arrangements ready, and I think the stage is set for your arrival. We have effectively scattered or taken down everyone on our list except one."

"Who's missing?"

"It's the doctor. Eve's in a little hot water over the article about the preacher, so she has to let the editor cool off a bit before she does the expose' on the doctor."

"Is she going to be able to do it?"

"She promised me she would do whatever it took to get her stuff in the paper."

"That's my Eve," he sighed appreciatively.

"I've made the reservations at the hotel, and I'll meet you at the airport."

"I guess I'll have to get used to riding in a cheap car," he said with obvious distaste.

"No, you better get used to driving yourself around."

"Oh, that's terrible. I haven't driven a car in several years."

"Well, you might want to practice. It can be quite busy around here, particularly when the military bases let out."

"What other bad news have you got for me?"

"I've gone to the trouble to order you some clothes so you can dress the part."

"Oh, why did Charlie wear such frumpy clothes?" he said looking at his picture on his desk. "You think I need to wear that kind of crap to pull this off?"

"Yes, but you really don't have to come down at all if you don't want to. I can take care of things myself.

"Oh no. I want the pleasure of taking that café off her hands personally. Have you got the demolition team ready to go?"

"Yes, Boss, but we have to take care of the legal matters such as the fake will, getting the court to transfer ownership to you first."

"You've got all the paperwork in line, don't you?"

"Yes, and we know which judge we want, too."

"Good. How long before you think we can watch that café get smashed to smithereens?"

"It could take a month, possibly longer to get it through the courts."

"Over a month?"

"We'll try to get it done as quickly as possible. You know how the legal system works…in slow motion."

"Alright. Send me the details on my flight plans, and I'll see you next week."

"Right, Boss."

****

Mike finished writing a speeding ticket for the motorist and realized he was just a short distance from Wendy's, so he decided it was time for lunch. He checked in with the dispatcher and made his way to Wendy's.

He sat by himself next to the window, thinking about Jenny. He knew he was wrong to walk away from a friend in need, but it was just too much to handle at the moment. If Mike was honest with himself, he really did love Jenny. The obvious problem was the baby. What if Steve returned and wanted to be with Jenny and his child? Jealous thoughts filled his head.

Mike decided he had to make another trip to see Jenny. He had to apologize and see if he could be of some help. He hoped Jenny could find it in her heart to forgive him. He was so lost in thought that he didn't see Scarlette standing right beside him. She finally cleared her throat to get his attention.

"Scarlette, I'm sorry I didn't see you. Please sit down." She was the last person he wanted to see right now.

"Well, how have you been since the other night?"

"Wonderful!" he lied. "And you?"

"Great. But I'm missing you. When you going to come pay me a visit again?" she said with a flirtatious little smile.

"Soon," he lied again. "I have to work some overtime to catch up on the emergency trip back to the beach." He lied a third time. Mike didn't like lying, but he felt he had to because he really didn't want to let Scarlette know he was really thinking about Jenny. After all, she was there for him when he was upset, although he wished that it had not been her.

Scarlette made some small talk, and Mike forced himself to join in. Mike was relieved when his lunch break was over. He gave Scarlette a quick hug and headed back to his patrol car. She followed him; and when he got to the car door, she planted a passionate kiss on him. Mike pulled away and quickly returned to duty.

****

"Jenny, this is Pastor Andrews. Would Thursday evening be OK to meet at the Bluebird?"

"That would be fine. What time are you coming?"

"About seven."

"No problem. I'll order a few extra pies for everyone to enjoy."

"Thanks, Jenny. I really appreciate this. Please pray that everyone will show up."

"I will. See you Thursday."

****

Mike walked into the Sheriff's office. "You are doing a good job, Mike." The sheriff said without any prompt. "You're meeting your ticket quota, and the locals find you to be a nice polite young man. I'm glad you're on our force here."

"Thank you, sir. What prompted that?"

"Just thought you might like a little feedback."

"I appreciate that."

"What can I do for you?" the sheriff asked.

"I noticed on the schedule that I'm working the morning shift on Thursday and then the late shift on Friday. I was wondering if I could cut out a couple hours early on Thursday. I'll be here for my shift Friday."

"Where is it this time? Back to the Beach?"

"Yes, sir."

"Got a woman back there?"

"No. I've got some fence mending I need to do."

"A woman?" he repeated.

"Yes."

"You better be careful, Scarlette can be a mighty jealous type."

"Thanks for the tip."

"Mend that fence and be back here ready to work on Friday."

"Thanks, I appreciate it." Mike took the cue and headed out of the office.

****

The Boss's plane landed at 7:30 sharp at Norfolk International Airport. He walked down the ramp and met Robb Thomas, who was waiting for him at the end of the concourse. The two men greeted each other and talked while heading down to get his luggage. Once they were safely in the car, the boss inquired about the plans.

"When is my first appearance?"

"Tomorrow at lunch time."

"Is that when I present the papers?"

"No, that's when you find out that Charlie passed away."

"Is that going to be all mushy? I hate mushy stuff. Do you think they'll want to hug me and all that crap?"

"I don't know, sir. We'll have to play that part by ear."

"Okay." Robb spent the thirty minutes it took to drive down to the Cavalier Hotel to bring the Boss up to speed on the details of the operation. The Boss seemed pleased. After they checked the Boss into his room and he freshened up, they decided to have a late dinner.

Robb drove the Boss down to Rudy's, a seafood restaurant at the other end of Atlantic Avenue. It's located right on the water offering customers a beautiful view of the ocean while they eat. Neither Robb nor the Boss appreciated the beautiful view because they were deeply involved in their conversation. Porpoises jumped and children played by the water, but neither was noticed by the two of them.

Chapter Fourteen

Wednesday lunch was busy at the Bluebird. Jenny and Carlos had to hustle to get all the food out, but they managed. The three old men, as usual, sat at the counter chattering away about sports as the crowd began to dwindle. Carlos headed to the back to get started on the dishes while Jenny began to break down the grill.

As the work was progressing, an older man walked through the door and set a suitcase down. No one seemed to notice that he had entered except Jenny. Without looking up from her work, she informed him that the grill was already broken down, but she would gladly to make him any kind of sandwich he would like. The gentleman said he wasn't hungry. That got Jenny's attention, so she turned to see who was standing in her café. When she saw him, she let out a scream. The three men turned around, and Carlos came running from the back room.

There standing at the door was the spitting image of Uncle Charlie. Tears were flowing down Jenny's face. Al's eyes moistened up at the sight. Joe just stared in silence. Jack was the first one to speak, his voice a little hoarse,

"Can we help you?" he asked a little hesitantly.

"I'm sorry to startle you all. You look as though I were a long lost friend who just walked through that door."

"No. No. We're sorry sir." Jenny worked hard to regain her composure. "Can I help you?"

"Well, I sure hope you can; I'm looking for the owner of this place."

"That would be me."

"Oh, that's right. I forgot. I know that the previous owner hangs out here and still works the grill; his name is Charles. I'm looking for him."

The tears returned to Jenny's eyes. "I'm sorry, he's not here." Jack answered in an effort to help Jenny, whose emotions were showing.

"Oh, well, I'm his brother. I was hoping to catch up with him."

"My God!" Jenny exclaimed. "He never told us he had a brother."

"I can't imagine why not. We were very close."

"Excuse us." Jenny said, wiping her eyes. "We've forgotten our manners. Please, come have a seat."

"You are very kind," he said to Jenny. He picked up his suitcase and moved to the counter, taking a seat. "Well, look up there, there's my brother's picture. I miss seeing him. How is the old chap?" To that question, there was total silence while everyone looked down as there wasn't a dry eye in the bunch.

"Please don't tell me something's happened to my brother," he said feigning concern.

Jack was the first to speak, "I'm afraid there is some bad news."

"Is he in the hospital? Nursing home?"

"No," Jack worked to steady his voice; "he passed away about eight months ago." And Jack put his arm around the old man's shoulder. The old man appeared stunned, but never shed a tear.

"How did it happen?"

"He was involved in a car accident."

"What a tragedy," he said, still trying to bring tears to his eyes. Everyone else in the place was crying openly. Jenny excused herself to the back room. Jack, Al, and Joe started at the beginning and filled the old man in on the details. When they had finished, there was a moment of silence in the café.

Joe was the next to speak, "I'm sorry for your loss...uh..."

"Butch. I'm sorry I should have introduced myself when I came in. I'm Butch Collins, Charlie's brother."

"I'm Joe, this is Jack, and that is Al." And they all shook hands.

"If you don't mind my asking, why weren't you at the service we had for your brother?"

"Why wasn't I there?" he repeated, as if surprised that they didn't know. "I've been on a mission trip. I was in South Africa and we only communicated by letter. When I hadn't gotten one in a while, well, naturally I was concerned. I scrimped and saved to get my airfare back to the states. I decided I needed to find out what was going on with my brother. And now he's gone. He was one of my major supporters." This particular lie pleased Butch the best. It sealed his story and made it complete.

They all accepted Butch's story, all except for Carlos. He seemed wary of the man, as if something just didn't ring true. He couldn't put his finger on it, but he was watching as Jenny returned from the back room and rejoined the group.

"Well," Butch continued, "I'm glad I have some time off. I guess I'll have to sell the café and close up Charlie's place."

"As far as Uncle Charlie's place, a police officer and I went over and cleaned it out not long after he passed away. We have most everything packed up in boxes." Jenny answered.

"Thank-you very kindly. Do I owe you anything for moving or storing his belongings?"

"Oh heavens, no. But you don't have to worry about the café; he sold it to me over five years ago."

"Oh, no. He told me he was leaving it to me in his will. The plan was I could use the proceeds to continue my work overseas." He liked his lie better with every passing moment.

"I've got copies of the contract we signed when I bought the café, if you would like to see them," Jenny offered.

"Didn't you all read the will after he died?" he said figuring there was no will in the first place.

"No." Jenny said. "We didn't know a will existed."

"Sure there's a will. I'll have to get a copy and bring it by for you."

"That's fine, but the café still belongs to me."

"We'll have to see about that. But not to worry, I'm sure we'll come to a fair and amicable agreement about this issue."

"What issue," Jenny thought, "the café is mine." She didn't say what was on her mind out of respect, but her emotions were starting to boil within her.

"Well, this has been an emotional day for me," Butch said with a sigh. "I think I better go find a hotel. I was planning to stay at my brother's place." He was still unable to get any tears to fall.

"Okay, there are plenty of good choices."

"I'll be back for breakfast in the morning, Jenny. This place reminds me of him," he said, faking a smile. Jenny waved at him as he left.

"What was all that about?" Jack said, when Butch was a safe distance from the building.

"I don't know. But one thing is for sure. He is not getting his hands on this café; not if I have anything to say about it."

****

Craig was working with Mary to decide the layout for the morning paper. There were no big stories at the moment, so the front page remained an unsolved puzzle. The smoke level was down as the excitement level was in slumber mode. No one was rushing around, and the telephones seemed to have gone silent.

"Hey Craig, you got a minute?"

"Oh, no. Eve, last time you came in here with a 'got a minute'. I almost lost my head. That preacher was hotter than Hades. Mary, keep working on what you've got, I am not sure, but I imagine this will be interesting," he smiled at her.

"Now, you know you are just exaggerating about that preacher. That series on the modern church was excellent. I am still hopeful I could win an award for that series."

"I admit that series was exceptional, all but that last piece."

"Well, we can't all be perfect. Anyway, I've got a hot new story."

"What's the story and do I need a lawyer?"

"You are funny. The story is an expose'…"

"Oh no!"

"Now give me a chance, will you. There's a local heart specialist who's well recognized and had an outstanding record until recently. Lately he's made some big mistakes, and the hospital is trying to cover it up."

"What kind of mistakes?" he asked with cautious interest.

"He has left instruments inside patients. He's fallen asleep right in the middle of surgery. He's had to do additional surgeries on several patients because his work was incomplete or he did something that the patient hadn't agreed to prior to surgery."

"Those are all strong allegations. I expect to see the proof before we run the story."

"The proof is there, you have to trust me."

"Not on this one, girl. Hospitals have big-time lawyers, and I really could lose my job if I ran a story like that without some kind of solid proof."

"What kind of proof you want? X-rays? Testimonials?"

"Yeah, both. Signed by the patient receiving the inadequate care."

Eve thought for a moment. "Okay, so if I can show you proof, you'll run the story."

"I want copies of the evidence. This could be a big story, one that could go national, and while we don't have to reveal our sources, I want to have them for the big boys upstairs."

"Copies," she said thoughtfully. "I am not sure I can get them."

"When you get them, we'll talk. If that's all, I have a paper to get out."

Two hours later, Craig was at his desk beginning to feel hungry. It was going on six, and he decided that he would run out for a couple of minutes and get a bite to eat. He talked to Mary and gave her directions as to what stories needed to be run. He was just about to leave the newsroom when someone said he had a call on line two.

"Yeah, this is Craig… Well, I was just heading out for a bite…I think I could do that…What time will you be there? … I'll see you there."

"Hey, Mary, I may be longer than I originally thought. Eve is on the trail of that story she told us about, and she wants me to check out a few of the facts. Hold the fort down while I'm gone. You know the routine if I don't make it back, right?"

"I'll take care of everything."

Craig arrived at the Olive Garden in the Pembroke area about 6:15. The wind blew sharply across the parking lot, causing Craig to reach back into his car for a jacket. He looked up and saw the crescent moon smiling back at him. He wondered if the moon wasn't so much smiling as it was laughing.

He told the beach-blonde hostess who he was and that he was supposed to meet someone there. The hostess was wearing her class ring, which revealed she was a senior in high school. She informed him that his party had already arrived and asked him to follow her to his seat. He noticed that the clothes she wore seemed about two sizes too small, but then decided that most girls her age wore them that way. She took him to the table, and there was Eve, dressed to kill.

"I hope you have some solid proof for me," he said as he took his seat.

"Pour yourself a glass of wine and join me." Eve said. He had a gut feeling that he was about to be taken, but the salad had already been delivered with the wine before he arrived at the restaurant, and he was plenty hungry and thirsty.

"Let's see what you've got, before I order. I want to know if we are really celebrating or not."

"You can't enjoy anything," she said, taking a sip of her wine. Eve switched sides of the table and slid up close to Craig. He put his wineglass down and took in the full beauty of the woman sitting beside him.

"I'll try to relax after I see the folder in your hand." She reluctantly handed him the folder. He glanced through the material. It was all there. There were x-rays showing the instruments, letters written that were signed by co-workers documenting the mistakes, and finally a patient letter documenting one incident. All the hard evidence that Craig wanted was right in the folder as Eve said it would be.

"I have to admit that I'm surprised to see all this evidence."

"I do good work," she said whispering into his ear. She leaned in close and kissed his cheek. "Are we going to run the story?"

"When I show this evidence to the publisher, I think we'll get the green light."

"You mean a great big editor like you has to ask the publisher?" She was tracing his ear with her finger.

"Well, no. But I would like to run it by him on a story like this one."

"What would it take to get you to make that kind of decision on your own?" she crooned to him.

"Well, I want to lock this folder in my office."

"I thought you trusted me, especially now that you've seen the evidence."

"I do trust you, but I want this to be able to show the boss where we got the story."

"What about my first amendment rights? And what about the privacy of my sources?" She was caressing his chest and purring in his ear.

"I believe in all that stuff, but I believe in keeping my job, too."

"So you'll run the story as long as that folder is locked up in your office?"

"Yeah."

"Good. Now that business is out of the way, let's eat." She filled his wine glass. He took it and drank up. Dinner was served and multiple glasses of wine were consumed. Craig had loosened up considerably. He was laughing and enjoying the company of a beautiful woman at his side.

"Would you like some dessert?" the waiter inquired.

"We have our own dessert." answered Eve. The waiter left the table, and Eve turned to look Craig in the eyes. "I would like some dessert, wouldn't you?"

"You just told the waiter you didn't want any."

"I'm not talking about that kind of dessert," she said seductively.

Craig asked the waiter for the bill, and they bolted out of the restaurant and headed over to Craig's apartment. In the morning, Craig awoke to an empty apartment. He showered, and then he headed to the office. When he arrived, there was Eve in a cubical working at a computer. He swung by to say,

"Good morning. Hey, you slipped out," he whispered.

"Somebody has to work," she said with a broad smile. "I see you remembered the folder."

"It's getting locked up in my file cabinet right after I show it to the boys upstairs. I have an appointment in fifteen minutes." He gazed at her with a besotted smile.

"You're staring," she said, playing with her hair.

"Can you blame me?" She smiled back at him. "Want to come over to my place for dinner tonight?"

"Yeah, that would be nice." Just then Mary walked up.

"Hey, what happened to you last night? You never made it back."

"Yeah, I got tied up, sorry. Did everything get out OK?"

"Smooth as clockwork."

"Glad to hear it," he said turning back to Eve, "when do you think you'll have that story ready?"

"It will take a couple of hours, but I will have it on your desk as soon as it done."

"You've got that big story?" Mary asked.

"You might say. I have a few loose ends to tie up before we go to press. This may not be ready for tomorrow's paper," she said.

"I was thinking about running it on Sunday anyway. We have a larger circulation on Sunday which would give us more exposure."

"It's about that doctor you were telling us about?" Mary inquired.

"Yeah, but you'll just have to wait to see it like everyone else," she said with a smile and then she returned to her work on the computer.

"I'm the assistant editor, shouldn't I know what's going on around here?" she said to Craig, as they headed for his office.

"Oh, you know more than anyone else. Now tell me what's brewing around here. What are we working on for tomorrow's edition?"

Chapter Fifteen

Nearby, in Jenny's house, two figures suddenly materialized: an angel accompanied by a man. The angel looked around at the pictures, fascinated by what he saw. The man immediately started to rummage through some of Jenny's drawers.

"We're going to be late, if you don't hurry up," the angel chided the man.

"Give me a minute, I have to find something," he answered.

"What are you looking for anyway?"

"Aaahh, here it is. Let's go." And the two of them vanished instantly.

****

It was Thursday evening, and Jenny was back at the Bluebird. She was rarely there in the evening; but this evening, Pastor Andrews was having his meeting. Jenny had a pot of coffee going and was warming the pies in the oven. The smell of apple and cherry pie permeated the cafe.

Pastor Andrews arrived early and helped Jenny set up. When he walked in, he almost melted as he smelled the wonderful aroma. He couldn't calm his nerves and was fumbling with the silverware and the coffee cups. He talked to Jenny about what he was planning to say, and Jenny offered a few tips.

After they talked a while, Pastor Andrews asked Jenny how she was feeling. She explained that the mornings were getting better and that, overall, she felt better. Then she told the Pastor about the newest visitor to the café, Uncle Charlie's brother. She told him that he was trying to make a plea for the place and was even thinking of going before a judge to see if he could take possession of the café. Jenny had hired a lawyer who thought that Jenny had a strong defense and that any judge should dismiss the case against her.

The people started to arrive, and by 7:30, everyone had enjoyed a slice of pie and something to drink. Pastor Andrews helped to serve everyone. When he slipped by Jenny, he whispered,

"I can't believe that they all came." Jenny nodded. "Please pray for me." She winked at him and he smiled. He put his notes on the counter and cleared his throat. The place quickly became quiet, and everyone turned their attention to Pastor Andrews.

****

Mike parked his car in Jenny's drive and took a deep breath. He looked out toward the ocean and looked at the clouds that seemed to be riding the horizon like a highway. He rolled down the window and listened to the ocean waves crashing on the other side of the dunes. The sound comforted his troubled soul and quieted his spirit.

He looked up at Jenny's place and thought about the last time he saw her and how he had failed her as a friend. He picked up the flowers that were on the seat beside him and started for her door. He rang the bell and rehearsed his speech once more. He stood there and waited, but no one came to the door. He rang the bell again, and still there was no answer. Then Mike checked for Jenny's car; it was gone.

Mike sat down on the steps and tried to figure out what to do. She could be grocery shopping and running errands so he wasn't sure in which direction to head. Mike got back in his car and started driving. He headed down toward Atlantic Avenue. When he arrived, he decided to just cruise the strip. This was a favorite pastime of the local teenage crowd in the summer. One would start somewhere near the Cavalier and then drive south to the loop at the end of Atlantic and then drive north and head back again. The cruisers drive round and round, moving only two or three feet at a time in bumper-to-bumper traffic. Horns blared and kids yelled to one another as they passed on either side. Kids loved it, but parents called it driving "Idiot's Circle."

Mike rounded the loop near First Street and then headed back down the strip. There were only about six cars on all of Atlantic Avenue, which made cruising not quite as much fun. As Mike drew near the Bluebird, he noticed that the parking lot was almost full. He turned in and saw that the place was packed. He parked and walked up to the door. The bell rang when he entered, and everyone turned to see who came in. Mike tried to be inconspicuous, but his entrance drew all their attention. Pastor Andrews looked up and smiled at Mike and then continued his speech. Mike sat down in the only empty seat he could find.

Jenny got up and asked Mike quietly if he would like a slice of pie and a cup of coffee. He nodded and she got it for him and returned to her seat.

Mike quietly proceeded to eat his pie and drink his coffee while Pastor Andrews explained his reasoning for thinking that there was a force at work that was bigger than any one of them could handle on their own. He explained the unlikelihood that they would all be going through major difficulties at exactly the same time. The trouble, he explained, was trying to find the common thread that tied them all together.

⁜⁜⁜⁜⁜⁜⁜⁜⁜⁜

Two more visitors entered the café. The bell didn't ring because the door never opened.

"What are we supposed to be doing here?" the angel asked his companion.

"We're sitting and watching," he said as he struck a match on the counter and lit his pipe.

"What's that?"

"It's something I miss very much up there."

"Are you allowed to have it?"

"Only if you don't tell," he said, giving the angel a stern look.

"See no evil, hear no evil, speak no evil." the angel replied.

****

The meeting ended with an agreement to meet again on Sunday evening there at the Bluebird. Everyone agreed to think and pray about the situation and to try to figure out what was going on. They all had something in common, and it was a spiritual enemy who was trying to destroy them. They needed to pray and ask God to reveal this enemy and who the enemy was using to bring about such havoc in all their lives.

Pastor Andrews hung back and talked with Jenny and Mike after everyone had gone. "Do you think it went well, Jenny?"

"Yeah, I do. I also think that they were open to your idea that there is something going on beyond the ordinary."

"I felt the same thing."

"You know something funny, someone was smoking this evening."

"I noticed that too." Pastor Andrews said.

"But I didn't see anyone smoking." Mike said.

"There had to be someone smoking, or else how do you explain the smell of smoke?"

"I don't know. I must have missed it," he said.

"Oh well, the important thing is we have everyone praying about this situation. There is real power in prayer. If there is something going on, I believe God will reveal it."

"I sure hope he does." Jenny added.

"Don't worry Jenny, I'm sure of it," he said, patting Jenny's shoulder. "Hey, I need to run. You two take care." Pastor Andrews shook Mike's hand and made his exit leaving Mike and Jenny in the cafe. Mike got up to help Jenny clean up things and wipe down the tables and the counter.

When they were done, Jenny looked at Mike and said, "It's good to see you again."

"It's good to see you, too."

"Are you here for a long weekend?"

"No, I have to be back for work tomorrow afternoon."

"Wow, what a coincidence you came tonight."

"Yeah, actually, I came to see you. I want to start by apologizing to you. I was an idiot the last time I was here. I am really sorry I acted that way."

"Thank you, Mike. That means a lot to me."

"Jenny, I like you so much…" he paused, "in fact, I wish we could be more than just friends."

"Wow, maybe I should sit down for this," she slid herself up onto a stool, and Mike sat down next to her.

"Jenny, I can't stop thinking about you. I hope you can find it in your heart to forgive me."

"Mike, I can and, in fact, already have forgiven you, but can you forgive me?"

"Yes, Jenny, I forgive you, too," he said, while reaching out to take her hand.

"I hope you realize that forgiving me is not just me alone anymore." she said rubbing her stomach.

"How is the baby? How are you?"

"According to the doctor, we are fine. I am starting to get a little bump, although it is hard to notice it yet."

"Have you heard from…"

"The father? No. He disappeared without a trace. I don't understand it. Pastor Andrews thinks it's part of all this stuff he's talking about, but I'm not sure. I think it was my own stupidity."

"Don't say that about yourself. You are a good person, and I want to be here for you. I want to be your friend through the whole process."

"Thanks, Mike. That's the best news I've had in quite a while."

"So what is our next step?"

"Well, you heard the pastor, we all need to pray…"

"That wasn't what I meant. What is OUR next step?" he asked while picking up her hand and holding it in his own. Their eyes met, and Jenny blushed and turned away. The two of them sat quietly for a few moments just enjoying the peacefulness and each other's company.

****

"That was neat to watch," the angel said to his companion at the counter.

"Yeah, I'm glad we stayed for that. I always thought they would make a nice couple."

"You played matchmaker with them?"

"In a way," he said with a chuckle. The old man put his pipe in his mouth and beamed while looking at the pair. Then he got up and walked over to the piece of a poster that hung on the wall. He allowed his hand to lightly touch the seeds that had been glued onto the poster board. Then he read the words once again, "Seeds of Faith."

"Come on," the angel said, "It's time we got out of this place. We've got some work to do." With that, the two of them disappeared.

Chapter Sixteen

It was Friday afternoon when Eve went into Craig's office and closed the door. Craig looked up from his work, pleased to see Eve there.

"I have the final copy of the story on that heart surgeon for you to read." Eve said.

"Can I read the Braille version?" he said motioning for her to come around his desk and to take a seat on his lap.

"I don't know," she said, laying the story on his desk and sitting in his lap and kissing him lightly. "Business first," she said stopping him. "When do you think you'll be able to run my story?"

"How about this coming Sunday?"

"Will it be front page material?" she asked, caressing his cheek.

"I haven't read the final draft but…"

"But I want it on the front page. Besides, I may have to head back to my lonely desk and work some more if you don't think it's worthy of the front page." She started to move away from him. He pulled her back.

"Okay, front page."

"I knew you would see it my way," she said, laying a kiss on his lips.

"Does that mean business is over, and it's time for pleasure?"

"I think it does," she said, kissing him again.

****

On Friday, Jenny was sitting quietly in her recliner listening to the evening news. She had just finished her dinner and set her plate on the coffee table. She was thinking about Mike and how glad she was that they had patched things up. She was wondering if they might have a future, when the phone interrupted her thoughts.

"Hello…Hello, is anyone there? … I can hear the noise in the background so I know someone's there. Do you want to speak or not? Last chance…"

"Jenny, don't hang up," came the voice from the other end of the receiver.

"Who is this?" her mind began to race. Silence again. "I think I recognize your voice."

"Jenny, it's me, Steve."

"Steve, oh my God, where are you?"

"I can't tell you that. I called because I was worried about you."

"Where the heck are you? What happened to your business downtown?"

"Jenny, you were set up."

"What? What are you talking about?" her heart was pounding so fast she could barely breath.

"I wasn't planning to open a restaurant. I was hired as an actor to play a part."

"Yeah, the construction guys told me, in some movie. Who are you anyway?"

"I'm not a professional actor, Jenny. They aren't making any movie from the restaurant down there."

"Then what the heck is going on?"

"I was hired to play the part you saw. The guy that hired me wanted me to get you involved with me so you would break up with whoever your boyfriend was at the time."

"What?" she exclaimed.

"The whole plan was to break the two of you up."

"So, you were acting. You have no feelings for me at all?"

There was a long pause. Jenny could hear the sounds in the background so she knew he was still on the phone. "I wasn't supposed to…" he said breathlessly.

"Well, do you or don't you?"

"I wasn't supposed to call you, but I am, aren't I?"

Jenny's head was swirling. "Was anything you said to me true?"

"My name. I wasn't supposed to tell you anything more."

"Great."

"I just called to tell you I am sorry. I wish I could get to know you for real. I think you are a great person. Anyway, I gotta go."

"Wait." Jenny yelled. "I need to tell you something."

"I'm not supposed to be talking to you."

"I'm pregnant!"

There was a short pause. "Is it mine?"

"I don't sleep around. Yes, it's yours."

"But we were being careful."

"Evidently some of your little swimmers found their way around the protection."

"Hey, I'm not ready to be a father!"

"Do you think I want to be a mother?"

"What are you going to do? Are you going to get rid of it?"

"I don't believe in abortion. No, I'm keeping it."

"Oh man, this wasn't supposed to happen."

"No kidding, Sherlock."

"This whole thing is a disaster. I knew I shouldn't have done it."

"You said someone put you up to it?"

"Yeah."

"Who is he? Why did he care about who I was dating?"

"I don't know who he is."

"What do you mean, you don't know?"

"The office we met in was all dark. I couldn't see his face."

"You took a job from someone you couldn't see?"

"Well, you know that picture that hangs in your café, the one with you and the previous owner? The guy looked similar to him."

"A guy who looks like Uncle Charlie hired you?"

"Yeah. Oh, God, I have to get off the phone."

"Wait. Don't hang up!" But it was too late. He was already gone. Jenny threw the phone across the room, and it landed in a chair. Jenny fell onto the couch and wept.

****

Mike had just finished washing his dishes when his phone rang. He dried his hands and picked up the receiver. "Hello."

"Mike, it's Jenny." she cried.

"Jenny, what's the matter?"

"Oh, Mike, I just got a terrible phone call from Steve."

"What did he say?" he asked cautiously.

"Oh, don't worry. He doesn't want anything to do with me," she cried.

"What did he want?"

"He told me I was set up. That he was hired to try and break us up."

"What? Did he know you got pregnant?"

"No. The pregnancy caught him off guard too."

"Start from the beginning and tell me everything."

Jenny started from the beginning sobbing as she told him about the call. She stopped several times to blow her nose and to get her emotions under control. Mike patiently listened to the whole story.

"Wow, I can't believe my ears," Mike said when she was finished. "So we were set up. And by someone who looks similar to Uncle Charlie. Kind of interesting that his brother would show up in town at this particular time."

"Oh, Mike, you couldn't be more off base. He's been in the café every day. He's joking with the other old codgers and everything."

"But he is trying to take the café from you."

"You're right about that. But he's a missionary."

"That's what he tells you. He could be lying."

"I guess that's true, too."

"I tell you what, I'll try to get some friends to help do a background check on this Butch Collins. Did your caller ID pick up on the number Steve called you from?"

"Yeah, but I checked with an operator. It's a pay phone."

"That's alright. If we have the place, we can assume that Steve didn't drive too far from home or work to make that call."

"You're probably right," she read the phone number to Mike who looked up the area code on his laptop.

"That's New Jersey. Huh. I bet our man is from New York. I mean, it wouldn't be that far of a drive for Steve to go from his office. And bigwigs are not going to live in some small place."

"Sounds like you are making some pretty big assumptions."

"I know, but I have to start somewhere. I think you should call Pastor Andrews and tell him what happened. This Steve may have helped us more than we know."

"Alright, I will. Hey, Mike?"

"Yeah."

"Thanks for being there and listening."

"You're welcome, Jenny. I'm going to be with you all the way through this. You can count on me."

"Thanks, that really means a lot."

****

Eve picked up her phone on the second ring, "Hello."

"Have you got confirmation about the article running?"

"Yes, Boss. It will be in the paper on Sunday morning."

"You check the morning paper to be sure it's in there, and then you're out of town. You got that?"

"Sure thing, Boss, but do you think I'll need to do anything else here?"

"I guess you better not close the door totally, but I think you're done. The article should spark a medical review, and you've left all the evidence with that editor, right?"

"Everything's in place."

"Then I guess you'll need to take your ailing mother up to John Hopkins."

"That works for me."

"I'll be in touch later."

"Bye." As soon as she hung up, she went directly into Craig's office feigning distress. "Craig," she said behind fake tears, "they want me to take my mother up to John Hopkins in Baltimore for some testing. Oh, what am I going to do?" she threw herself into a chair with great flair.

"Oh, I'm so sorry. Come here," he said and held her in his arms. "When do you need to go?"

"They want me up there on Monday. Oh my, I'm so worried about her."

"Look, you just take off and don't worry about things here. As for me, I will be here for you."

"I thought this was the beginning of something special?" she cried.

"I believe it is, but you need to go and take care of your mother. Just promise to keep me informed. If you need me, I could fly up for a couple of days."

"That means so much to me right now." She put her arms around him, and he held her tight. "I need to go home now, but maybe we can have some dinner later."

"That would be great. Give me a call and let me know when you can meet me."

****

"Jenny, I'm glad you called," Pastor Andrews said after she explained what had happened to her. "This could be more important than we all realize. Is Mike going to call you when he finds anything more out about this Steve or Mr. Collins?"

"He said he would."

"Good, hopefully you will hear from him before our meeting tomorrow evening."

"Let's hope so. Do you think I should treat Mr. Collins any differently tomorrow at breakfast?"

"No, but I would be careful what you say around him."

"Okay, I guess I'll see you tomorrow."

"I think God's working, Jenny. I'll see you there."

Chapter Seventeen

It was eight o'clock in the evening, and Pastor Andrews was sitting at home in his study. He had closed his door and was thinking and praying about the meeting he had scheduled for this coming Saturday evening. He was looking over the list of people who were facing unusual circumstances. Many were from his flock, but there were others who didn't attend his church. He kept looking at the list and trying to figure out what they all had in common.

"Lord," he prayed, "you can see everything and I am blinded. Help me see the connection. Help us find out what is going on. Then give us the wisdom to respond in the way you desire to the situation. God, I feel in my spirit that you are up to something, please show me." He opened his eyes and studied the list some more. His wife gingerly tapped on the office door,

"Yes dear, come in," he called to her.

"You have a call from Mike Milton. Do you want me to take a message?"

"No, I'll take the call. Thanks, sweetheart." He reached over and picked up the receiver, "Mike, what have you got?"

"Nothing concrete yet. My friends say we should have something in the morning. But I was just thinking about all those people who were sitting at the Bluebird the other day. Do you know what they have in common?"

"That's what I've been trying to figure out for the past couple of days."

"It was right in front of our eyes, and we didn't realize it. Did Jenny tell you about the call she got?"

"Yeah, but what does that have to do with it?"

"The common thread with all those people is that they were at Uncle Charlie's funeral. Uncle Charlie is the one who ties all these people together. I bet if we looked through his pictures from his Wall of Fame, we would find every one of those people in those pictures."

Pastor Andrews's mind was racing. He read down the list of people, and sure enough they had all attended the funeral. "Mike this is great. I'll do some checking on my side. I think you are on to something. Please try to get back to me if you find anything on that background check. I have a feeling Mr. Collins has something to do with what's happening."

"I think you're right."

"The meeting starts at 7:00 in the evening. I want to give Jenny a chance to get through the day before we barge in. Have you got my cell number?"

"Yeah, I'll call the second I have anything to report."

"Thanks, keep up the good work." Pastor Andrews hung up the phone and got out a couple of clean sheets of paper. He began to list all the bits and pieces he had received over the past few days. Each piece individually meant very little; but, when put together, they were beginning to form the pieces of a puzzle. The only problem was that the picture wasn't clear yet.

****

At five o'clock on Saturday afternoon, Pastor Andrews was sitting in Hardee's at the corner of Laskin Road and Virginia Beach Blvd. The sun was shining brightly in the late winter sky, but Pastor Andrews hadn't even noticed. His mind was preoccupied with the meeting that would soon take place at the Bluebird Cafe.

"Good afternoon, pastor," Dr. Emanuel Everheart said as he set his tray down at the table where the Pastor was hunched over his notes.

"Thanks for coming Dr. E." the Pastor said, hardly looking up from his notes. Most people called Dr. Everheart, Dr. E., after a sixteen-year-old patient referred to him that way in an article that appeared in *The Virginian-Pilot.* The girl had a rare infection that caused her to need a valve replacement, and the doctor also repaired a slight hole in her heart that she had lived with her whole life. The two of them were pictured together in the paper after the surgery.

"Have you got it figured out yet?"

"Are you kidding? This is such a puzzling situation. It is hard for me to believe that anyone would want to tear down the good work of Uncle Charlie, but that's the way it appears to me. I just can't seem to figure it out."

"Well, maybe the good Lord will open your eyes today."

"I hope so. Thanks again for coming to support me," he said putting his notes aside and turning his attention to Dr. E. "You know I appreciate it."

"No problem, but I am on call tonight," he said, tapping his phone.

"We'll just have to pray that no one needs you." The pastor shared what he knew with Dr. E., hoping that by going over it something might jump out at him. Before leaving for the Bluebird, Dr. E. offered to pray for the pastor and the meeting. Pastor Andrews accepted his offer.

****

"Good evening everyone, I want to thank you for coming. As I told many of you the other night, I don't believe all the misfortune that we are experiencing is a coincidence. I believe that there are a number of things coming together to work against us, some of which I believe is spiritual. I believe that spiritual forces, both godly and those of the devil can work in our physical realm. God's forces can make our lives better, and the enemy tries to tear us apart.

"Sometimes I believe we come to a place where those two forces are meeting head on in a spiritual battle. Let me be clear, God will win the battle. The trouble is that so many of us believe that we just sit around while God works, that we don't have an active part in the process. Nothing could be further from the truth.

"Don't misinterpret that to mean that God can't work without us, because He can. But I firmly believe that sometimes God intends to work in and through us to achieve spiritual objectives. The enemy has a plan, and God has a plan to thwart all that the enemy plans to do. Sometimes those plans involve our lives, and we need to sit up and pay close attention.

"I think that is what is happening in our current situation. I don't believe that all of us are having a bad time in our businesses and personal lives, just because fate is working against us. I believe there are spiritual forces at work to weaken our businesses and in some cases close them for good. I don't believe God is behind this, because we did something bad or wrong, I believe we are being attacked at the spiritual level." A hand went up. "Yes."

"If what you are saying is true, how do you fight such a thing? I mean we can't get a gun and shoot spiritual forces, can we?"

"No, you're right. But we can fight through prayer."

"How do you do that?" another question rang out.

"I hope that's what we're here to talk about."

"Who's behind all this stuff that's happening to us, a spirit or a person?"

"Another good question. Actually, in our present situation, I believe it's a combination of the two. I believe it's an evil spirit working through a person."

"So are you suggesting we attack this person?"

"Not physically, although it could make all of us feel a lot better," he said with a chuckle, which spread around the cafe.

"Do you know who this person is?"

"That's part of our problem."

"If you don't know, how do we find out?"

"We pray."

"Do you actually believe that God will tell us?"

"Yes, I really do. If we pray, I believe with all my heart that God will reveal whom we are up against and how to pray for them."

"How will we know?"

"You all are asking some really good questions. We'll know, because when God reveals something, he will confirm it to us. Now, I'm not positive how he will reveal it or confirm it, but we'll know when it happens."

"How do we start?"

"I think the best place to start is with what we know. I have been working on collecting little tidbits from many of you and while the puzzle is a bit fuzzy, it is taking shape. So let's begin with a few facts that we already know. I'll list them on this whiteboard that I brought and that way we can all look at the facts together."

As he set up the whiteboard, Jenny walked around and offered refills of coffee and tea. As she made her way through the café, she distinctly picked up on the smell of smoke. It wasn't from a fire but from a pipe. The aroma was distinctive; it smelled like Uncle Charlie's pipe. She looked around the café and saw that no one was smoking. She whispered to the pastor that she could smell the smoke as she passed by him. He, too, could smell that distinctive aroma.

He smiled and asked, "Does anyone smell anything unusual?"

"I smell the coffee, if that is what you mean?"

"No, anyone else?"

"I smell tobacco smoke like from a pipe." Everyone began sniffing the air. It didn't take long for everyone to recognize the aroma as Uncle Charlie's pipe.

There was total silence, and everyone stared at the pastor who picked up a marker and wrote on the chart paper; Uncle Charlie.

Does everyone here know whom I am referring to when I say, 'Uncle Charlie'?" Everyone nodded. "Were all of you at his memorial service?" The group nodded in unison again.

Jenny jumped up; "Did all of you speak at his memorial service?" The group nodded in agreement a third time.

"Good work, Jenny." Pastor Andrews said as he added that point to his chart. "Jenny will you tell everyone what you have experienced and tell them about your newest customer here at the café?"

Jenny stood up where she was sitting and turned to the group. "I was dating Officer Milton, who got a new job out in Emporia. After we were apart for a while, a guy came to the Bluebird pretending to need help starting his own café. Naturally, I wanted to help him out. He worked here and I went to his new place and helped set things up. We became close but he suddenly disappeared from my life. After sometime he called to say our relationship was a set-up to make sure Mike and I broke up."

There was some slight murmuring in the crowd. Jenny continued, "While we were talking, he told me that I was set up by an older man who had some similarities to Uncle Charlie. He had seen the picture hanging on the wall," she said pointing to the picture behind the counter. "Last week, a man came into my café who nearly made me faint right on the spot. It was Uncle Charlie's brother." There were several "Wow's" from the crowd. Jenny sat back down.

"Why wasn't he at the memorial service?" someone asked.

"He claims that he is a missionary and that he was in Africa and that he had no idea his brother had died." Pastor Andrews answered. "I'm not sure I believe it," he continued adding these facts to his list.

Cindy Morris raised her hand and said, "I work down in the clerk of court's office. I did a little bit of checking on some of these new businesses that have suddenly come to town and are trying to put most of you out of business. While each of the businesses is operating as separate corporations, one man filled out and signed the papers for all of them. His name is Robb Thomas."

"That's new and it shows purpose and intention." Pastor Andrews added this fact to his list.

"Interesting that she would mention that name," George King chimed in without being called upon, "That's the guy who bought the first three houses that Randy Stumps sold. I drove by those houses the other day, and they are still empty. But the fact that his company sold those properties so quickly caused some of my customers to jump ship to his company."

"Robb Thomas is playing a big role in this then." Pastor Andrews starred the name.

"Pastor Andrews, this seems really stupid…"

"Don't say that, we need every little piece to try and figure out what's going on."

"Well, I've been sitting here for ten minutes; and all I keep hearing in my head is '*Time* magazine page 27'. I know that's dumb."

"No, it's not. And here is five dollars. Walk across the street there to the 7-11 and buy a copy. Let's see what you are hearing." Todd headed out.

"Pastor, I have something silly, but maybe like you say it's important." Margaret Johnson offered. "I was in the new flower shop the other day and noticed that most of the employees were from New Jersey or New York."

"That fits, right Jenny?"

She nodded. "That's where Steve's telephone call came from."

For the next ten minutes, people offered little things that they had uncovered, things that seemed insignificant at the time, but in this context seemed important. The excitement in the cafe was almost electric as the sharing continued. Suddenly, Jeff came running back into the cafe.

"I got it! I got it! We are all going to feel so stupid for not seeing it. Jenny, what did Uncle Charlie's brother claim his name was?" he was panting trying to catch his breath.

"He said Butch Collins."

"Wrong," he said with so much excitement. "How about Fred Collins!" he exclaimed while holding the magazine in the air.

"What?" Pastor Andrews said, taking the magazine from his hand. "You mean the multi-billionaire from New York?" Jenny came running forward to see the picture too. They both looked at it, and their jaws dropped. Everyone wanted to see it, so they passed the magazine around the café. There were a few moments of stunned silence, while everyone sat back and considered the implications.

Jenny's cell phone rang. She grabbed it quickly to turn it off but then noticed it was Mike.

"Hey, what's up?"

"Am I interrupting the meeting?"

"Yeah, but what do you have for us?"

"Please tell Pastor Andrews that we can't find out anything out about Butch Collins. It's like he doesn't exist."

"Are you sitting at a computer?"

"Yeah."

"Search for Fred Collins."

"Oh, my God," he said when he saw the images.

"That's what we just now figured out," she said. Jenny stepped into the backroom for a minute to talk to Mike and then quietly slipped back in.

"What do we do now?" came a question as Jenny sat back down.

"Well, we need to pray."

"Should we ask God to send down fire to consume Robb Thomas and Fred Collins? Or would it be better to pray for his business to fail?"

"No," Pastor Andrews said. "We need to pray for their salvation."

"What?" yelled George King. "That jerk has ruined my business as well as a number of others. And you're telling me that we need to pray for his salvation? I hope they rot in hell." Pastor Andrews didn't immediately respond but gave George and the others a moment to calm down.

"If you really knew what hell was like, you wouldn't want anyone to go there, even your worst enemies. Hell is total separation from God, love, truth, faithfulness, civility, and any good quality that you can name. I think the first thing we need to pray is for his salvation, and then we need to pray that God will give us the wisdom so we can thwart his plan."

"More importantly, we must remember what scripture teaches us, 'For our struggle is not against flesh and blood, but against the rulers, against the authorities, against the powers of this dark world and against the spiritual forces of wickedness in the heavenly realms.' This means we are not fighting Fred Collins or Robb Thomas; we are fighting the principalities that are directing their lives. We want to see their souls saved, and the enemy's plans thwarted. So let's start praying those things and see what God releases from heaven."

There were no further objections, so they all bowed their heads and began to pray. Pastor Andrews began leading the prayer for Fred Collins, and everyone joined together in unity for his salvation.

****

"We are going to be late," the angel said.

"Hush, I want to hear what's going on." The old man responded.

"Hey, what are you doing with that thing?"

"I told you before, if no one knows I'm enjoying it while I'm down here, there won't be any problems when we get back." Then the old man stuck the pipe in his pocket.

"You better hope I am not asked. Shouldn't we be going to our appointment?"

"Let's just be quiet and listen for our signal to go." The two sat quietly in the back.

"It was you that whispered about *Time* magazine into that young man's ear. I saw you do it. Why did you do it?"

"I was just trying to help the process along."

"How come they could smell your smoke from the pipe, but not be able to see us?"

"It's magic. I don't know. But if it works, I'll do it. Besides, I am not interfering with anything or anyone."

"I think you are helping them."

"Do you think that's wrong?"

"No, I guess not."

"Quiet now, let's listen for our cue."

As soon as they heard the group start to pray for Fred Collins, the old man told the angel that it was time to make their move. Instantly they were gone.

Chapter Eighteen

Fred Collins was sitting in his hotel room enjoying a mixed drink. He was feeling good about how his plan was progressing. The newspaper would be running the article on Dr. E. in the morning, and that would begin the downward spiral of his career. He laughed to himself at the thought of Dr. E.'s career going down the toilet.

The phone rang, and it was Robb Thomas.

"I just got off the phone with the judge for your case against the café."

"Do you think he will see things our way?"

"When he drives that new boat out on the bay, I'm sure he won't even remember one stinking little café that had to go in order for him to enjoy such pleasure."

"Ah, that's great. Everything seems to be falling into place. Have you got that wrecking ball lined up? I want that café destroyed as soon as possible."

"Should be down within twenty-four hours of his ruling."

"When did he say he would decide our case?"

"Looks like it might be two weeks."

"Okay. How goes the property acquisition around the café?"

"Moving along nicely, Boss. We should be able to get started on that resort fairly quickly."

"Are there any problems in our plans that I need to be aware of?"

"None that I can tell. Pastor Andrews seems to be trying to organize a group of followers. He's got about thirty-five, so no big deal. They've met once."

"Are the elders still in favor of his dismissal?"

"I think we'll have him out within a month or two."

"Good. Keep up the pressure."

"Will do. Anything else?"

"Not tonight. I'll talk to you in the morning."

"Good night."

Fred hung up the phone, reveling in the failings of those weak people. He walked over to get the remote and felt the sting of acid in his throat. He detoured to the bathroom and grabbed some antacids. He popped a few, picked up the remote, and headed for his bed. He clicked the remote, surfing through the channels.

Suddenly, Fred felt like his left arm was tingling. He got up and rubbed his arm. Then he pulled his shirt off and began to massage it harder. The tingling didn't seem to subside. Then his chest began to burn again with the feeling of acid in his throat. He popped a few more antacids and returned to the bed. He tried to lie back and relax.

All of a sudden, he noticed that the room felt really warm. He went over and adjusted the thermostat down. He returned to the bed, feeling worse. He tried to lie down again, but the pain in his chest seemed to increase. He tried sitting up, but the pain continued to build to almost intolerable levels.

He reached for the phone and noticed that the room was starting to spin around. He pressed Robb's number,

"Get in here, I don't feel good all of a sudden."

"I'll be right there." By the time Robb entered the room, Fred was lying on the bed out cold. Robb dialed 911.

****

Dr. E. was praying with the group that had gathered at the Bluebird. Several people were interceding with God for Fred Collins when Dr. E. felt his phone vibrate in his pocket. He pulled it out quietly and looked at the number. It was the hospital. He slipped away from the group and went outside to take the call.

"This is Dr. Everheart, what's up?"

"We have a possible heart attack on the way to the hospital now. He's a tourist staying down at the beach. The gentleman's assistant called and asked for our finest surgeon to be on hand. Said money was no object."

"Don't I feel special. Assemble a team in case we have to do emergency surgery. I'll probably try to stabilize the patient and wait on the surgery until later, but I am not sure what we'll need at this point. What is the ETA of the patient?"

"The paramedics said they had just arrived and would have the patient here in about 10 to 15 minutes."

"Great, I'll be there in about ten."

"We'll get things rolling, and we'll be ready when you get here."

Dr. E. slipped back in the cafe, quickly located Pastor Andrews and whispered to him that he had to leave for an emergency at the hospital. He turned to leave, but Pastor Andrews grabbed Dr. E's wrist. Pastor Andrews interrupted the prayer and asked,

"Could we take a moment and pray for Dr. E.? He just got an emergency call from the hospital, possible heart attack." The group quickly gathered around Dr. E. and began praying. It was a powerful and profound minute. Dr. E. thanked the group and hurried out the door. The group returned to praying for Fred Collins.

****

The ambulance arrived at the Cavalier Hotel in Virginia Beach. The rescue workers were quickly escorted up to Fred Collins' room. When they entered the room, he was immediately hooked up to an EKG machine. Fred was having difficulty breathing and was unresponsive. He was floating between a conscious and unconscious state. Finally, he blacked out completely.

A moment later, he was sitting over on the couch observing the workers from across the room. There he was lying on the bed with the paramedics talking to him, but he was sitting over on the couch.

He got up and walked over to take a closer look. Sure enough, there he was on the bed, gasping for breath. He looked at the monitor and watched it indicating that his heart was beating. He tried to speak to the paramedics, but they couldn't hear his voice.

"It's a strange feeling to watch yourself lying on the bed, isn't it?" came a voice from over on the couch. Fred straightened up and looked over at the couch and saw Charlie sitting there.

"Charlie, what am I watching?"

"You're having a very serious heart attack."

"Oh," he said looking back at himself on the bed. "What are you doing here?" he said in sudden surprise. "I thought you were dead."

"I am," he replied, as he struck a match to light his pipe.

"If you are dead, what are you doing here? And for that matter, why can I see and talk to you while I am clearly lying on the bed?"

"I'm here to see you. And right now, your spirit is outside your body."

"Am I dead?"

"Not yet."

"Am I going to die?"

"I don't know."

"A lot of help you are," he said, returning his gaze to his body lying on the bed. Charlie took the moment to take a few puffs on his pipe. The paramedics packed everything up and moved the body onto the stretcher and then out of the room, leaving Charlie alone with his brother Fred. "Am I supposed to be going with my body?"

"Not right now," he said taking another long drag on his pipe.

"What happens now? Are you the grim reaper?" He feigned fear.

"No." he said with a chuckle. "I'm here to talk to you."

"Are you going to escort me to heaven?"

"I'm afraid not."

"Well, what's going on?"

"Want to sit on the balcony? We can enjoy the ocean."

Charlie got up and walked right through the window and took a seat on the balcony. Fred stopped short and tried to open the door. He was unable to open it. He looked through the window at Charlie and shrugged his shoulders. Charlie smiled, got up and poked his head through the glass.

"Sorry, I forgot you aren't used to being in your spirit. Just walk right through the window, come on." Fred tentatively approached the window and stuck his hand through and then he slowly pushed himself through.

"That was strange," he said as he took the other seat on the balcony.

"How have you been, Fred?"

"You should know, aren't you all-knowing now?"

"No, that is reserved for God."

"I'm fine, I think," he suddenly became uncomfortable.

"Have you missed me?"

"Sure," he lied.

"Really?"

"No, you know I haven't missed you. I never cared for you when you were alive, why would I care about you now that you are dead?"

"That's not exactly true. We were very close when we were younger."

"We were both naive. You went your way, and I went mine."

"It seems you've taken a lot of interest in me since I died."

"Oh really? How would you know that?" he asked sarcastically.

"I know what you are up to."

"Well, good for you. You can't do anything about it because you're dead."

Charlie chose not to respond to Fred's taunt. Instead, he took a deep breath and enjoyed the ocean air. "What happened to you?" Charlie asked.

"Life changes people."

"There was a time in your life that you believed in God."

"That was when I was naïve. I believed in God, and I thought we were going to conquer the world. I even thought about becoming a missionary or a pastor at one time in my life. Did you know that?"

"No, Fred I didn't. What happened to change all that?"

"You know darn well what happened. We were the perfect middle class family, husband, wife, a beautiful daughter, a nice house, the family dog and cat; and yeah, we were active members in church. We had it all, and life looked hopeful. Then one day, God took all that away from me," he said with bitterness in his voice.

Suddenly, they were sitting in a bedroom. Fred was startled by the change in scenery, but the place brought a comfort to his soul. He looked over to a beautiful woman lying in the bed, his very own Claris. Fred quietly walked over to the bed and looked at his beautiful bride. CRASH. Claris bolted up in bed. She ran over to the window and looked outside at the torrential rainfall. CRASH again. The thunder shook the house. Claris shook it off and returned to the comfort of her bed.

Deborah, their daughter, came running into the bedroom. Fear and panic filled her eyes. Fred tried to pick her up, but she ran right through him. Claris picked up their daughter, and they got into the bed together. There were several more loud crashes as the storm waged its war outside. Claris sang a sweet lullaby to Deborah, and the two of them slipped off to sleep.

"Get out!" Fred yelled at the top of his lungs. "The house is on fire. That lightning bolt hit our house. Don't fall back to sleep." He pleaded with her, but the two of them nestled up on her side of the bed.

The room filled with smoke. "Run!" Fred screamed at his wife, but she didn't move. Suddenly, the room was filled with blinding light, and an angel then touched Claris' and Deborah's shoulders, and their spirits came peacefully out of their bodies. Claris walked over to where Fred was standing and caressed his cheek ever so tenderly,

"I miss you, my love," she said. "I'm OK, and Deborah is with me. We are waiting for you up in heaven."

Tears rolled down his cheeks. He reached out to touch Claris; but just as he was about to make contact, she was gone. In an instant, Fred found himself sitting in a church, tears still staining his cheeks. Charlie leaned over and said to Fred,

"The accident wasn't God's fault."

"He could have prevented it."

"God still loves you."

"If God loved me, He wouldn't have burned my wife, child, and home up." Charlie had to turn his head to hide his own tears. A moment later he said,

"That was a terrible tragedy." There was a long moment of silence.

"Where are we now?" Fred asked trying to see through tear-filled eyes.

"We're at the Bluebird."

Fred got up and looked around. "I think I know these people," he said. "Yeah, I do know them. There's Jenny."

"Why don't you listen for a moment to what they are praying about?" Charlie suggested. Fred walked among the group and listened.

"Father, I ask you to forgive Fred Collins for what he did to me. I forgive him for ruining my flower business."

"She forgives me! How could she forgive me? I crushed her." Fred asked with a huff.

"The forgiveness of God is deeper than the sea; it's hard for us to understand. But you are right, for her to ask God to forgive you because she forgives you is a big step in her life," Charlie responded.

"Father, we ask you to extend your mercy to Fred Collins wherever he might be right now. I also want you to know that I forgive Fred for what he did to me in getting that woman to write those libelous articles in the paper about me," Pastor Andrews prayed.

"Well, you can't blame a pastor for forgiving me, they're supposed to forgive," Fred said.

"They are human, too, Fred. It's not easy to forgive others, especially when they wronged you for no apparent reason." Charlie reminded Fred.

"God," Jenny began, "I ask you to save Fred Collins' soul. I intercede for him, pleading with you to intervene on his behalf. Nothing is too hard for you. No soul is out of your reach until the end; please do something in this situation. Father, if you can use me,

I am a willing vessel. Father, if you can forgive my sins, and I know you already have, please forgive Fred and extend your grace to him."

The prayers continued. Fred was silently stunned by the earnestness of the people gathered to pray for him. After a few moments, Fred and Charlie were sitting on the balcony again in silence.

Fred was the first to speak, "Are they Ok now?" Fred asked in a hoarse voice.

"Yes, your lovely wife and beautiful daughter are doing just fine. They eat regularly at my little diner up there. They wanted me to tell you that they love you and miss you very much." Charlie said with a smile. He wiped his eyes and continued, "They also want you to come back to God, to have faith once again."

"I've got no room for a god who steals."

"God didn't steal them from you. Besides, they are in a much better place right now."

"Can I talk with them?" he asked timidly.

"I'm sorry, you can't."

"Then what are you doing here, anyway?"

"I asked God for the chance to come talk to you, to see if I could convince you to turn around and to serve Him once again."

"Ha. Ha. Ha." he laughed out loud. "What a waste of your time. I don't want anything to do with your god. I'm serving a much better god right now."

"Yourself?"

"I'm the only one I can depend upon."

"If you die today, where are you going to go?"

"Heaven. Everyone who dies goes to heaven."

"Wrong answer. Everyone doesn't go to heaven."

"I lead a pretty good life. I help people. You should see the list of charities that I give big bucks to every year. That's got to count for something."

"I'm afraid not. Don't get me wrong, it's very important that we do good deeds. But if just doing good things could get us into heaven, why would God have to send His son to die for us?"

"I don't know. Besides, that's just one way."

"No, that's *the* way. You know how much it hurt you when you lost your wife and daughter, just imagine how much it must have hurt God when people like you and me nailed His son to the cross?"

"I bet He was ticked off."

"Yeah, I bet He was. But He allowed it so that He could have a relationship with all of humanity."

"If I were God, I would have blown those ignorant fools away and rescued my son."

"Good thing you aren't God. If He had done that, He wouldn't be able to have a relationship with any of us because we are all sinners. We need the blood of Jesus to pay the way for us to have that relationship with a loving God."

"It's a pretty tough God that demands the blood of His own son."

"Some people think of God as this gushy love. He is love, but He is so much more. He is a God of righteousness and holiness. Sin can't even be in His presence. But the key is that sinners can be in His presence because of the blood of Jesus. There is incredible power in the blood of Jesus to wash away our sins and to grant us forgiveness."

There was silence on the balcony. The ocean waves crashed in on the beach. The breeze off the ocean was a bit cool. Families were walking along the boardwalk in the early twilight. Children were squealing as siblings chased one another. Charlie refilled his pipe and lit it once again. The two brothers sat silently on the balcony.

"Do you believe we can be forgiven for things we've done deliberately?"

"If you are asking, can I forgive you for what you've done to all my friends, the answer is yes."

"How can you do that?"

"That's simple. I consider all the sin God forgave me for, and forgiving you becomes very easy. As far as all the stuff you've done to my friends, the Bible says that in all things God works for the good of those who love Him, who have been called according to His purposes. So, no matter what kind of evil you dig up, God can turn it around for something good."

"How can anything 'good' come out of the fire that stole my wife and child?"

"I turned my life over completely to God after that." Fred looked shocked at that. "Yep, I decided I needed God to help me get through what happened to you. It was hard for me to accept what God allowed in your life."

Fred looked shocked at Charlie. "You're kidding, aren't you? You went to church before that fire."

"Yes, I did." Charlie said looking directly into his brother's eyes. "But it took that fire to help me make a full commitment to following God. I went to church and I read my Bible, but I am not sure I really believed it until I made a fresh commitment after the fire. Look at the result in my life from that one terrible thing that happened."

"Tell me, did God do that? Did God burn my house down?"

"No, but as you saw He sent an angel to rescue your wife and daughter before the fire got to them. What you couldn't see was the angel that was there trying to comfort you in your horrific loss. Do you know that God wept with you at the funeral?"

"I still don't see how anything good can come out of it. Look at my life. I walked away from a relationship with God because I blamed him."

"Look at my life. Look at all the people's lives I touched because of my faith in God. You've been working for close to a year, and you still haven't gotten everyone whose life I touched. Not only that, but consider all the lives that those people touched because God used me in their lives. The ripples go on forever. All that because of one horrific accident that shook my life to its core."

There was silence again on the balcony as the two men sat quietly. They watched the first stars make their twinkling appearance. The full moon had just risen over the horizon while some wispy clouds floated past. Charlie lit his pipe and took a few puffs.

"I always hated the smell of that thing. I liked the cigarettes you smoked better."

"I switched because the cigarettes were killing me. I really never smoked the pipe that much. It helped to keep me from smoking cigarettes." There were a few more minutes of silence while Charlie smoked his pipe. "Do you think you could forgive God now that you know He was with Claris and Deborah?"

"It would be hard, but considering that He helped them, maybe."

"God loves you in spite of all you have done."

"God seems so harsh."

"I think you are confusing God and the enemy."

"But if they had only lived..."

"I would do anything to change the past for you. Fred, you suffered an unfair blow. God didn't do it. But God is here now to help you heal, to help you live again, and give you a reason to hope."

There was another long silence. Charlie watched a family light some fireworks on the beach. The children cheered with delight. He gave Fred another moment and then said,

"It's time. We need to go."

"Where?" Fred asked.

Instantly, they were standing in the hospital. Fred looked around the room and saw a body lying on the operating table. He walked over and looked at the person. He looked into his own face.

"Will I make it?" he asked grimly.

"I don't know."

"What happens to me if I don't"

"That's not determined yet. I need you to listen. I've only got a couple more minutes. The first thing you need to know is that nothing is impossible with God. No matter how bleak a situation may seem; there is always hope! Don't forget that there is always hope."

"Hey, Charlie, things are beginning to turn dark. I'm starting to feel...cold...and strangely hot at the same time."

"Listen carefully to me. When Jesus was dying on the cross, one of those men who died with Him cried out for mercy. He asked Jesus to remember him when he came into his kingdom. That man deserved to go to hell, but in the last moment he sought forgiveness and he found it. No matter where you are, you are not beyond the reach of God."

"Charlie, something's happening to me."

"I know."

"Charlie, I'm…I'm afraid. Charlie! Charlie! Where are you, Charlie?"

Chapter Nineteen

"Where am I? I can't see. My skin is burning. The air stinks. Oh, it smells of sulfur. Ouch, what is happening to me? What is this emptiness in my stomach?"

"Hey, buddy. Welcome to hell." The large demon smacked Fred in the back and knocked him to the ground.

"Ouch! What's the matter with my skin?"

"It's burning, but you'll get used to it."

"What if I don't want to get used to it?"

"Ha, ha, ha." The big demon laughed. "Hey, buddy you're in hell."

"I don't want to be in hell."

"Well, you lived your life the way you wanted to live it, now it's time to pay for your decision."

"But I was a good person."

"I love that one. Everyone thinks that if they are good enough they might get a ticket to the other place. But you're wrong!" he said with fury in his voice. "You are a scumbag, and you are here. This is your destiny."

"Why can't I see it?"

"It's total blackness here. You'll learn to feel your way around."

"What if I don't want to learn?"

"What else are you going to do? You're stuck."

"What's the matter with my stomach? It feels empty?"

"That's the way it always feels down here. There are no warm fuzzy feelings down here. Your stomach will always hurt here where we are."

"I can change."

"It's too late for that. You're dead."

"What do you mean?"

"I mean you are dead, it's time for processing. Let's go."

"I'm not going." The demon picked him up off the floor, piercing him with his talons. "AAAHHHH!" he screamed. "Put me down."

"You don't give the orders around here."

"I don't want to go."

"You're dead."

"They might revive me up there."

"Fat chance."

"God, have mercy on me."

"SHUT UP!!" the demon yelled.

"Charlie said your mercy endures forever."

"SHUT THE HELL UP!" the demon yelled and threw Fred across the ground. The pain was almost unbearable. He struggled to get his breath. He could feel his skin boiling. The stench of sulfur was overpowering.

The demon picked him back up again. He heaved Fred into a chair that sat at a small desk. The demon struck a match and lit a candle. The small light illuminated the desktop. The demon went around the desk and pulled out a piece of paper.

"Sign it," he demanded. Fred scanned the document quickly and discovered that this document would seal his destiny to a place he would rather not go.

"I am not signing that document," he said with all the strength he could muster.

"I don't know how you ran your show up there, but you are going to sign that document because you aren't going anywhere until you do." The demon folded his arms and stared at Fred, his dark eyes piercing his soul.

Fred whispered a few words, "God, I'm a sinner, and I deserve to be here, but I'm asking you to help." A ray of light pierced the darkness like lightning across a night sky.

The demon pounced on Fred from across the desk. He grabbed him and began to choke him. "You are going to shut up and sign the document. Do you understand me?"

Fred fought with all his might. "Jesus…" he got out and the demon flew across the room. A second shaft of light entered the dark room, but the darkness swallowed it up. Fred cleared his throat and tried to form the words again; but before he could utter a sound, the demon was on top of him. The force of his landing took the wind out of his lungs.

"You are going to shut your mouth and sign that thing, or I'll sign it for you."

"That would be a forgery, and therefore worthless." Fred squeaked out.

The demon grabbed Fred's hand and forced the pen in it. "Now sign it!" he screamed in Fred's ear.

"Jesus, please forgive me of my sins." Fred managed to utter as the demon tried to force him to sign. The demon lost his grip and was thrown across the desk into the wall. This time the light penetrated the darkness, and the darkness could not overpower it. Fred fell to his knees and cried,

"God, please help those doctors to revive me. I want the chance to fix things in my life. Please pour out your mercy on me."

The demon screamed and pounced on Fred, winding him. "Shut up, it's not going to do you any good. You are already processed into hell."

"I'm not processed into hell. If I were, you wouldn't be so upset. I believe God is going to win this battle." Once again, he cried out to heaven for mercy, "God, Jesus, have mercy on me and those doctors up there. I don't deserve it, and I would totally understand if you chose not to have mercy on me, but please forgive me. Please, I beg you to have mercy on me." The demon smacked him across the face. The pain was excruciating and took his breath away. But the demon was tossed against the wall again as the light broke through the darkness and remained brighter and stronger.

The demon yelled, "It's over, now come on. Face your destiny. God can't hear you, and He doesn't care about you."

"No, there is still hope, and I believe God will rescue me. God, please forgive me and remember me when you come unto your throne." The prayer came effortlessly back to his memory.

"There is no such thing as hope." The demon argued with Fred. "It's over, come with me." The demon picked Fred up over his head and started to carry him away.

"God," Fred yelled as the demon moved toward the door, "pour out the blood of Jesus on me and forgive me." The demon threw Fred on the floor and screamed in agony.

"Don't ever use that name or His blood here. Do you understand me?"

"What, the blood of Jesus bothers you?" The demon screamed again. "Oh God," Fred cried out earnestly, "I don't deserve your mercy or forgiveness, but I am asking for it. Please help those doctors to save my life. I need the power of the blood of Jesus to deliver me."

The light broke through the ceiling; and this time, the darkness couldn't overcome it. The demon cowered in the corner. Fred opened his eyes to see an angel holding out his hand. The light blazed brightly from every pore of his body. The wingspan would have made an eagle jealous. The angel lifted Fred to his feet, and then effortlessly the two of them seemed to be lifting off the ground. The darkness was unable to defeat the light.

The next thing Fred knew, he was standing in the hospital operating room. The angel gently set him down, and Fred walked over to check the heart monitor. Yep, his heart was still beating. He turned to thank the angel, but the angel was gone.

Fred smiled because he was alive; and for the first time in many years, he felt hope. It had been so long that he had forgotten the buoyancy that hope gave life. Fred bowed his head and thanked the Lord for His forgiveness and mercy. Suddenly, Fred felt something else inside his heart: peace. "Thank you for the peace," he added "and thank you for my brother, Charlie."

Chapter Twenty

"His pulse is getting weaker," one of the doctors said. Fred turned and looked at the man lying on the table.

"Come on, hold on. Keep fighting!"

"Do you think I should continue? There is massive internal bleeding; and by the time we get his rib cage split, he'll probably be gone. There is so much damage that needs to be repaired," the doctor said.

"His pulse is weak, his blood pressure is dropping," the second doctor responded.

"God help me." Fred heard the first doctor whisper. No one else seemed to have heard the doctor's plea.

"Yes, Jesus, please help the doctor with his work." Fred cried out.

Immediately, Fred felt someone enter the room, but the doors had not budged. He looked around, and saw a man. He was standing off to the side, but he was looking intently at the man lying on the table.

Fred approached him, and the man made eye contact. His eyes glowed with a warmth and love he had never known. His expression was intense, yet he felt the most accepted and clean he had ever felt in his life. He knew without asking that this man held the power of life and death in his hands.

Fred wondered if he needed to bow or if he even had permission to speak. Both the power and the compassion of the man transfixed him. The man returned his gaze to the person lying on the table. Fred looked at him too. The doctors were huddled around the table working feverishly to save his life. Instruments were being passed between doctors and nurses. The machines were clicking and humming away.

The man finally broke the silence and spoke to Fred, "What do you think the outcome will be? Will the man on the table live or die?"

Fred didn't answer immediately, "Only you know the answer to that," he finally spoke without anyone noticing. Then one of the doctors spoke,

"His vitals are weakening. We are losing him."

"They have no control over what happens, do they?" Fred asked the man.

"They can impact it, but the decision is ultimately someone else's," he answered without looking up.

"That man lying on the table deserves to go to hell. But you've extended your mercy to him…to me." The man didn't look up. "With all due respect, I would like to ask a favor."

"What is your request?" the man asked Fred.

Fred looked down at himself on the table before asking, "Would you allow me to go back…to live?"

"Why?"

"To be honest, I've messed up a lot of your people's lives, and I would like a chance to fix that."

"He's about to flatline," a doctor who was watching the vital signs interjected. "I think he's gone!" As soon as the words left his mouth, time stopped. The monitors and the doctors all froze in position. It was just Fred and his Savior.

"That's not a good enough reason to go back," the man answered Fred, establishing eye contact with him again. "God has the ability to bring good things to those people whom you have tried to destroy. To be honest with you, I am afraid you would return to your old ways. It's a hard thing for a man to change. You are set in your ways, and you walk among people with whom there is no hope."

"Are you telling me that these people are beyond your saving grace?"

The man smiled at Fred. He looked at him with an intensity that caused Fred to lower his eyes. The man reached out and lifted Fred's head so he would look the man in the eyes once again. "Do you know what you are asking me?"

Fred paused and considered his question, "No."

"Your salvation is frail, and I see in you the ability to walk away."

"Every man and woman has that choice, but I hope with the things I've seen and experienced today that I would not make that choice. I want the chance to see if my light could shine for you, for Charlie and for Claris."

The man reached out and embraced Fred. The sweet smell of his robe enveloped him. His love was so powerful that Fred began to change his mind. He never wanted to leave this man's side. They parted their embrace. Fred looked into the man's eyes once again, seeing a tear drop from his cheek. The desire to return to life on earth burned in Fred's heart once again.

Suddenly, several other people appeared in the room: Charlie, Claris, and Deborah, who all stood around that operating table. Fred turned to see the three and felt joy in his soul. The feeling washed over him like a wave crashing down on the beach. He stepped away from the table and went over and embraced Charlie. Tears of joy streamed down both their faces.

"Thank you," Fred whispered in his ear. "You saved my soul." Charlie just smiled. Then he embraced Claris so tightly she lost her breath. They laughed and kissed. "You are the love of my life, and I have missed you dearly. My life has not been the same without you." Tears were streaming freely down both their faces. He picked up Deborah and twirled around with her in his arms. She squealed with delight. He kissed her cheek and told her to take care of her mom. She nodded emphatically. He set her down and embraced Claris again, "Please don't give up on me. I need your faith to survive. While I don't want to leave you ever again, I feel that I must."

"I understand and I will be waiting for you. Fred, I love you dearly." He caressed her cheek, ran his fingers through her hair, and kissed her once again.

Fred turned to face Jesus, "Jesus," he began with a slight tremble in his voice, "you saved my soul and I thank you. I want to go back to prove to them and to you that I can indeed live for you. I can turn my life completely over to you and the Father. I ask that I keep the memory of this time that I have shared with you and my family. If I go back without this memory, I believe you will be right; I am too weak of a man. But if you will let me remember this time, I will endeavor to be faithful to you. I want to prove my love for you."

Jesus smiled and embraced Fred. Jesus prayed for him, and he felt the power of the prayer deep within his soul. "I will let you go back. I have placed the memory of everything that has just taken place in your heart. Now be faithful and keep your word."

"Thank you again. I know that I do not deserve it."

"It is grace and mercy, and I want you to learn much more about it."

"I promise, I will."

Jesus turned to the body on the table. "You need to get back in there again." Fred paused and turned to look at his family once more. He ran to Claris for one more kiss. He touched Charlie's shoulder and rubbed Deborah's head. He took one last look at his family before walking over to the table and looking Jesus in the eyes. The love he felt enveloped him. He hopped up on the table and sat back into his body. He looked back at his family and waved to them one more time. They waved back. He looked up at Jesus who was looking at the man on the table. He reached out and lifted Jesus' gaze, and their eyes met once again.

"I want you to know," Fred began, "I really appreciate all you have done. Thank you for believing in me and giving me this chance. And one more thing, Jesus, I love you." Jesus smiled and his teeth shown like the stars in the sky. Fred lay down, re-entering his body and looking up as Jesus reached into his chest to begin working.

A couple of minutes passed as Jesus worked on Fred's body. Fred lifted his head twice and peeked over at his family. Fred heard three things as the world where Jesus was, faded, and time started to move forward...

"Good luck, we love you," came from his wife and Charlie. "I love you, Daddy," came from Deborah his daughter. "Go in peace," Jesus said and their world was gone.

"Wait a minute," the doctor watching the machines said, "his blood pressure is coming back up. His pulse is returning to normal."

Dr. Everheart said to the other doctors, "Look at this." They looked into the man's chest and gasped at what they saw. The leaking artery sealed itself. "Give me some suction." The nurse placed the instrument in Fred's chest and sucked out the blood and other fluids. His heart beat slowly returned to normal. Within a minute, everything looked normal and healthy; all that remained to be done was closing up. Each of the other doctors looked up, not believing their eyes. Dr. Everheart just smiled as he recognized the handiwork of God.

****

"Welcome back. I thought we were going to lose you." Fred blinked several times at the brightness of the lights. He was not in the operating room any longer. He was back in his body and lying in the hospital.

"Where am I?" he mumbled.

"You are in recovery."

"What happened?"

"You had several heart attacks, and an artery rupture. I thought you were going to check out on us."

"Who are you?"

"I'm Doctor Everheart, the chief surgeon."

"Howdy, Trail Mate," he got off with a weak laugh.

The man's eyes became big, "What did you just say?"

"I know all about you, Trail Mate," he mumbled.

Dr. Everheart was visibly stunned. He reached back for the chair and collapsed. There was a long moment of silence in the room. Fred drifted back to sleep momentarily. He awoke with a jolt because the doctor was sitting on his bed.

"Do you remember anything from your surgery?"

"I wish you could have seen your face when Jesus started to work on me."

"You saw that? He was in the operating room?"

"Yes…we'll have to talk about it soon." Fred said groggily, but Dr. Everheart pressed him for information.

"I've heard of people who remembered things about their surgery, like they woke up in the middle of everything. Was that what happened to you?"

"Nope. I was standing right beside you…even heard your prayers for help."

"You heard my prayers?"

"Of course." Fred was tired, but he wanted to tell the doctor what he saw. "I felt Jesus reach into my chest and heal my heart. I don't know all he did; I just know it was Him who brought me back to this world. I wish you could have seen your eyes when that happened. I saw the doctors and nurses looking down in my chest while he worked."

"What else did you see?"

"I remember," he said taking a shallow breath and trying to focus his mind, "He touched my chest after he fixed everything. What happened then?"

"Your artery healed itself. You're supposed to have a drainage tube coming out, but the once we suctioned the fluids off your chest cavity was clear."

Fred gave a weak smile and closed his eyes. The doctor realized that Fred needed to rest more than he needed answers. Dr. Everheart got up to leave, but Fred stopped him before he left the room, "What's today?"

"It's early Sunday morning." Fred winced at the information. "What's wrong?" he asked.

"Have you seen the morning paper?"

"I've been working on you all night. It's a little too early for that. Why?"

"You and I are going to need to talk when I wake up."

"You can be sure that I plan to talk with you a whole lot more when you recover from the anesthesia." The doctor turned and left the room.

"OK," Fred continued after the doctor left, "we'll get that fixed when I get to feeling better. I think I need to sle…" and he was gone.

Chapter Twenty-one

Dr. Everheart arrived home at two a.m. exhausted. He took a shower and crawled into bed just before three. He decided he needed to sleep after the emergency surgery, and he would have to miss church. His family got up quietly and went to church without him. After they got home, the smell of bacon, eggs, pancakes, and a fresh pot of coffee interrupted Dr. Everheart's sleep. As he lay quietly in bed, he heard his children playing at the door. Then he heard his wife whisper, "OK, go see if he's awake."

The kids came over to the bed and said quietly, "Daddy, are you awake?"

"No" he said without moving a muscle.

"We know you're awake because you answered us," they said and then jumped on the bed with him. He scooped the kids up in his arms and gave them a growling bear hug. He looked over at his wife who was standing at the door. She laughed and said,

"You've got a few minutes before we're ready," then she headed back to the kitchen.

Dr. Everheart tussled and played with his kids on the bed, and they squealed with delight. He got himself up, dressed, and was sitting in his place at the table in a few minutes. His hair was disheveled, and he needed to shave; but he gave his wife a genuine, loving smile. They shared a nice, quiet breakfast that was filled with laughter and smiles.

When breakfast was done and the kitchen cleaned up, the kids went up to the play room, and Dr. Everheart and his wife retired to the family room. They had just started to flip through the paper when the phone rang.

"Hello." Dr. Everheart said as he answered the phone. "Good morning, Dr. Corin... Yes, it is a beautiful day... No, I had an emergency procedure last night so I am just getting up...Page three, yeah I've got it..." He flipped the front page back and saw the headline,

Heart surgeon Dr. Everheart. Is he an asset or a liability?
He scanned the article quickly. "Oh, my God," he sighed. His wife curled up beside him to see what he was reading. Her mouth hung open as she read.

"No sir, I don't know anything about this. Yes sir, I can see how this could be damaging to the department as well as the hospital... Yes sir, they were my patients... At their last check-ups, everything was fine... Yes, I imagine we have some film on these patients back in the records department... Yes sir, I can meet you there in about an hour."

Dr. Everheart hung up the phone visibly shaken. He re-read the article that was full of accusations about improper procedures and incidences of leaving instruments inside of patients during surgery. Within the hour, he was back at the hospital digging through the records department to find the files for the patients who were mentioned in the article in the paper. Dr. Corin was working at his side.

The media circus began within hours. All three networks had local correspondents at the hospital pumping the story out on the local news. Thankfully, the story didn't garner national attention. While the news stations repeated the allegations that were mentioned in the paper, they also mentioned Dr. Everheart's long time good standing with the hospital. The administration made statements in support of Dr. Everheart and told the media that he would not be placed on administrative leave unless or until these allegations could be substantiated.

While the media pressed for every angle on the story, the administration dug hard to try and get to the bottom of the mess. After three days, the hospital board called a meeting to discuss the situation and what outcomes might be considered. They were in the middle of the meeting when someone barged into the room and told the board members that they needed to watch what was going on in the news. There was a news conference being broadcast live from down at the entrance to the hospital.

"Thank you for showing up today. I appreciate the interest the media has in my recovery. I want you to know that I am feeling fine. I guess when a man worth a few billion dollars goes in for surgery, everyone wants to know if he came out alive…especially those listed in the will." The press members chuckled. "Well, here I am. I want to thank this hospital staff for being so wonderful to me. I want to thank God for rescuing me from death. I would also like to thank one of the best surgeons in the world, Dr. Everheart, or Dr. E as he likes to be called.

"I understand that there has been a terrible media campaign going on against this doctor for some alleged errors in his surgery. I want the media to know that there is not a finer surgeon in this hospital than Dr. E. I plan to offer my assistance to him, and we will get the best legal team in this country to help him if it comes to that.

"So, thank you very much for coming to check on me, and you can be sure that there will be more news on Dr. E. in the coming days. I put my name and reputation on the line that his good name will be restored. Thank you again."

****

Five minutes later, Fred was wheeled before the board. The chairman spoke first, "Mr. Collins, thank you for coming. I also want to thank you for the positive PR that you just provided. Sadly, I have to inform you that the allegations are strong, and they can be substantiated. We have solid proof that Dr. E. has made some serious mistakes."

"Would the board consider taking a thirty-minute recess to allow me to talk with Dr. E. and to get a few other people here that might help clear this matter up?"

"I am not sure you are going to be able to clear up such a matter in thirty minutes," the chairman responded. "However, if you think you can present some evidence that might sway our opinion within thirty minutes; we will grant you that time."

"Thank you, Mr. Chairman. Dr. E., may I see you in your office, please. Robb, wheel me around to the elevator, we have a few calls to make." While they went to Dr. E.'s office, both Robb and Fred stayed busy making calls. When they arrived, Fred gave Robb some final instructions as he prepared to meet with Dr. E. When Robb left, he closed the door.

"Dr. E.," Fred began, "first, I want to thank you for the outstanding work you performed on me."

"We're supposed to talk about that, but life has gone a little crazy."

"Do you remember a patient of yours by the name of Charlie Collins?"

"Uncle Charlie," he said with the first smile he had in three long days. "I miss Uncle Charlie. How do you know him?"

"He's my brother." Dr. E. was visibly shocked. "I know you operated on him when he had his heart attack."

"Yes sir; that was a unique situation."

"I now know how unique that was. My brother and I did not see things eye-to-eye. I considered my brother to be a weak, religious nut. When he died, I made a vow to get back at anybody's life he touched or influenced. You, being the last doctor to treat him, were on my list.

"The article in the paper that started the firestorm in your life is my fault. I take full responsibility. I am also coming to you to ask you to forgive me. I know I do not deserve it after what I have done, but I am asking for it nonetheless."

"You created this problem for me, and now you want me to forgive you? Why did you do this to me?"

"I was trying to destroy everything my brother did. I was wrong."

"So you expect me to forgive you after you made a total mess of my life?"

"Expect is a big word, I was thinking more like hope. I will tell you right now that within the hour this whole mess will go away. You will be restored to your position, and I will take care of the media as well. I will fix this problem to the best of my ability. But I am still asking for your forgiveness." There was total silence in the room.

"You are saying that when we go back before the board in fifteen minutes all of this will clear itself up?"

"Yes, it should."

"If you can wave that magic wand, then yes, I will forgive you. But this mess had better disappear."

"That's good enough for me," and he reached out to shake his hand. Dr. E. was hesitant at first, but he did shake his hand.

****

"Mr. Chairman, I want to thank you for the thirty-minute recess. I believe we have all the information that you will need to clear this matter up. My associate is passing out some information that will help in this matter.

"If everyone will look down at page one, you will discover that I am the source that created this negative campaign against Dr. E. The details of my plan are included for your benefit. If there is anything that is unclear in the matter or you would like to see the supporting evidence, we can provide that for you within twenty-four hours.

"I realize that my actions have brought a dark shadow on this hospital. If you will turn to page two, you will see the promotional campaign that will be undertaken to restore the good image of this hospital to the community. Please note that the cost for this campaign will be funded entirely through my corporation."

"We could sue you for your actions. What you have done to both this doctor and our institution is reprehensible. We should have you arrested," one of the board members suggested.

"That's correct, but I believe we can put our resources to a much better use. The cost to take me to court would be astounding because I have very deep pockets. I believe it would be far better for us to spend that money as described on page three.

"I am proposing an expansion of your current facility. I want to create a world-class heart center right here at Virginia Beach General. I am proposing up to a one hundred million dollar expansion with state-of-the-art technology. We will create a board to guide the construction and staffing of the new facility. The staff for the new facility will be headed up by our very own Dr. E." he said with a smile and a wink in his direction. Dr. E. stared at him, stunned.

"It says here that you are putting up fifty million of your own money?"

"That is correct."

"Why are you doing this?" the chairman asked.

"Dr. E. is a good man, and he deserves to work in a state-of-the-art facility. I also want to right a very bad wrong. Mr. Chairman, can we take a vote on whether you will accept my terms? I hope everyone notes that the terms of this agreement include the fact that none of you will ever discuss the terms of the agreement and that all malice lawsuits would hereby be dispensed."

"I think your proposals will sail right on through..."

"Mr. Chairman, we can't just forget that this man libeled our hospital and one of our doctors."

"John," the chairman said controlling his ire, "did you read what he plans to do for us?"

"Yes, but..."

"There are no buts, vote! All in favor? And it carries."

"Thank you, Gentlemen," Fred stated. "I will need those sheets back from you, wouldn't want any of this out in the public. Mr. Chairman, my lawyer will be in touch in the next couple of days to start the legal work for our deal."

"Sounds great. I think this meeting is adjourned." Everyone took time to speak to Fred who was feeling a little tired from the meeting. Dr. E. and Robb were the only two left when Fred began to feel the full effects of the exhaustion on his body. They wheeled Fred back to his room and helped him get back into bed. Robb stepped out into the hall, leaving Dr. E. in the room with Fred.

"I don't know how to thank you for today."

"Forgiving me, remember?"

"No, I haven't forgotten. I can't believe you told them that I will be leading this new facility."

"You'll see it in writing when my lawyer gets done with them."

"Thanks again. Now, it is time for you to rest…Doctor's orders."

"One more thing before you leave. I think you could use some time off after all you have been through and before all the expansion excitement begins around here. I have made arrangements for you to fly in my private jet down to my residence in the Florida Keys. I have some staff there who will take care of your every need. You've got the place for a week. Don't worry about things here, I talked with the chairman of the board and made the arrangements with him. The plane will be gassed and ready for your departure from Norfolk International Airport at nine a.m. tomorrow morning."

"Are you serious?"

"Yeah. And again, I'm very sorry."

"For what? You just gave my family the vacation of a lifetime, and you have also given me the best job I could ever imagine."

"So you forgive me?"

"From the bottom of my heart," he said as he shook hands with Fred. "You've done too much, now it's time for you to rest. No arguments. Rest!"

Fred closed his eyes and smiled for the first time in many years. There was a peace that washed over him like a spring rain. He welcomed the peace in his heart, and, within a few minutes, he was sound asleep.

Chapter Twenty-two

"Marge, can you come in here, please?" George King called to his secretary.

"Yes sir, I'm on my way." She came quickly into his office and stood in front of his desk. He motioned for her to sit down, which she did. He came around the desk and sat next to her.

"Marge, I guess you know things aren't going too well around here…"

"Oh my, that plant went dry, and I need to water it," she said jumping up and going over to the plant.

"Marge, please come over and sit down. The plant can wait. I need to talk to you." Marge returned to her seat, but she would not look George in the eye. George noticed that she was crying. "Oh, Marge, we've made a good team for many years. You know I think we're both going to miss this place." She still didn't respond; she just turned away.

"This has been the best job anyone could ever have wanted," she said with a sob.

"Yeah, you said it." He noticed his own emotions were a little too close to the surface. After a long moment, he continued, "There is no sense beating around the bush, I think I will close the office at the end of the month. You can stay on and help me clear everything out. I have a few more closings next month, but I will handle them from home. I would appreciate your help in cleaning this place out. I want to leave it in the best shape possible, and I know you do, too." He stopped because the lump in his throat was preventing him from going on. They sat silently there avoiding each other's eyes and neither knowing what to say.

The phone rang and broke the silence. Marge dutifully got up and returned to her desk to answer it. By the time she arrived at her desk, her professional tone was impeccably back in place.

"Mr. King, the phone's for you, a Charlotte Cranford."

"This is George, how can I help you?"

"Hi, Mr. King. I don't know if you remember me, but my name is Charlotte Cranford, and I live over in Kings Grant."

"I think I remember you, aren't you on Webber Avenue?"

"Yes sir, that's correct."

"What can I do for you?"

"Well, I was thinking about listing my house, and I wanted to know if you would come by and give me your suggestions about listing my place. You helped me find this house, and I will probably list it with you. I do want you to know that I am meeting with three other agents and then making my decision."

"Charlotte, I am closing my office and doing my work from home. I will give you great service just as I always have; but I want to be sure you know up front that I am closing the office, if that affects your decision."

"I still want you to come by."

"Great. How does tomorrow evening about seven sound?"

"Perfect, I will see you then."

"Marge, can you come back in here, please. We need to finish our conversation." She took her time and sat down across from him. "Look, this is unpleasant for me, too."

"You would never have talked in a negative tone like you did to that woman if things weren't this bad. I hate it for you."

"Thanks, Marge. I want to talk to you about one more thing. I set up an interview for you."

"You what?" her indignation rang out.

"Yeah. I called the Stump Brothers agency, and they said they could use someone like you to help organize their office."

"You got me an interview with the enemy. Are you crazy?"

"Marge, you are the best. You deserve to have a good job. I have been assured that they will meet your salary requirements and maybe include a little raise."

"I would never…"

"Thank you for your loyalty, but I am asking you as a friend to go down there."

"You want me to spy on them?"

"No. I want you to do your job just the way you did it here. Give his office the class it needs. I set you up an appointment for this afternoon at 4:00. Please go and live up to the recommendation I gave you."

Tears rolled down her cheeks, and she didn't make an attempt to hide them from him. "You are the kindest man I know. And you are a great boss." Then she ran out to the restroom.

****

Marge was seated at precisely 3:55 in the Stump Brothers' realty office. While their offices were nice, they did not have the class of King Realty. They were missing the beautiful details that she would need to bring to the office. The furniture, while nice, had some bumps and scrapes. No one had bothered to use a cover stick to make them look nicer.

The main desk would have to be moved. She liked to face the customer as they walked in the door and not have them enter to her side. By turning the desk ninety degrees, she would also be able to enjoy looking out the window which was currently to the main receptionist's back.

"Where was the receptionist anyway?" she thought. She had been sitting here for five whole minutes, and no one had greeted her. Actually, it seemed that no one was in the office because the phone was ringing off the hook. George had a policy that if a phone rang three times, someone else in the office needed to pick up the line because obviously Marge was away from her desk.

Marge waited fifteen minutes, and still no one came to greet her. The phone's incessant ringing was driving her crazy so she got up and walked around the receptionist's desk and answered the line. "Stump Brothers' Realty, how may I help you?"

"Is this Marge?" came the voice over the line.

"Yes, who is speaking please?"

"It's me, Steve Stumps, I was hoping you would pick up."

"Where are you? We were supposed to have an interview ten minutes ago."

"I'm very sorry about that. There has been a change in our situation."

"You've decided you don't want to hire me?"

"Absolutely not. The problem is with our family. Our father has had a major heart attack, and the family is rushing home to be with him."

"I am so sorry to hear that. Please forgive my outburst."

"Don't worry about it. We have a slight problem on our hands. You see, our father runs a very successful real estate company in his hometown. So we are going to have to move back home and run Daddy's business. Are you with me?"

"Yes, sir."

"Well, that means we are going to have close up shop there in Virginia Beach. All of our closings that are ready to go are in the filing cabinet directly in front of you. They are in order by date of closing, not alphabetical."

"Should I be taking notes?"

"Yeah, we are going to need you to run through all our closings for us."

"I can't do that alone. Besides, I am not a licensed real-estate broker."

"Well, we were hoping you could convince your old boss to help out."

"You mean, you want Mr. King and me to close your deals?"

"Yes, and King Realty keeps the commission, too. Actually, there is a folder on the desk in front of you that has several important documents in it. It says 'critical docs'...do you see it?"

"Yes," she said, opening the folder and inspecting the papers inside.

"You will find the lease agreement on the building, the furniture and equipment, and some legal documents that allow you to complete the sale of the properties in question. There is another legal document which transfers all the properties we have listed to King Realty. Once the customer's current six month contracts run out, you can put them back on the standard six percent commission."

"You are transferring all of this over to King Realty? Why?"

"I told you, Daddy had a heart attack, and we can't run two real estate companies. Now if there are any other questions, I will get our lawyer to contact you. I need to run." And the line went dead.

Marge sat and studied the papers trying to process what had just happened. There was a letter to George explaining everything that Steve had just covered with her on the phone. The contracts for all the leases were standard lease agreements. After about five minutes, she picked up the phone and called George.

"You need to get over here right now," she said, when he answered his phone.

"I'm not coming over there. If they are looking to hire me and humiliate me further, I am not interested."

"Shut up and just get in your car and get over here. No more questions, just do it!" she exclaimed, and hung up the phone.

George was absolutely stunned by the way she spoke, but something made him get in his car and drive over to Stump Brothers' Realty. He arrived to find Marge going through the closing files. She looked up at him when he walked in and apologized for her abruptness.

"Well, I don't think you have ever spoken to me like that. I was so stunned I just came over. Where is everybody?"

"You and I are it."

"What are you talking about? Should you be going through those files?"

"You better have a seat, and let me explain things to you."

For the next couple of minutes, she explained what had happened. Then she gave him the folder with the important papers, so he could read everything in there for himself. His shock was thorough. He kept saying, "I don't understand," and "I don't believe this." When things finally sank in, and they both realized that King Realty had been saved, they started to dance. Then they jumped up and down, and finally they both gave an undignified, "Whoopee!" and pumped their arms in the air.

All the while, Fred smiled broadly, sitting in a limo across the street watching the pair as they celebrated.

Chapter Twenty-three

There was a rap at the door, and Margaret Johnson yelled, "I'm closed! Can't you see I am going out of business?"

The disheveled old man knocked once again and motioned for her to come to the door. Margaret reluctantly went to the door and explained to him one more time,

"Look, I am going out of business. I don't have any more flowers, go over there to Flower World, they can help you."

"I wasn't lookin' for flowers, I was hopin' for a little money to buy some food."

"I just told you, I'm going out of business. I don't have any money."

"Folks tell me that they can always count on you for some food."

"Not today." She said and turned to go back in the store. The disheveled old man turned to walk away. His clothes were torn; his hopes dashed. Compassion gripped her so she went back to the door and called to him,

"Hey, I'm going to have a bowl of soup. If you want to join me that would be fine." The old man brightened up and went into the store. "Excuse the mess; when you are closing up shop after almost thirty years, it's hard to get rid of things."

"What happened, if you don't mind me asking?" He set his knapsack down on the floor.

"It's that Flower World over there. They just ran me out of business," she told him, while opening the can of soup and putting it in a bowl to heat in the microwave. "My husband and I started this business together, and now it's just me. I lost him six years ago."

"I'm sorry ma'am," he said while pulling a table and a couple of chairs together. He found some paper towels and made place mats out of them and then folded a couple more to make napkins. "So what are you going to do now?"

"I don't know, flowers are all I really care about."

"Why don't you go buy those guys out?"

"Ha, ha," she laughed. "That takes real money, something I don't have."

"You have a nice laugh ma'am."

"Thank you. Probably the first time I've laughed in a month."

"Shouldn't wait so long between laughs."

"Yeah, you're right. Hey, look at the table, you have it fixed nice for us." She put their bowls of soup and some crackers on the table. She picked up her spoon, but he reached across the table and touched her hand gently. She looked up at him, and he said,

"Gotta thank the man upstairs, don't we." He pulled his hat off and prayed, "Dear Lord, we thank you for taking care of our every need today. We lack nothing because you supply everything. For that, we are deeply thankful. We ask that you bless this food which we are about to eat. Amen."

"Amen. And thank you. I don't normally forget I've just been distracted lately with closing this business."

"That's alright. So what you gonna do now that this chapter of your life is over?"

"I don't know. I have a cousin who has a flower shop, I might go help her."

"You know Mama used to tell me that when one door closes another one opens. I believe that God is gonna be looking out for you."

"Thanks," she said with a smile, "I needed to hear that." They sat eating and talking for the next twenty minutes. The old man encouraged and lifted Margaret's spirit in a way she couldn't explain, so she was disappointed when the old man got up and said he had to leave.

"Can I get you anything?" she asked as he prepared to leave.

"No ma'am. You just met my daily needs. What more could any stranger ask? Thank you, very kindly, I pray God's richest blessing upon you." And with that the old man was gone.

Margaret went back to clean the table where she found a dollar bill hidden under the bowl from which the old man had eaten. Next to it, on the napkin was written a note, "God will provide. Thanks." Margaret ran to the door, but the old man was nowhere to be found. She put the dollar in her pocket and cleaned things up.

A few moments later, there was another rap on the door. Margaret looked up expectantly. It was her UPS man with some packages. "You need to sign for these, Mrs. Johnson."

"I didn't order anything. You know I am going out of business. What have you got?" she said, as she opened the door.

"Two packages. You need to sign here and here, plus there is a $1.00 delivery fee that you have to pay and then sign right here that you paid it."

"I am not signing for any packages that I didn't order. Who are they from? Look, there is no return address. I don't want them and heck if you think I am going to give you a dollar for something I don't want."

"Mrs. Johnson, they are addressed to you. You have to take them."

"No. I can refuse to accept delivery of those packages."

"Well, I have specific instructions to bring these packages to you and to get you to sign these papers. The packing slip even says to find you here at this address."

"Let me see those." she said abruptly, taking the packages from the UPS driver. "They are addressed to me here at this address, but I didn't order whatever is inside those packages. Take them back," she said, handing them back to him.

"I've been your UPS delivery driver for years; it's just two more packages."

"Can we look inside to see what's in them?"

"Mrs. Johnson, I have several more stops before the end of my day. Will you please sign so I can get going?"

"Oh, alright. I wouldn't want to hold up your deliveries."

"I hate to mention it, but there is the matter of the dollar delivery charge…"

"Look, I don't have any money," she said as she pulled out her pants pockets. Then a dollar floated out of her pocket and landed on the floor. Then she remembered the dollar the homeless fellow had left beside his plate. The delivery man reached down and picked it up and waved it in the air as he turned to leave the store. At that exact moment, one of the packages started to chirp.

"Hey, what is that? Is that your cell phone?"

"No. Check one of your packages," he said, as he hopped into his truck to leave. "I think one of them is ringing." And he drove away.

He was indeed right. One of her packages was chirping. She pulled a stool over to the front counter and picked up the larger package and ripped it open. Sure enough, a phone was inside the package, and it was ringing. She flipped it up and answered it.

"Hello."

"Hello, is this Mrs. Johnson?"

"Yes it is. Who is this?"

"It's Kelly Shores, I'm the assistant manager of the store. I am sorry to bother you, but a supplier is here with some extra roses and wants to know if we want them. I figured with the Hampton funeral orders coming in we might need them."

"What are you talking about? My store is closed."

"I'm sorry about your old store Mrs. Johnson, but I am talking about your new store."

"You're talking about my what?"

"Maybe I should start from the beginning. This is Kelly Shores from Flower World, the store you bought today. I am the current assistant manager, and I hope to be able to keep my job. Anyway, I am calling about the extra flowers, do you want me to go ahead and get them?"

"I own Flower World? You must be mistaken. They are the ones who put me out of business."

"The previous owner of Flower World called an employee meeting this morning to say he and the manager were heading back up north to take care of some other business interest. Anyway, they told us that you had bought the place, lock, stock, and barrel."

"How on earth could I afford to buy that place?"

"I don't know. I am just going by what they told us."

There was a moment of silence. Margaret poured the remainder of the contents of the envelope onto the counter. She found keys with tags for Flower World. She also found an address book with suppliers listed in it. Her mind was reeling.

"Mrs. Johnson, what do you want me to do about the flowers?"

"Honey, if you think we need them; and they are a good deal, take them."

"Thanks. I'll do it. Looking forward to meeting you."

"Thanks, bye." Margaret hung the phone up. She looked through the keys one more time. The keys were to everything at Flower World, including front door, back door, and the safe. What is going on? She opened the other package and discovered legal documents. She tried to focus her mind so she could read. She scanned down the first page; it was a contract to buy the Flower World business. The terms and agreement all looked right until she got to the very end where it listed the selling price…$1.00.

"What?" she shrieked out. "I bought the Flower World for one dollar? This has got to be a mistake." Then she looked at the papers that the deliveryman had put in her hand after she had signed for the packages. They weren't standard UPS papers; they were the final contract to purchase the Flower World which she had signed.

She read the contract again. It was legitimate. She was not going out of business at all, she was getting into a huge business venture, bigger than she ever imagined. Tears streamed down her face as she looked across the parking lot at Flower World.

A young man walked out of the store to the big sign in front of the business. He took down the words of the old message and put up the following one:

WELCOME NEW OWNER, MARGARET JOHNSON

Fred sat back smiling in the comfort of his limousine. The driver was the first to speak, "The sign changing out front, that was great!"

"I liked that one myself. Did you see her face as they put her name up there?"

"I was afraid she might have a heart attack."

"I know, I better be careful how I go about helping people in the future. But I have to confess, it sure is fun." He looked over at Margaret Johnson who had left her store and was walking over to Flower World. He could see a sense of awe and wonder in her eyes.

"Take me back to the hotel, I need to get out of these rags and get cleaned up."

"Did you really let her make you a cup of soup?"

"Yeah, why not. I wanted to see if she had the character people said she did."

"Boss, you are crazy, but I like this side of you better than the old you."

"I like me better too. Now back to the hotel for a much-needed shower."

"Right Boss."

Chapter Twenty-four

Jenny arrived home from the supermarket, tired. She could feel the extra weight of the baby dragging her down. After putting the groceries away, she made herself a warm cup of herbal tea. She sat at the table and was glad to get the weight off her feet. She did some paperwork; but after twenty minutes, she was just too tired to do any more.

She crawled onto the couch, pulled the afghan over herself, and was asleep before she was barely settled in. An hour later she woke up and lay there half listening to the evening news and half in a dreamy state. When she finally pried herself off the couch, she stumbled into the kitchen and made some something to eat. The news went off, and a rerun of Cheers came on while she ate. When it was over, she picked up her dishes and headed to the sink to clean up the kitchen.

When she was done, she settled back at the table to get her paperwork done. She wrote checks for a few bills and got them ready to mail. She went over to her computer, read through her email, updated her Facebook page, and commented on a few of her friends' pages. Even though she had a nice nap before supper, she was ready to go to bed.

Jenny showered, washed her face, and, then before heading to bed, put a load of towels in the washing machine. The machine offered a gentle hum as Jenny climbed into bed. She picked up the book that lay on her bedside table but only read a few pages before she turned her light out. Jenny drifted off to sleep with the hum of the washer machine doing its job.

The dreams came like a cold front passing through an area. She was at the Bluebird, when three hundred customers walked in and demanded service. She was by herself and she couldn't handle the crowd or the stress of the moment. Next, she found herself moving into a dinky apartment with no bathroom. She had to ask her neighbor if she could use her bathroom. On the third trip, the neighbor lost patience with her and told her to go someplace else. She walked over to the gas station but had to go again as soon as she got home. She woke up because she realized that all the trips to the bathroom in her dreams were actually signals from her own body that she needed to go.

The washer was done, and her place was quiet when Jenny got back into bed. Before she was comfortable, she reached over and opened the window so she could listen to the ocean. She had to strain slightly, but she could hear the rhythmic crashing of the surf, which was a soothing sound to her soul. Soon she was drifting off into a gentle sleep.

She found herself walking up a sand dune and over to see the ocean. It was a warm summer day, and there were few people out enjoying the beautiful day. She walked down by the water's edge and allowed it to wash over her feet. The sun was warm, but the water was still cool. She walked along the beach feeling the peace and tranquility in her soul.

She looked up and saw an umbrella with someone sitting under it. It was odd because there were no other beach umbrellas around. It was the only one. She looked again, and there appeared to be a man alone under the umbrella. The other chair was empty. She felt drawn to the man, but was uncertain why. As she drew closer, she saw a puff of smoke come out from under the umbrella. She knew immediately it was Uncle Charlie.

She ran up and sat down beside him. The shade of the umbrella was comforting. She turned and looked at him. It was Uncle Charlie sitting there smoking his pipe. She didn't know what to say, so she started with, "Hi stranger, how you been?"

"Heavenly," came his answer with a smile. The two sat quietly taking in the beautiful day. Then he asked, "How are things down at the Bluebird?"

"You were right about Carlos. He's been a great help since you left…" her voice trailed off as she said it. He pretended not to notice.

"I told you I saw some potential in him. What about the old boys, they still coming around to see you?"

"They haven't missed a day. How's heaven?"

"Sweeter than you can ever imagine. Loraine and I have a café and a whole new crowd of regulars. I have more fun than you can imagine."

"I'm glad to hear it." Jenny turned and watched a ghost crab come out of his hole and run down by the water. He captured something and ran back to his hole. A seagull drifted by and landed a short distance away on the sand.

"Whenever you come to see me, there is something on your mind. So what's up?"

"Getting right down to business, I see."

"I am figuring this is a dream or a vision or something, but it is obvious to me that you have something you want to talk about. By the way, are you really here, or is this just my way of trying to understand what's on your mind?"

"Questions…that's a good thing." Uncle Charlie took time to light his pipe again because it had gone out. He wasn't in any hurry, and that agitated Jenny slightly.

"Well?"

"I guess you could say that I am here, at least I am aware of our time together even though I am up there. I am fortunate to be a part of this vision or dream."

"So why have you come to me?"

"It's complicated, but it has to do with all that you have been going through lately."

"I've been through a lot, so you'll have to narrow it down. You know, I could have used your help and guidance with some of these things. I don't have anyone to turn to for help."

"That's not true. Someone has been with you throughout this whole process."

"You mean you have been with me?"

"Not me silly, the Father has been closer to you than you could imagine," he said tenderly as he reached out and took her hand. Jenny held his hand. It felt so real. Just then a nice breeze began to blow. Jenny closed her eyes and allowed the breeze to blow through her mind. It carried her burdens away and left peace in her heart. The nice feeling was interrupted by Uncle Charlie as he squeezed her hand. "I do want to talk with you about something."

Jenny opened her eyes and looked out at the ocean. She wanted to stay right here in this moment. She wanted to live with this kind of peace.

"Jenny?" his soft voice interrupted. "Can we talk?"

"I suppose…"

"I would like to talk with you about my brother…"

"Absolutely not!" she responded throwing his hand back in his lap. Jenny turned away from Uncle Charlie. She tried to restore the peace, but her mind was running.

"Jenny, we need to talk about my brother."

"Your brother caused Mike and I to break up. He sent Steve into my life and I think it's your brother's fault that I am pregnant," she yelled at him.

"No, it's not," he pleaded.

"You're not going to blame me, are you?"

"Well, I guess he did have a hand in the matter," he conceded. "I know he sent Steve down to break you and Mike up. What he did was wrong and you have every right to be mad at him."

"Thank you," she said deflating. "I know I have some responsibility for my condition, but I also know he had a hand in setting up the situation."

"True. But being mad at him doesn't fix the problem. Blaming him doesn't help the situation."

"It helps me to blame him."

"No, Jenny, it hurts you," he said gently. "Unforgiveness only helps to build roots of bitterness, resentment, anger, you name it. Those things can destroy your life. I want you to be free."

"You want me to forgive your brother. Let him off scott free?"

"Not exactly. I want you to release him to the Lord. When you forgive someone, you release them to God, and you release it from yourself. It's like mailing a letter, you are sending it away. Don't let unforgiveness poison your life. Mail it to God."

"But if I forgive him, give it to God as you say; what if God decides to forgive him? Then no one has to pay for what he did to me…"

"Your part is to forgive, let God do whatever He decides is best."

Jenny got up and walked down by the water. Uncle Charlie followed. She let the water wash up on her feet. It felt cool and refreshing. Uncle Charlie picked up a shell, admired its beauty and then released it back to the water.

"What if I tried to forgive and the feelings come back?"

"Like a letter sent to the wrong location, you must return to sender. You can't forgive and then go get it back. The truth is the feelings will come back to you, but you have to refuse to let them find a place in your heart. Forgiveness is releasing the feelings, the hold that unforgiveness has on your heart."

"I want to but… it's hard Uncle Charlie."

"That's right, it is the most difficult thing you have to do. Forgiveness costs you all those feelings, but it gives you peace, joy, and righteousness."

"Why righteousness?"

"Righteousness is right standing with God. Unforgiveness doesn't allow you to be in right standing with God. If you can find it in your heart to forgive someone as undeserving as my brother, then you will be like your Father in Heaven. When you can forgive, then you will be in right standing with Him because you will be doing as He does."

Tears streamed down Jenny's face, "I want to forgive, but it is hard. Pray for me."

"How about if I pray with you?"

"I would like that." He held her hands and she started, "God, I want to forgive Uncle Charlie's brother. Please help me to release all these bad feelings. I want to be free."

"Now proclaim it," Uncle Charlie whispered.

"I…I forgive Fred Collins." The tears flowed freely, and Uncle Charlie embraced her. She cried, and he allowed her to release it. A few moments later, Jenny released her hold on him and reached into her pocket for a tissue she didn't know she had. She blew her nose and wiped her eyes. The warmth of the sun radiated on her, but it also seemed to radiate from her heart.

Uncle Charlie and Jenny walked down the beach together just enjoying the peace between them as two old friends. Neither spoke; they just walked in silence. It was Uncle Charlie who stopped when they saw a man up in the distance. Jenny turned to see what was wrong, but Uncle Charlie just stared up at the man.

"What is it, Uncle Charlie?"

"I have to go," he said.

Jenny looked up the beach at the man and then back at Uncle Charlie. "Why?" she asked.

"You need to talk with Him."

Jenny looked up the beach again. "Who is it, Uncle Charlie?"

He didn't answer. He walked up to Jenny and put his hands on her cheeks. He had the biggest smile she had ever seen. His face seemed to glow as she looked at him. "Jenny, I love you, and I will be watching over you."

"Uncle Charlie, I love you, and I miss spending time with you." They embraced. Jenny shed some fresh tears. Uncle Charlie wiped them from her cheek. Then he turned and started to walk up to the dune. "Thank you." Jenny called out to him. He turned and smiled at her one last time before he disappeared over the dune.

Chapter Twenty-five

Jenny looked up the beach and saw the man who was still a pretty good distance away. She ambled down to the water and allowed it to wash over her feet. She knew she should be walking toward the man...running to him. She stood looking out at the water, working in her heart to close all the doors where she did not want him to look. She made sure the doors were locked tight and then swept the halls of her heart clean.

She looked down the beach at him approaching. She gave her heart one last inspection; and when she felt it was safe, she started to walk toward the man. As she walked, she rehearsed what she wanted to say. She wanted to steer him clear of some topics, those doors she tightly closed, because she hoped to keep them secret from him.

The distance between them was closing. When he was merely one hundred yards away, something happened. At first, she couldn't put a finger on it. She felt calm. He was two hundred feet away. A peace began to flood her soul...a peace that was beyond understanding. He was one hundred feet away. What was it she wanted to talk with him about? Her mind was clear. There was no worry, no fear, no concern about what he might think or say.

When he was ten feet away, he stopped and so did she. She looked at him; he was not what she expected...maybe better than she expected. She looked into his eyes and tried to see the color but found herself lost in the pools of love that emanated from them. She could swim in those eyes for hours. She had to struggle to pull her gaze away.

She looked at his face, and he was smiling. It was the biggest and warmest smile she had ever seen. His teeth gleamed in the light. In her heart, she realized he was smiling because he was with her. He was glad to be in her presence. He had joy in his spirit because they were together. She felt that he wanted to spend time with her. When the questions tried to rise in her heart, they were smothered by his love and abiding peace.

She looked at him, and he stood there with his arms spread open wide. She hesitated only for a moment, and then she leapt into his arms. He twirled her around and around. He whispered softly into her ear, "I love you, Jenny." The words brought tears to Jenny's eyes, and they flowed freely. He set her down gently on the sand, but she refused to release her grip on him.

He started to laugh. An unspeakable joy filled his soul and overflowed into her heart. Suddenly, she couldn't help but join him in his laughter. She broke the embrace and wiped the tears from her eyes. She looked at him and found acceptance in his eyes. They stood together and looked out at the ocean just in time to see a porpoise jump out of the water and land with a big splash. They looked at each other and laughed.

Jenny reached out her hand and took his as they began to walk along the shore. Nothing was said; nothing had to be said. Occasionally, they bent over and picked up shells. He always tossed his back in the water after admiring it, but Jenny put hers in her pocket. He finally came to a stop and looked out at the water. Jenny stopped and took in a deep breath of salt air.

As they stood there, the abiding peace began to lift; and Jenny could feel its departure. "Why does the peace have to leave?" Jenny asked breaking the silence.

He didn't respond. He just looked out at the water and watched the waves break and wash up over his feet. The peace did not entirely depart, but the questions she had earlier began to find footing in her thoughts. "Why do you want to talk with me?" He remained silent. He watched the water and allowed the sunlight to wash over them. "There is an important reason I am having this vision or dream. So why have you come to me?" she asked curiously.

With eyes filled with compassion and love he said, "Forgiveness."

Her spirit sprang to life; "Uncle Charlie already dealt with that. I know I have to forgive Fred, and I told him like I will tell you, I will work to do it," she said defensively.

"I have no doubt that you will complete the task," he answered while admiring a shell.

"So we are done here, right?" He shook his head. Jenny thought, "If you are concerned about my parents, Uncle Charlie helped me deal with that many years ago." He shook his head again. "Is it my grandparents? No. Oh, it's Mike. I think I can forgive Mike…" He made no acknowledgement of her confessions. He just looked peacefully out at the water.

Jenny pondered deeply, and, almost out of habit, she rubbed her tummy. She thought she detected a little movement as she did. Then it came to her, and anger swallowed her as she formed the words, "If you want me to forgive Steve who got me pregnant, well, you are going to have to use some of that peace stuff to work it out of my heart. He wasn't being careful, and I ended up pregnant. It's not my fault. I am still mad at him for agreeing to break Mike and me up. If you think I should forgive him, well…"

Jenny looked at him. He hadn't reacted to her outburst. He just stood there looking out at the water. Then she saw it. It was almost unnoticeable, but it was there. A tear had formed in the corner of his eye. Then she saw it fall. It rolled down his cheek and trickled into his beard.

"Jesus," she dared to say his name for the first time. She grabbed his arm and turned him towards herself. "What is it? Who do I need to forgive?"

With tears rolling from both eyes and a love that he could not contain, he said, "Yourself."

Jenny reeled as if she had been punched in the gut. She fell on the sand unable to take a breath. The pain was unimaginable. Jesus was knocking at the door she had hoped he would never find. She forced herself to her feet and ran down the beach a little way and collapsed and wept bitterly.

Jesus gave her a moment before approaching her. He sat down on the sand next to her and put his hand on her back.

"How can I forgive myself when my sin is right here for all to see?" she said as she slapped her protruding stomach. "How can you come to someone as ugly as me? I thought the Bible said you couldn't abide in the presence of sin. Look at me! I am the worst of sinners." She screamed and lay on the beach weeping uncontrollably.

Jesus sat quietly and rubbed Jenny's back as she wept. He gave her the space to grieve. When the sobbing eased, Jesus said softly, "I am still here. I will never leave you, nor forsake you."

"Why?" she said in a barely audible voice.

"Because you are my sister, you are the Father's daughter. Jenny, you are family. We don't turn our backs on or walk out on family."

Jenny sat up, wiped her eyes and looked at Jesus. His eyes were still pools of deep love; his smile at her remained constant. She laid her head on his shoulder and wept some more. When she again regained her composure, she sat up and looked out at the ocean. The waves washed up on the sand, and just then a group of pelicans flew by, skimming the crest of a wave.

"Jesus, how do I forgive myself? I know that is what you want, but I don't know how I can forgive myself for doing something you taught us not to do."

Jesus reached out and took Jenny's hand and placed her fingers on his scars. He rubbed her hands over the scars on his hands. Softly and gently he said to her, "I paid a high price for your forgiveness. I gave my life up for you. I did it, Jenny, because I wanted you to have what I have with the Father, a relationship with Him that's free from sin and guilt."

Jenny put her hands back on Jesus' hands. She caressed the scars and allowed the tears to roll freely down her cheeks. "Why...why would you do such a thing for someone like me?"

He gently lifted her head until she looked him right in the eyes, "Love. Jenny, I love you with a pure agape love."

Again, Jenny rested her head on Jesus' shoulder while she continued to gently caress Jesus' scars. She whispered to him, "I am trying to accept your love and forgiveness. And," she paused to wipe her eyes and to sit up and look at Jesus, "I want to forgive myself, but I should have known better. My sin is written in your word. It plainly says don't do it. Yet, I did it. And I can't deny it; it was pleasurable. And in spite of this awesome experience here on this beautiful beach, given the right circumstances, I think I would fail you again. I know that I will sin again. I hate myself," she said tearing her eyes away from his and looking down.

"First, let me say that I understand. You are human, fighting the temptation that tries to lure you away from me. Sometimes you act out of rebellion and other times you are disobedient to my word which can lead to some interesting results," he said, as he reached over and caressed her stomach. The action gave Jenny the courage to look back at Jesus. "Neither the Father, the Spirit, nor I expect perfection from you. You were born into a broken world. It is not the one we originally created for you. Because you were born into a broken world, you are going to sin. Does that give you a license to go out and sin whenever you feel like it? No. We gave you the power to resist temptation. If you will resist, the temptation will leave you. You also need to seek God's grace. Grace is where you draw the power to resist. Many people do not understand how much power there is in grace. If you can connect your faith to God's grace, nothing will be impossible for you."

"You're saying that you know I am going to fail, that I am going to sin."

"Yes."

"That's not fair," she protested.

"You have the power to overcome by grace through faith."

"Then why do I feel so bad when I fail?"

"Do you think you might be feeling guilt for your sin?"

She thought about that for a moment, "Yes," she hesitated, "because I know you hate me when I sin."

"That's wrong," he said gently, but firmly. "We hate sin because it keeps you away from us and from your destiny. It makes you feel like," he paused, wanting to be sensitive, "like you are a failure. We hate everything that takes you away from us and makes you feel like you can't come to us. But, are you listening, Jenny?" She connected with his eyes that held her gaze and nodded. "We love you. We hate sin for its power to pull you away from us, but we love you unconditionally. We love everything about you."

"How can you love me when I sin?"

"We love you, and we hate the sin. Got it?" She nodded and looked out at the ocean. The sea breeze blew gently across Jenny's face. The sun's warmth caressed her body. Jesus gave her a moment to let his words take root in her heart before he said, "Jenny, can you believe and accept that you are forgiven? Do you understand that you are forgiven and that we are holding nothing against you?"

"So you and God forget about it?"

"Totally."

Jenny took a deep breath. "It may take a while, but I'll try to get it."

"We're not done yet, Jenny. I want to go a step further." She looked at him with a furrowed brow. "I also want to take away the guilt from your sin. I don't want you to feel bad."

"Easy for you to say, I am the one who failed. It's like you gave me a test, and I failed. You are giving me back my paper with a failing mark on it, and then say I should feel good?"

"You have that wrong. To use your analogy, when you confess your sins, you are turning in your paper. When I get it, I erase all the wrong, the sin, and I return to you a clean sheet of paper. Your sins have been wiped away. You are clean before the Father."

"Wow. I want to live like that. I want to walk free of the sin, to be clean. But I can remember my failures. I know I will fail again."

"You have to let me have the guilt, Jenny. My blood covers all your past sin. And when you sin again, and we have agreed because you live in a broken world, you will sin again, I will forgive you of that sin as well. If you confess your sins, I will forgive you. Once you have confessed, I want you to get back up, brush off the dust and start moving forward again. Return to me and get about doing the things the Father would have you do."

"OK, let's say I say something profane, a curse word. I can see repenting of that, accepting your forgiveness and then moving on.

No one was hurt. I let my tongue move without controlling it. Confessed, forgiven, done. But…" she turned away to hide her tears.

Jesus picked it up, "But what about the consequences of your sin? Let's take gossip. Suppose you told a friend that you say a group of other friends skinny dipping in the ocean. Nothing happened except that you created a juicy story. But if you told a friend that you saw two people out skinny dipping who were each dating other people, there could be a huge consequence for doing that. You could be forgiven for your sin of gossip, but the consequence for those two people would not be wiped out. Is that what is bothering you?"

She couldn't look back at him; she could only nod. Jesus leaned back and looked up at the sky. He gave it a moment before responding,

"Jenny, you know that I drank wine with my meals here on earth. Having a social drink or a glass of wine with a meal is not sin. Drinking until you are drunk is sin and can easily lead to additional sins. Sometimes people will take a few drinks and then get into their cars and end up hurting themselves or worse, someone else. Those are real consequences. There is forgiveness for their sins, but the lasting effects, the consequences of those sins will still be there."

Jesus paused and allowed those words to hang in the air. A big wave crashed and washed around them. They both jumped up to avoid getting soaked. They started to walk along the beach continuing their conversation.

"How do you get over the bad feelings from the consequences of sin?" she asked.

"There is only one way, and that is through me. People will tell you that time heals all wounds, but there are some that time just won't heal. It takes coming to me and allowing the Spirit to work in your heart to heal and, yes, to help you forgive yourself."

"I need that kind of help."

"I agree. I don't want your son to be…"

"I'm going to have a son?" she interrupted.

Jesus smiled at her in a warm and wonderful way. "Yes, and he will grow up to make you proud. He is destined to touch many lives for my sake."

Jenny looked down and rubbed her stomach saying softly, "I'm going to have a boy. You are going to be a very special boy."

"I'm worried about him," he said. Jenny looked up to Jesus. "If he is born with the guilt you are feeling in your heart right now, it will be passed on to him; and he may not fulfill his destiny."

"How do I forgive myself, and let you take the guilt away too? I know better than to go away with someone. But I went away with Steve, and I committed sin. I knew what I was doing and sadly, I knew it was wrong in your eyes. I deserved to be punished. That will help the guilt to go away."

"I was punished for you. If you can open your heart and receive the forgiveness that I have to offer, you will be cleansed from the sin; and you can let me have the guilt too. If you do it, then you can look down at your stomach and see the son you will have with joy and peace in your heart."

"No one has ever taught me this at church. In fact, people at church point at me, and I know they are saying things behind my back."

"That's because they haven't accepted my forgiveness for themselves. They think that their sins are better, less dirty than yours. All sin is evil to me; no sin is less bad than any other sin. When they see other people's sin …or the consequences of those sins, it makes them feel less guilty for their own sins. What they need is to be forgiven and to allow me to wash away the guilt for their sin as well. If they could accept that, they would be comforting you and encouraging you instead of pointing at you."

"We really don't understand how our sin separates us from you, and how your grace can repair that brokenness."

"There is a place in the Bible that says, "Those who have been forgiven much, love much and those who have been forgiven little, love little.""

"You said that," Jenny smiled.

"Yes, I did. I believe there is something deeper here that people miss. It is those people who understand how sin gets in the way of our relationship who repent and are forgiven. They love much because they have received forgiveness for their sins and allowed me to take away the guilt of their sin, too. Those people are living free and forgiven. Their love abounds to no ends. The people who believe their "little sins" are not so bad, rarely seek forgiveness for their sins because they aren't "bad sins." Their conscience is scarred, and they can't walk in complete freedom because they are still carrying their sins around. Therefore, their love is not as strong, and they spend their time comparing their sins with others to make sure they can feel alright."

"I don't want to be like that," Jenny said softly.

"You don't have to…" he said with his arms open wide.

Jenny ran into his arms and wept. "Jesus," she sobbed, "please forgive me for my sins. Please forgive me for my wicked behavior. I'm so sorry. And please take away the guilt of my sin. I don't want to live with that. I want to live a free life… free from sin and guilt."

"You are forgiven, Jenny. Your guilt has been washed away." She clung to him and cried. When the sobbing ceased, she pulled away and looked at Jesus' face. There were tears trailing from his eyes, but a huge smile was on his face. They both wiped their tears simultaneously. Then they began to laugh. Jesus reached out and hugged Jenny again. Her heart felt clean and fresh.

Chapter Twenty-Six

Jenny and Jesus walked down the beach together. The sun was hanging low in the sky, and she sensed that this symbolized a closing of their time together. She wanted to ask if her assumption was correct, but she was afraid. She had so much she wanted to talk with him about but didn't know which question was the most important. She was working through her list when Jesus interrupted her thoughts.

"Jenny," he asked, "how do you think we see you?"

"That's a tough question, especially since I feel so clean right now. Thank you very much," she said with a slight bow to him and a big smile.

"Seriously, think about it for a moment and describe the best you can how you think we see you."

She considered it for a moment. She sat down in the sand and started to play with it between her fingers. A wave washed up around her feet, causing a ghost crab to race down after the water to find a tasty morsel. She was trying to decide how to best answer his question. "The truth is," Jenny started, "I guess I thought you three saw me as a sinner."

"OK," Jesus said, without reacting. "Now describe how you see yourself."

"Sometimes I feel like a failure, constantly struggling with sin. I just can't seem to get it right. I want to be good and to do good things, but I just seem to trip up and make some bad choices along the way. I guess I don't see myself as a rotten sinner, just someone who struggles with sin. I am certainly not as bad as a murderer or anything like that."

"So, in your mind there are degrees of sin."

"Yeah. Take a guy who looks at a girl and lusts after her. He isn't as bad as a guy who sleeps with a girl. Or a person who is only angry with someone is nowhere near as bad as a person who kills someone. I always thought certain sins were worse than others. But you just finished teaching me that sin is sin. A little gossip is just as bad as a murder to you. I guess I am going to have to rethink all this stuff."

"Good," Jesus said. "You also need to understand that there is a difference between sin and the consequences of sin. Take your example, the guy who lusts after a girl is just as wrong as the guy who sleeps with a girl, but there are certainly more possible consequences for committing the act. Does that make sense to you?"

"Yeah, it does. Sin is sin, but the consequences for our acts remain." She rubbed her belly and continued, "I think I learned that lesson."

"Do you feel forgiven for your sin even though you have to live with the consequences?"

She thought about that for a long moment. A seagull landed up the beach and began preening his feathers. The sea breeze blew her hair off her face as she looked out over the water. She looked at Jesus and said, "I think I get it in my heart, but I have to get my head on the same page. I remember my sins and failures…"

"But we don't. When you are forgiven, we throw the memory of your sin away. To us, it is just as if you never sinned before in your life."

"If you think I never sinned, how do you explain the baby?" she retorted.

"Grace and mercy," he responded with love in his voice.

"I don't feel worthy," she said and a tear slipped out of the corner of her eye.

"You are my sister. You are the Father's daughter. And you are the temple of the Holy Spirit. You are plenty worthy." There was silence as Jesus allowed her to drink in his words. Then he continued,

"Let me go back to my original question, how do you believe we see you?"

"I guess not as a sinner, so I don't know."

"Good. Are you willing to trust me and learn how we see you?"

She signed deeply, "OK, how are we going to do that?"

"First, let me say that each one of the three of us sees you differently, but the same. I know that sounds confusing, but let me explain. Let's begin with a small favor on your part. Will you close your eyes for a moment, please?" Jenny complied. "Now open them."

When she opened her eyes, there was an exquisite mirror sitting beside her on the beach. Her reflection was crystal clear. The wood along the sides looked hand carved by a master craftsman. She admired it and ran her fingers along the carved edges.

"Step back here," Jesus directed her. "Now, when we look in this mirror, we can see ourselves." Jenny nodded in agreement. "Now, close your eyes again, and I want to show you something. Open them again and look at your reflection in the mirror."

When she opened her eyes this time, she was horrified by what she saw. There she was in the mirror covered in black splotches, deep oozing sores, her clothes were ragged and torn. She saw cancers on her skin. She reacted violently. Jesus quickly grabbed her and told her to close her eyes again. When she opened her eyes again, everything returned to normal.

"What was that?" she demanded.

"That is how you see yourself. You think you are ugly in our sight. You see your sin as cancers that have no cure. The deeper and worse the sore the more you believe that there is nothing that can be done about those sins. What you don't understand is that you can apply my grace, which is really my power to overcome, and change those circumstances. My grace has the power to break the chains of darkness and set you free from sin."

"Do I really see myself that way…full of the cancer of sin?"

"Yes, but I want to change that. I believe that if you can see yourself the way we see you, it might help you see yourself in a better light."

"Now I want to show you how I see you. Close your eyes."

She did, and when she opened them, she saw a reflection of herself with dirt on her hands, her hair looked like she had been driving down the road with the windows down. Her clothes were disheveled, and she was missing one shoe. "Do you see me this way?" she asked. "I thought the Bible said you couldn't see my sins and failures. The world has stained my appearance."

"The truth is that I am different from my Father and the Holy Spirit. I can see your sin; not all of it, only that which you have not repented of yet. Unrepented sin is still visible to me. The good news is that once you repent of your sin, you will look like this. Close your eyes again."

When she opened her eyes this time, she saw a reflection that was absolutely pure. Not one hair was out of place and her clothes, hands, and face were absolutely spotless. "Wow, I look beautiful," she said of her reflection.

"Yes, you do. When you repent, all your sin is gone, including the guilt of your sin if you will allow me to have it. I am the only one of the three that can see you both ways. I want you to come to me and allow me to wash you and cleanse you from the stains of the world. I never expect a person to clean himself up before he comes to me. I love and accept each person right where he is when I find him. I want him to come to me. He doesn't need to hide because of his sin, that's why I came into the world, to take away his sin. Then when he repents, I clean him up completely. My blood washes away every stain. Every person who comes to me just as he is can look as beautiful as you do in that mirror."

She admired herself. She didn't have a blemish anywhere on her skin. There were no crow's feet in the corner of her eyes. She had never seen her hair with such a beautiful sheen. The reflection brought a smile that could last a lifetime. "Could I have this mirror for my bathroom?" she mused to Jesus with a chuckle.

"That mirror would change so many people's lives for the better. If they could look into it and see themselves as I see them, they would be brighter lights for the Kingdom." She saw his reflection in the mirror, and all his scars were gone. The sight was so stunning she immediately turned and looked at him. The scars were all there, each and every one of them. She returned her gaze to the mirror and saw a younger looking Jesus, one that had not borne the weight of the world on his shoulders. A pang of sorrow rose from her heart. "It's OK, Jenny; I did it willingly." She reached over and embraced him, thanking him again for paying the price.

"Look in the mirror again," he said, after kissing her on the top of her head. She turned and there she was with a royal crown on her head and the most beautiful robe she had ever seen in her life. She twirled and watched the royal garment flow with grace as she spun. The crown was covered in jewels and sparkling gems. She reached out and touched the mirror, wishing she could feel the magnificent robe. The crown fit her head perfectly. She looked like a princess.

"I didn't think I could look better than before, but I was wrong. I look like royalty!"

"You are a princess. If only people could see themselves as God sees them. You are the Father's daughter, and He loves you far more than you can possibly understand. Do you see one stain of the world on you?"

"No!" she said still twirling about in the mirror.

"Nor does the Father. He sees you as you will someday be…a royal princess in His court. The Father is always trying to move you to where He sees you. When you pray and ask for His will, He tries to move you into your royal position. He wants you to rise up and fulfill your purpose for His Kingdom in your world."

"Does that mean he wants me to go on a mission trip?"

"Think about that. In a way, each person goes on a mission trip every day in his life. Some people go a long way from home to take the Father's message of love, while others go to places like the Bluebird Café. There are so many people whose lives you touch in your little corner of the world. Don't discount that. You never know how changing one life can change so many others."

"How can I change a life?"

"It's complicated, but it works like this. You being the royal princess have access to your Father's throne room 24/7. You don't have to wait to be summoned, and He is ALWAYS glad to see you.

You place your requests before the Father, and then He activates the Holy Spirit who does the work to bring about the answer to the prayer request. So the Holy Spirit is the agent of change, but he is being moved to help bring about the change because you prayed, if they are according to the Father's will."

"God wants to see me and answer my prayers?"

"More than you will ever imagine."

"So what if I pray for something that is selfish or wrong?"

"That's praying for the flesh versus for the spirit. God knows your heart. I will say that sometimes people pray for things that God doesn't think are a good idea. For example, the people of Israel begged God to give them a king. God told them through Samuel it was not a good idea. They insisted they wanted a king. So God gave them a king."

"There were some good kings like David and Josiah…"

"But there were plenty of evil kings who lead the people away from God. What I am telling you is that you need to pray and be honest with God. If what you are praying is not in His will, listen and He will guide you to what is better for your life. That means He will say no to some of your prayers. Remember, He is a good Father. When you pray, allow the Spirit to guide you, and then He will help you pray better prayers that line up with the Father's will."

"How do you know that?"

"Because the Spirit of God lives within you, and He will guide you."

"Jesus, did all your prayers that you prayed on earth get answered?"

"Some of my prayers have yet to be answered…"

"Two thousand years later and they still aren't answered!" she exclaimed.

Jesus held up his hands. "Slow down there. Some of my prayers were for the saints who aren't even born yet." Jenny relaxed. "I think the question behind your question is did I always get a 'yes' answer to my prayers?"

"Yes, did you get everything you requested?"

"Let me give you one example from the Bible. In the garden of Gethsemane, I prayed a selfish prayer." Jenny looked shocked. Jesus continued, "I asked God to let the cup pass from me. I didn't want to go to the cross…in my flesh. I knew it was going to be painful."

"Obviously, no one would want to face that kind of pain," she added.

"So, in my flesh I prayed and earnestly asked God for a different way out of that situation. I couldn't have been more intense with my request if I had tried. My flesh wanted out. Do you think God could have granted that prayer request for me?"

"Well, I guess so, but that would have left us in a big mess down here."

"That's exactly right. If I had asked the Father, even while I was hanging on the cross, He would have sent thousands of angels to rescue me. But it was God's will for the redemption of man that I endure the cross. So, you could say in a way that God answered my prayers with, no. Did you hear what I said? The Father answered me; it just wasn't the answer my flesh wanted. I was willing to go to the cross; in essence, I submitted to God's plan for my life."

"But you finished that prayer with, 'nevertheless not my will but yours be done.'"

"That's correct. My flesh was weak, but my spirit knew what I had to do. I had to live in obedience to God. I was afraid, and I felt weak in my flesh."

"That's hard to imagine."

"Do you know what those Romans could do with a whip? Let me show you," he said as he began to lift his robe.

"No," she said, "I believe you. I just never thought about you being afraid or praying for something out of your flesh."

"Does that help you?"

"Strangely, yes. It's better for me to pray and make a mistake than for me not to pray at all. And if I pray asking for the Father's will in all circumstances, He will do what is best."

"I think you are catching on. Hey, look," he said, "the sun is about to set." The two of them stood there on the beach and quietly watched it set. "I have one more thing to show you," he said after the sun sank behind the horizon. They turned and looked at the mirror. He put his hand over her eyes; and when he pulled it away, she looked at the mirror again.

This time light shone from her body. It was temporarily blinding; but then as her eyes adjusted, she saw herself. She was absolutely radiant. She felt excited and hopeful. She felt as if she could do or accomplish anything. "How do you like it?" he interrupted her thoughts.

"Is it me? Is it really me? Wow, I can't believe it."

"This is the way the Holy Spirit sees you. He sees you full of hope and promise. You are enveloped in his love."

"And I glow," she added. "Why am I glowing?"

"The Holy Spirit sees you as you can be. He sees the best in you and is always trying to bring that out. The Holy Spirit is trying to make you like me. He's taking out the old you and putting in the new you. He is regenerating you into the woman of God you have been created and called to be. He is always creating a bright future for you."

"What happens when I sin or things feel like they are going wrong, or when tragedy strikes?"

"We've talked about sin, you have to repent. But that is when the Holy Spirit begins to create a new future with infinite possibilities." Jesus reached out and touched Jenny's stomach and said, "When the unexpected comes our way, the Holy Spirit is a master at taking something that seems bad and making it into something good. Mind you, we are not the ones who bring tragedy or sadness into your lives, but He is the one who makes all things work out for the good."

"Are you telling me that the Holy Spirit has written a future for my son?"

"Yes. If you can accept the forgiveness of God in your life and give me the guilt you feel for your sin, then the Holy Spirit can come along and write a new and bright future for you and your son. You begin that process by repenting and accepting the goodness of God in your life. God is the author of everything good in your life through the Holy Spirit."

Jenny turned and looked in the mirror. "Does the Holy Spirit really see me this way?"

"He sees you filled with love, hope, peace, joy, faith, and the list goes on. He sees your future, and He desires to bring you into that good place."

"He doesn't see me as a sinner, but rather as a pure daughter of God, or a princess..."

"He sees you as you will be. He is always creating a positive and a good future for you. He is always trying to lead you in the paths of righteousness because they are the ones filled with the promises of God for your life. He sees you as overcoming and victorious."

"And when I fail?"

"He believes you will succeed. And then he starts rewriting the future again. He's so creative and energetic; nothing seems to slow him down. Your mistakes are opportunities for him to write something better...to make a stronger testimony if you will."

The mirror disappeared right before her eyes. Jesus reached out his hand for her. She grasped it, and they began to walk down the beach together. "I don't want you to go," she said softly.

"I am always here, and I will never leave or forsake you."

"But we will never have a time like this again..."

"Don't say never. You don't know what the Holy Spirit might have planned for your future. Come, let's sit down for a minute." They walked up on the dry sand and found a good spot. The sky was beginning to turn dark, and a few stars were beginning to wake up. They sat quietly enjoying the roar of the ocean and watching more stars find their place in the sky.

"I would like to pray for you and your son, if you will allow me," Jesus asked. Jenny nodded and lay back so Jesus could put his hands on her stomach. Jesus began to pray, and the words were like the most beautiful song you have ever heard. Jenny closed her eyes so she could drink in every word, every blessing Jesus pronounced over her and her son. Her spirit began to soar, and she allowed his words to carry her away.

Slowly, she became aware that she was no longer on the beach. She could feel the blankets on her bed, and her head was lying softly on her pillow. She tried desperately to hold onto the image of the beach, but it faded along with the sound of the surf. A moment later, the vision or dream came to an end, and she was lying alone in her own bed, looking up at the ceiling. She closed her eyes trying to savor the feelings, trying to remember every word he spoke to her. How she wished she could bottle and preserve the experience and never let it slip away.

Chapter Twenty-Seven

Fred had an early morning appointment with Pastor Andrews, and he didn't want to be late. He actually arrived fifteen minutes ahead of schedule. He decided to go for a walk and ended up in the private outside chapel with a beautiful garden surrounding it. Fred sat down and started his day with a word of prayer. He hadn't been praying long when Pastor Andrews walked up.

"A beautiful and peaceful place for prayer, isn't it?"

"Yes. I feel a special closeness here?"

"You should, your brother did about all the work around this chapel until his passing."

"I like it. Do you know that I would have missed things like this before? I was too busy to slow down and even notice something this beautiful."

"I am glad that you have changed. This new life seems to be fitting you well."

"This is a safety zone for me. I'm not dealing with the sharks that live up north yet. I have plenty of trials to go through in the future. That brings up a couple of things I want to talk to you about."

"Would you like to go to my office, or would you rather talk here."

"Here's fine with me." Pastor Andrews settled into the seat next to Fred and took a deep breath of refreshing air.

"What's on your mind?" Pastor Andrews said, opening the door for him to speak.

"I'm afraid to go home to the sharks. I am afraid I'll fall away from my new found faith or fail entirely. I need a support system to keep my feet grounded in the faith. So I am asking you for some help. I know I don't deserve any help after the article in the paper and everything else I did, but I need it."

"What do you propose?"

"I have to come down and check on the resort that I am building down at the beach about once a week, maybe every other week. I was wondering if you would have lunch with me and hold me accountable to keep up my new walk."

"I would be honored to do that."

"You would?"

"Of course. Fred, you have to understand that you are going to fail, you are going to trip up, you are going to make mistakes, and yes, you will sin."

"I don't recommend using that in any motivational speech you plan to give."

Pastor Andrews laughed out loud. "Fred, I fail, I sin. But just like you, when I fail I have to repent and try to make things right. The Christian walk was never designed to be easy. It's by grace that you have been saved. I believe God will help you; but you are right, it's very important to have accountability, someone who can speak directly to you. And as I said, I would count it an honor to serve in that role for you."

"Why?"

"Because I have had many people who have done it for me, and several who hold me accountable right now in my life. Don't think that just because I am a pastor that I have this whole thing figured out. I struggle just as much as anyone else does to walk the walk."

"You mean it doesn't get easier the longer you do it?"

"Some things do come easier, some temptations you know to avoid so they aren't as tempting to you. But you are still in the flesh and subject to the rules of the flesh. Also, I will need to work with you on building some good habits in your new found life. Some will be hard to start, but they will become easier the longer you walk with the Lord."

"Like what?"

"Well, take prayer and reading your Bible. That's something you should do every day. In the beginning, that will be a tough thing to do every day, but over time that will become a natural part of your everyday life, like putting on a pair of shoes."

There was a moment of silence while those thoughts settled in. The morning sun was beginning to warm up, and its rays felt comforting after the chilly morning.

"You said there were two things on your mind, what's the other one?"

"I've worked really hard to fix and restore all the things I did to the people who loved my brother."

"Let me tell you that the reports that I've been hearing are very generous on your part. I am sure God and Charlie are smiling down on you right now."

"Thank you, but I have so much more I need to do, but that's not what is troubling me right now. It's Jenny. I've ruined her life and no amount of money or kind words are going to be able to fix it. I lay in bed at night and try to figure out what to do, but nothing comes to mind."

"You took care of the lawsuit and had the big crane removed that was set to destroy the Bluebird: those were very nice things."

"It's the baby…What was I thinking? … I didn't mean for her to get pregnant… How can I fix that?" He turned to face Pastor Andrews; tears were streaming down his cheeks.

"The baby is a big challenge for her, you, and the father. Have you been by to see her since you got out of the hospital?"

"Are you kidding? I can't face her," he said turning away to wipe the tears from his face.

"Here's the first piece of advice that I am going to give you. You need to go down and talk to Jenny, face to face."

"Oh, no! What would I say?"

"I don't know, but I would encourage you to pray hard. I will give you one little hint. The best place to start is by saying, 'I'm sorry'." There was a long silence between them. Pastor Andrews knew this was the first real test of Fred's faith. "I'll give you one more hint," he said. "Jenny usually does inventory on Wednesdays. That might be the best time to go by and see her."

Fred didn't respond; he just sat and stared out into space. He finally turned to Pastor Andrews and said, "I would rather go speak to a corporate board than to do this, but I know it's something I have to do."

****

It was Wednesday afternoon, and Jenny was working on her weekly inventory. She was learning that carrying extra weight around could certainly slow her down. She was also learning that she couldn't easily bend over to count the cans on the bottom shelves anymore; she needed to squat down. She had a sneaking suspicion that she had many more things to learn about the process of bringing a child into this world.

Fred's car pulled up in front of the Bluebird. Jenny was so engrossed in her work that she didn't see it pull in. Fred walked up to the door and tapped on it. Jenny couldn't hear his tap over the sound of the music and air conditioner. Fred turned to leave. As he started to walk away, he turned himself around and paced right up to the door. He tapped again too light for Jenny to hear. After taking a big breath, he finally knocked on the door.

Jenny looked up from her work. The two of them established eye contact through the glass. Neither one flinched or moved. Finally, Fred motioned to Jenny to let him in. Jenny put the pencil between her lips and just looked at the man. After a moment, she took the pencil out of her mouth and placed it and the clipboard on the counter. She walked over and unlocked the door planting herself firmly in Fred's way.

"Can I help you?" she asked.

"I was wondering if I might come in and talk to you for a little while?"

"I'm kinda busy, I'm working on inventory," she said coldly.

"I don't want to take you from your work, but I would like to talk to you sometime. If another time would be better, mention it."

"No," she relented "come on in. Would you like some coffee or tea?"

"A glass of tea would be nice. And how about a slice of one of those delicious pies you've got?"

"Have a seat over in the corner booth; I'll be with you in a minute." Jenny went behind the counter and made them both glasses of tea. She got a fresh blueberry pie and cut two slices and then carried everything over to the booth.

"Thank you both for your time and your hospitality."

"Well, I am having to take breaks more often now. I assume you didn't come down here for a slice of pie and a glass of tea after hours for no reason; so what's on your mind?" she said abruptly.

"No, I suppose not," he said taking another bite of pie attempting to stall for time. Then he set his fork down, wiped his mouth and said, "Jenny, I'm the one responsible for sending Steve down here, but I never intended for you to get pregnant."

"I knew you were behind it all," she said rather coolly.

He stopped, took a deep breath and began again, "I heard your prayer for me the other night."

"What?" she said, slightly deflated. "How could you have heard my prayer?"

"A very dear friend of yours, my brother, brought me here that night. I want to thank you for asking God for my salvation when I imagine what you really wanted to ask God to do was send me straight to hell. I almost ended up there. If it hadn't been for you and those people praying that night, that is exactly where I would have gone. The truth is, Jenny; I deserved to go. So I want to thank you for your prayer that helped to deliver me from that fate."

Jenny's guard was down; she wasn't expecting this from the man who betrayed her. She averted his eyes and looked out the window, trying to appear casual.

"Jenny," Fred continued, "I want you to know that I am very sorry for what happened to you. It's my fault, and I want to take responsibility. I have been working hard to fix some things: the suit against the café is over, the crane is gone, but I can't wave a magic wand and make the baby disappear. I want you to know how deeply sorry I am for what happened to you."

Jenny turned her head to conceal a tear that fell from the corner of her eye. Fred turned his head and pretended not to see. A tear seeped out of the corner of Fred's eye; he wiped his nose to catch it.

"I won't lie to you; it's been hard." Jenny said in a soft and broken voice.

"Is there anything I can do for you?"

"Yeah, you can call and explain this to my parents," she said with a little laugh, hoping to break the tension.

"Jenny, I would be glad to call your parents and talk to them for you." He pulled out his cell phone and prepared to dial. "What's the number?"

Jenny looked across the table at him and realized that if she called the number out; he would not only dial it, but he would explain the whole situation to her parents for her. In that moment her heart softened toward the gray haired old man across the table. She looked into his eyes and saw the family resemblance on the inside with Uncle Charlie. This was no longer a lying imposter sitting across from her, but a changed man, a man who had been given a new heart. Suddenly the tears flowed freely down Jenny's cheeks.

Fred put down his phone and grabbed some napkins. "Please don't cry, I'll help you, just tell me what I need to do." There was a moment of silence while Jenny tried to pull her emotions back together. "Would you like me to send Steve back down to see you? Or would you like me to pull some strings and get Mike back on the local force?"

Jenny looked at Fred again. She realized that whatever she asked him to do right now, he would try his best to accomplish it. He would move a mountain if it meant winning her forgiveness. She could feel his love and compassion, and it reminded her in a very pleasant way of Uncle Charlie. That thought naturally brought more tears. The more tears that fell, the more helpless Fred felt sitting across from her.

Jenny fought to get her emotions under control. "I don't want anything right now. But I want to give you something. It's something you need and that I need to give so we can both move on from this moment. But first, I need to confess that your brother came to me in a dream a few nights ago." Fred's countenance lightened slightly. "Uncle Charlie and I sat on the beach and we talked. He wants me to forgive you, but you can imagine I was not willing to cooperate. But he convinced me that I had to let it go." She paused to take a deep breath, "Fred, I forgive you. Please don't feel badly anymore."

Fred stared back at Jenny. Tears erupted from his eyes and cascaded down his cheeks. He made no attempt to catch them or to stop them. Jenny quickly added,

"Now, don't you start. We can't both sit here and cry." Jenny reached over and passed him some napkins.

"I don't deserve that," he said through his tears.

"I can't withhold it from you. If I do, how could I ask God to forgive me for my sins and failures? I have to forgive you; I want to forgive you." That brought a fresh supply of tears for both of them.

"What are you going to do?" Fred asked.

"I'll manage."

"You'll need some help to keep this place running. And you'll need child care."

"Those are all details that I'll have to iron out in time. I don't know how I am going to handle and deal with any of those things, but with God's help I will."

"What about your parents? You said they wouldn't understand."

"Parents are parents, Fred. They'll never believe this story, even if you were there to verify every detail. My parents have always thought I was a bit promiscuous. The truth is, maybe they were right. But after they get over the shock and dismay, I imagine they will come around. Mom loves babies, and I'm Daddy's little girl."

"I want to help you, but I don't know what to do."

"You have. You've taken care of the café. That's a huge load off my mind. You've also gotten me to the place where I can begin the healing process on the inside. I have to be able to forgive you in order to heal."

"How you can see all the positive is beyond me."

"If you think this baby is a negative, you're wrong. God has a purpose for this child, and He chose me to be his mother. It just goes to show that God has a lot of faith in me. I just have to live up to it."

Fred sat silent for a moment. He looked out at the ocean waves crashing in on the shore. Some seagulls were floating just above a child and his parent out on the boardwalk. Fred watched for a moment while they tossed bread in the air to the birds. The sight brought the hint of a smile to his face. Jenny turned to see what he was looking at and smiled too.

"Jenny," he said breaking the silence, "I want you to make me a deal. When this child comes along, I want you to let me take him for walks along the beach," he said, pointing to the parent and child. "Second, I want to take your child to a Yankee's game. Maybe I would like to take him or her to a Knicks game at Madison Square Garden, too. And oh, I would love to see a child's eyes at the National Zoo." Fred's eyes were dancing with the possibilities. Watching him brought a big smile to Jenny's face.

"And you know," she said taking one of Fred's hands, "I was thinking maybe he or she could call you, Uncle Fred." Fred beamed at the thought and squeezed Jenny's hand.

Chapter Twenty-Eight

It was several weeks later in the middle of the afternoon at the Bluebird. Carlos had finished cleaning up and had gone home for the day. The place was finally quiet, and Jenny fixed herself a glass of tea and cut a slice of blueberry pie. She sat in a booth where she could look out at the ocean. It was hard to hear the ocean over the roar of the air-conditioner.

The weather was warming up, and business was picking back up. Spring was arriving and with it the joy of pollen and stuffy sinuses. It was a simple trade-off; you lose the cold air and get a head cold. Jenny's cold was ending with the last vestiges of a runny nose. She actually felt better today than she had in quite a while. She was still looking forward to a nap when she finished her paperwork for the day.

She wasn't really sure what was making her tired, the pregnancy or the exiting cold. Either way, she wasn't planning to be long doing the paperwork. The pie disappeared quickly, and her stomach growled for more. She drained her glass of tea as she filled out her bank deposit. She got up for a refill of tea and was heading back to her seat when she noticed a car pulling into the parking lot. She watched as Fred emerged from the car.

He smiled and waved to her. She went over and unlocked the door. They greeted each other, and she offered him a piece of pie and a glass of tea which he gladly accepted. She got herself an extra piece of pie and sat them on the table on the opposite side from where she was doing paperwork. He apologized for intruding, but she explained that his visit was a nice break.

They talked about Uncle Charlie while they ate their pie and sipped their tea. He shared childhood stories, and she shared more recent ones. They laughed as they shared warm memories of a friend and a brother who was sorely missed. Fred asked about the Bluebird, and she updated him on sales and a budding tourist season. He listened intently as she talked about traffic patterns, and how sales slumped to a crawl from December through late February. He updated her on the progress at the new resort he was building. The city had approved his plans, and demolition would begin within a week; and he was hoping that construction would ensue by mid-summer.

The conversation slowed when the pie was done. The hum of the air conditioner filled the air. Jenny started with, "I've heard all about what you have been doing for folks all over town."

"It isn't exactly all over town. It's focused on those whom I had intended to hurt."

"Still, word is circulating that things have changed for the better."

"Do you think the economy will get the credit?"

"Some will never acknowledge God even if He stood in front of them and performed a miracle. Others will see His hand in anything good."

He sighed, "I've been able to fix almost all the bad things I have done."

"Well, I for one would like to thank you for all that you have done for me," she said with a smile.

"I don't think I have done very much for you, especially since I robbed you of your innocence."

"Let me stop you right there. My innocence was lost long before I met Steve Leaks. I am not loose, mind you; but I have been around the block a few times. As far as Steve goes, I put myself in that situation. I could have chosen not to go away with him. I have to bear some of the responsibility for my behavior."

"I just wish there was something I could do to help you, to make things better for you."

"Better for me… Let me tell a little story, and you determine if you think that life hasn't gotten a little better for me. I went to my family doctor and asked him to help me find an OB doctor. He came back in a few minutes with the name of a doctor who will treat me at the hospital. I thought that was a little strange, but I went to my appointment which was made for me. The doctor treated me like a queen. I had a small problem between appointments and called to ask some questions. The nurse told me that my doctor was out of town but says she will get me an answer. Within the hour, my doctor calls me long-distance to answer what I discover are regular questions for first-time mothers-to-be.

"Then after one of my check-ups, I was talking to the nurse about my doctor. I asked about his patient load, and she explained that I was his only patient. When I asked for an explanation, she told me that he is the best OB doctor on the East Coast based out of the Mayo Clinic. I asked how I was assigned to him, and she said she had no idea.

"On my way out, I stopped at the billing desk because I hadn't received any bills yet. The lady pulled up my account and said that everything had been covered. When I asked how that was possible since they hadn't billed my insurance company yet, she said not to worry. I pressed the issue and explained that I can't get a big bill and be expected to pay it. She said my account was paid in full. When I demanded to know how, she said it was a privacy issue.

"To sum up, I have one of the best doctors in the country who flies into town for my appointments, and it's not costing me a dime."

"Wow, this new health care system is wonderful!" he said trying to hide the little smile on his face.

"That smile looks good on you, but allow me to continue. I asked Mike, the police officer, to go down to the baby store with me so I could get some new furniture and a car seat. It was over five hundred dollars' worth of stuff. Then a few days later, I checked my charge account on-line, and the charge didn't appear on my statement. I called the store, and they had no record of my purchase.

There was a purchase that included all the same items I have, but it was charged to some corporate account. I asked whose, and they could not reveal that information."

"That's billing privacy. They couldn't reveal that information," he said with a wry smile.

"Do you want me to continue?"

"No," he said grinning a little bigger. "I just feel so guilty for what has happened, and I want so badly to fix things for you."

"You have been doing plenty. I know you have been doing all this stuff, and I want to officially thank you for everything."

"You are welcome. Honestly, I am worried about the baby – he won't have a father."

"He does have a father, Steve. He and I have talked, and I am not sure what role Steve will play in my child's life, but Steve will be a part of his life. He is going to be raised with three grandpas, the three regulars here at the Bluebird. I think Mike, the police officer, is going to play a role in his life. And finally my child will be blessed to have a great uncle, Uncle Fred."

Fred's eyes began to moisten at the thought. "How could you consider…"

"How could I not consider that. Your life has changed. I believe you could be a good and godly influence on my child. Maybe you could take him to a Yankees or Mets game…"

"Yankees! The Mets can burn in…pardon me."

"You should come in and have lunch with the three old guys; they love baseball. Well, high school football is their all-time favorite, but major league baseball is their second favorite."

"Do you think they would even want to talk to me?"

"If you mention baseball, they will include you in their conversation before you know it. Just be ready to argue your point, and I mean with quotable stats."

"How would you feel if I came by and had lunch once in a while?"

"I would love it, Uncle Fred."

"I am not worthy of that title."

"Yes, yes, you are," she said taking his hands in hers.

Chapter Twenty-Nine

Jenny was locking the door to the Bluebird when her phone rang. It was Mike; so she answered, "Hey, Mike, what's up?"

"I was just wondering if you would like to go out for dinner this evening?"

"That would be great. Do you want to swing by my place about seven?"

"I'll see you then."

Jenny drove home and barely made it to the bed before she was fast asleep. She slept for two hours, much longer than she intended. She dragged herself out of bed and hit the shower. She was just finishing her makeup when Mike arrived. She let him in and returned to the bathroom to finish getting ready. Mike popped the TV on and watched ESPN until she was ready.

He took her down to Lynnhaven Fish House where they enjoyed a delicious seafood dinner while looking out over the water. Jenny told Mike about her visits from Fred. He was surprised to hear about her willingness to forgive so easily, mainly because she hadn't told him about her dream yet.

He told her about some personnel changes that were occurring at the police department, and the possibility of a promotion in the near future. She caught him up on some of the antics the old men were pulling at the Bluebird.

After dinner, he drove her back home where he suggested they take a walk on the beach. They both put on sweatshirts and walked down to the beach. The breeze was cool, but the sweatshirts provided enough warmth for them. They held hands and, while looking up at the stars, a meteor split the sky. It was a romantic sight.

"I've been meaning to thank you," she began, "for all the help with the baby stuff. You did a great job painting the nursery, and I couldn't have put all that furniture together without your expert help."

"You are welcome; I was just glad to be there. Is there anything else you need help with?"

"No, I think I am in pretty good shape, but thanks for asking,"

They sat on the sand, and she leaned back onto his chest to look at the stars. He took the moment to enjoy the intoxicating aroma that surrounded her and then lightly kissed her on the head.

"What was that for?" she asked.

"Nothing, sorry if I offended." The ocean crashed, and the sky shimmered with the stars. He continued, "You said something this evening that I just wanted to follow up on."

"Sure, what is it?"

"You said that Steve wasn't going to assume the responsibilities of being the boy's father. How do you feel about that?"

"Well, Steve is up there, and I am down here; he can't be really active in my child's life. Steve says he really doesn't want to be a dad either. Why do you ask?"

"Well, the child ought to have a positive male role model in his life."

"I'm not going out looking for husband material just so I can give him a positive male role model. He'll have lots of male role models. The three old men at the Bluebird will probably spoil him rotten. Uncle Fred will be there some. And I was hoping that maybe you might come around some and be a good role model for him, too." She gave him a little squeeze and kissed his cheek.

"Well about that..."

"You aren't planning to move again, are you?"

"No, it's nothing like that. I just wanted to play a bigger role in his life, provided you agree."

"I think it would be great to have you in my child's life," she said sitting up and looking at him.

"I want to become more of a part of your life and your child's life, too."

"Mike, I want you to be around as much as you want to be around. But to be honest with you, I am not looking for a relationship right now. I am about to become a mother, which is a huge responsibility. Trying to figure out a relationship with you, or anybody else for that matter, is just too much for me right now. I guess I just don't want to lead you on. Maybe in time, things could develop for you and me, but I can't promise anything for right now. I need to focus on being a mom and running the Bluebird. Do you understand that?"

"Completely. I just want to be close to you, to help you as you begin this new adventure in your life. As far as my expectations about a relationship in the future, we know who holds our future, and if it is His will and we can work it out; that will be great. I understand that we are just going to be friends, being there for each other as any good friend would be."

"Wow, Mike. You are a great guy. I am not sure I deserve to have you in my life." She leaned in and gave him a kiss on the cheek.

He caressed her face ever so gently. They looked into each other's eyes, and he moved in slowly, but deliberately, and gave her a tender kiss on the lips. She kissed him back and then put her head on his shoulder. The stars twinkled in the sky. The waves crashed, and the soft evening breeze blew as the two of them cuddled on the beach.

Chapter Thirty

Spring's warmth was in the air on Saturday morning when Jenny slid the key in the lock at the Bluebird. Before she turned the key and unlocked the door, she removed the key. She walked around the building and over to the railing on the boardwalk. She took a deep breath of the salty ocean air and watched the puffy white clouds sail through the brilliant blue sky.

The sky was bright from the glorious sunrise. She looked down the boardwalk at the many hotels that were temporarily silent but would soon be active with fun-loving tourists. She watched as the early morning shell seekers sought out their treasures. Jenny realized that she had made it through another long winter, and she was anticipating the arrival of summer. Some people don't like the heat and humidity, but Jenny and the Bluebird Café thrived on it.

Some pelicans glided over the water riding the curl of an ocean wave. Jenny had to force herself to walk back to the café. As she walked, she rubbed her tummy which was protruding, revealing signs of the new life growing within her. Things were definitely going to change, she thought. She made her way inside the Bluebird and got the morning routine going. It didn't take long for the place to fill up. As usual, the three old men held down their end of the counter.

The bell rang over the door, and Fred walked in. "Hello, Uncle Fred," rang out Jenny's voice from behind the counter.

"Good morning," he said with a smile. "Can I have a special?" Jenny nodded. He approached the counter where the three men looked at him with suspicion. "May I join you, gentlemen?" he asked.

The three of them looked at each other, and none of them answered right away. Jenny jumped in with,

"Yes, sit yourself right down there." She gave the three men a harsh stare. "Don't mind these old goats," she said with a wink. There was an awkward moment of silence as Jenny started to prepare his food. She poured him a cup of coffee and said, "Do you know that these old goats don't think the New York Yankees have a snowball's chance at making it to the World Series this year?"

"Are you kidding? With that new pitcher they got from California and the short stop from the Phillies, I think they have as good a chance as the Braves."

"The Yankees aren't in the same category as the Braves unless the Babe or Mickey Mantle joined the team." Al responded.

"Hey, you could give them the Babe, Mantle, Ty Cobb, and Ted Williams, and the Braves would still whip their butt."

"Now hold your horses there," Joe chimed in. "If you gave the Yankees all those guys, any team would have a hard time beating them. Besides I think…"

"Have you seen the stats on some of the players for this year?" Fred interrupted. "That new pitcher had three shut outs last year. Then you got that shortstop who hit 321 last season. That's nothing to sneeze at."

The three men argued aggressively with Fred, defending the Braves' chances at going to the World Series. Jenny winked at Fred as she set his plate in front of him. All the men were quoting stats to each other defending their teams' chances to make it to the World Series. There was obviously no winner in their discussion as the three men cleared out of the Bluebird.

Fred sat at the counter drinking coffee and reading the paper as Jenny went about cleaning up from breakfast. She looked over at Fred who was buried in the business section of the paper. She had to laugh at the sight of him. Fred heard her chuckle and asked what was so funny.

"It's you. You are so much like your brother that you don't realize it."

"What?" he said. "We are as different as night and day."

"You both love to read the paper; him sports, you business. And both of you could argue for your baseball team until the cows come home."

"I could argue a little longer than that if given half the chance," he said with a chuckle of his own. Fred folded the paper and placed a ten on the counter to cover his meal. Jenny went to get him change, but he waved her off. "Can you take a minute and talk to me?" he asked.

"Sure," she said.

"I want to thank you for that delicious breakfast and your encouraging words the other day. They meant a lot to me."

Jenny smiled and said, "You're welcome."

"I've got something else I want to tell you. I had a dream last night about Charlie." Jenny's eyes widened. "He said you would understand." Jenny nodded. "What we talked about, you and I will talk about some day in the near future. We both have things we need to get done. He left a little package for you, and I wrote you a personal note," he said handing them both to her. "Read it later and open the package later, too." Jenny set them on the counter. Fred turned and walked toward the door. Stopping, he turned back to Jenny and said,

"You don't know this about me, but I lost my precious wife in a house fire many years ago. She and our little girl died from smoke inhalation. That loss devastated me. But Charlie reminded me last night that you are about the age of my daughter, or how old she would have been. I want you to know that if my daughter were alive, I hope she would be a lot like you. You have done well for yourself, and you are a godly woman. You would make any man proud to be your father." Tears began to stream down Jenny's cheeks. Fred stepped back and took out his handkerchief and wiped her tears.

"I'm proud of you, Jenny. I want to thank you for letting me come into your life. You've changed me for the better, and I want to thank you again. I hope you'll allow me to stop in from time to time and have breakfast here." Jenny smiled and nodded. "You make sure you tell those 'old goats' to leave a seat open for me." Jenny laughed. "I was thinking about them. Do you think if I got some box seats at a

Braves' or Yankees' game that I could fly those guys in my helicopter to see it?"

"It would be impossible to stop them, although I think they would prefer a Braves game," she said.

"Good. I'll arrange it," he said with a smile. He looked deeply into Jenny's eyes. He opened up his arms to receive her. She immediately reached out and gave him a huge hug. She could tell he was slightly uncomfortable, but she assured him that he did a good job.

"I'm not the most affectionate fellow," he admitted.

"Don't worry, you'll learn," she assured him.

With that, he left, and Jenny went back behind the counter to get ready for the lunch crowd. The lunch crowd arrived, ate, and departed like clockwork. Jenny cleaned up and headed for home. Once there, she filled the bathtub with hot water and got in for a long soak. When she was done, she dried off and decided to take a little nap.

She awoke feeling refreshed and headed out to the living room to do some straightening up. She piled the papers in the recycle bin, picked up the dirty dishes, and took them to the kitchen. Jenny took a few moments to wash the dishes. She gathered up the garbage and walked it down to the can. As she turned to head back up the stairs, a car turned in the drive. It was Mike in his patrol car.

"Wow, what a surprise," she said giving him a hug. "Come on in."

"I can't stay, I'm on duty. How do I look in my uniform?"

"My, Officer," she said fanning herself and using a mock Southern accent, "You look so strong and handsome, I think I might faint."

"Thank you, my dear," he said with a slight bow. "Actually, I came by to bring you an ice cream sundae."

"What, just because I am pregnant, you think I might have food cravings or that I might be hungry all the time?"

"Well, if you don't want it, I am sure I can find some kid who would be glad…"

"Hand that ice cream sundae over, Officer, if you know what's good for you." He gave her the sundae, and the two of them walked down toward the beach. They climbed over the sand dune and sat on the towel that Mike had brought, while eating the sundae. They laughed and talked until Mike had to head back out on patrol. Jenny hugged Mike and thanked him for the treat. As he drove away, she thanked God for such a good friend.

Jenny went back inside and motivated herself to get some laundry going. She sat down in the kitchen to the hum of the machine and did some paperwork. When she was done, she moved the load of laundry to the dryer and started a second load. While she was waiting for the laundry to finish, she cleaned her bathroom and swept and mopped the floors.

With the laundry folded and put away and her place smelling fresh and clean, Jenny was ready for a quick shower before getting ready for bed. The shower was warm and relaxing. She put on some fresh pajamas and climbed into bed. She reached over for her book, when suddenly she realized that she hadn't read the note from Uncle Fred or opened the gift from Uncle Charlie.

She got up and went to the kitchen where she had put the two items on the counter. She picked them up and returned to her bed. She fluffed her pillows behind her back and opened the letter from Uncle Fred.

Jenny,

Words cannot express how sorry I am for all the trouble I brought into your life. Your positive attitude about the whole situation blesses me beyond words. Your faith in God to bring something good out of this situation challenges me to a deeper walk with God. You give me hope that God can use me to affect change in a positive way in the many people I know. It will be an uphill battle, and many will never be able to receive it because they know who I was before I gave my life to God. Please pray for me.

I want you to know that I contacted the hospital and told them to forward all bills related to the birth of your child to me. I have given them my private telephone number and told them to contact me in case of an emergency. (I've included my number at the bottom of this note for you, too; call me if you need me. I promise you, I'll be there.)

The gift is from Charlie. He said you would understand, because I certainly don't. He said to tell you that he's proud of you, and I am too. I look forward to breakfast at the Bluebird when I am in town. Maybe we can talk a little after the breakfast crowd is gone; I know I would enjoy it.

Warmest regards,
Fred Collins
(I know, Uncle Fred! I am trying to get used to that. The truth is, Jenny, you feel more like a daughter than a niece.)

Jenny wiped a tear from her eye and put the letter down on the nightstand. She picked up the package and put it close to her nose and took a deep sniff. The familiar aroma danced within her nostrils. She lifted the lid of the box and lifted the contents out carefully. She held the object up to her nose and once again took a deep breath. The aroma filled her lungs, and there was a sudden sense of peace that enveloped her. She lay back on her pillow and allowed the peace to permeate every part of her body.

She sat back up in bed after a minute and looked again at the object in her hands. It was Uncle Charlie's pipe. She looked at it lying in her hands. Oh, how she missed the old guy, but now she believed she had found a new friend, Uncle Charlie's brother, Uncle Fred. With that pleasant thought, she put the pipe back into the box and placed the box on the nightstand. She leaned over, turned out the light, and laid her head on her pillow.

"Good night, Uncle Charlie," she said out loud, and closed her eyes peacefully. She knew he was there even though she could not see him.

Uncle Charlie stood at the end of her bed, smiling and filled with love and pride as she lay there silently. In a voice that she could not hear he said,

"Good night, Jenny. Sweet dreams."

Also by Doug Creamer

Encouraging

Thoughts

Encouraging Thoughts is a collection of short stories, essays, and articles that were written to strengthen and challenge the reader to a deeper walk with Christ.

I write about my struggles, doubts, and fears and how God helps me overcome. I want you to see how I interact with God. I try to make the Christian experience real and tangible.

I write about the beach, a place where I feel the closest to the Lord. I share with you how God speaks to me through my surroundings.

If you are an animal lover you'll enjoy the stories about the animals in my life. I believe you'll be touched by these personal and true experiences.

Some of the stories come from working in the public schools. So many people think that this generation is out of touch with God, but I see that there are many kids who not only know their creator but want to honor him.

One section of my book deals with the news events from the early 90's. My most powerful piece was written after the Oklahoma City bombing. It could have been written after any major tragedy, especially 9/11.

I find things in nature very inspiring and there is a section in my book about nature. I believe God is all around us revealing His beauty and creativity, but we are often too busy to notice.

I wrote about my parents' divorce from my perspective as an adult child. I am painfully honest about what I went through and how I felt. I have given this section of my book to many students who were struggling with their parents' split and they have been grateful for the help and comfort it offered.

Throughout my writing career I think I have written many columns about holidays. I look for a unique perspective and hope to discover encouraging insights for each one. My child-like heart comes out at the holidays and I enjoy writing about them each year.

Finally, I end the book with a few special pieces, some of which are not necessarily inspiring. They were pieces I wrote and never published in another format. I included them in the book because I liked them and I thought they were fun. The inspirational ones at the end were my favorites, pieces that I promise will touch your heart.

If you would be interested in ordering a copy of **Encouraging Thoughts** check on Amazon or please include your name and address in a short letter. Also include $11.45 to:

Doug Creamer
Faith Farm Publishing Company
PO Box 777
Faith, North Carolina 28041

Also by Doug Creamer

The Bluebird

Café

It is not necessary to read The Bluebird Café in order to understand and follow Revenge at the Bluebird Café, but it helps.

The main character, Uncle Charlie has devoted his life to helping people deal with the difficult hand that life can sometimes deal us all. He's the kind of friend we all need, the kind that sees the good in everyone he meets, even if he has to dig deep to find it.

The problem is how will the people in Uncle Charlie's life deal with the tragedy that is about to befall them? Where will they turn for answers? Will they learn the lessons that he has worked so hard to teach them? Will they find the source of his strength and draw from that life-changing power? Will they be able to follow his example and help others find the good in themselves?

Many people's paths cross at the Bluebird Café, but the lucky ones cross paths with Uncle Charlie.

Check at Amazon or send 11.45 to:

Doug Creamer
Faith Farm Publishing Company
PO Box 777
Faith, North Carolina 28041

Thank You

There have been so many people who have helped and encouraged me in this endeavor. If I listed each person who influenced or touched this book in some way I would need many more pages to include them all. If you are one of the unsung helpers, please accept my heart-felt thanks. No writer completes a book like this on his own.

Special thanks must be given to Wayne Finney, Linda Branch, and my wife for reading and editing my book. Each of them offered invaluable insight and helped to shape the characters and the story. Each helped to correct my grammar so you could enjoy the story. I am a storyteller, not an English major.

The following people spoke encouraging words or helped to bring this dream to life. THANK YOU!!!!

Tim Austin
Sydney Byerly
Dennis Creamer
Mary Elkins & Paula Elkins who prayed for me and encouraged me to complete this book. God answered your prayers!!
Jim & Wanda Howard
Andrew McCarn
Dan Patton
Elaine Smith
Is Smith
Jean Smith
And my Mom and Dad who continue to believe and encourage me in my writing endeavors.
Again, I want to thank my wife who puts up with me while I chase my dream to write.

ABOUT THE AUTHOR

Doug Creamer has been teaching Marketing Education for nearly thirty years. He earned his National Board Certification in 2002 and has helped to develop and write two curriculum guides for the state of North Carolina. He was recently honored with the North Carolina Marketing Education Association's Marketing Education Teacher of the Year. His previous books were Encouraging Thoughts and The Bluebird Café. He lives with his wife in Salisbury, North Carolina where he can be found outside working in his yard if he isn't working on his website or writing.